QUEEN OF ALL

BOOKS BY KATHRYN ANN KINGSLEY

THE MASKS OF UNDER SERIES

King of Flames

King of Shadows

Queen of Dreams

King of Blood

King of None

THE IRON CRYSTAL SERIES

To Charm a Dark Prince

To Bind a Dark Heart

To Break a Dark Cage

To Love a Dark Lord

For a full list, visit www.kathrynkingsley.com

KATHRYN ANN KINGSLEY

QUEEN OF ALL

SECOND SKY

Published by Second Sky in 2024

An imprint of Storyfire Ltd.
Carmelite House
50 Victoria Embankment
London EC4Y 0DZ
United Kingdom

www.secondskybooks.com

The authorised representative in the EEA is Hachette Ireland
8 Castlecourt Centre
Dublin 15 D15 XTP3
Ireland
(email: info@hbgi.ie)

First published by Limitless Publishing in 2019.

ISBN: 978-1-83618-446-1
eBook ISBN: 978-1-83618-445-4

FOREWORD

The Masks of Under was the first series I ever officially published, back in 2019. And getting a chance to revisit it, polish it up, and republish it now has been like returning to old friends. It has been such a wonderful opportunity to be able to bring this story back to life.

I hope you enjoy reading the conclusion of this tale as much as I enjoyed (re)writing it.

To you, reader, I say thank you. And I truly hope this isn't the last dark adventure you follow me on.

Happy nightmares.

ONE

Lydia had lost.

They had all lost.

To be fair, any war against the King of All was going to be *pointless*. And they had known that. And she had gone into the fight knowing that she was the sacrificial lamb.

Something that both terrified her and... yet...

As his arm banded round her waist, as the King of All took them from the battlefield and the world dissolved around her in a swirl of darkness?

It wasn't just fear that coiled deep in her stomach.

There was also an anticipation that made her feel more like a monster than anything else. She had just seen him kill Ylena—he'd just mopped the floor with her. Taken her *prisoner*.

But damn it all to hell, if the look in his spilled-ink eyes—the darkness, the power, the *desire*—didn't make her want to forget it all and lose herself in him.

They reappeared in a room that she barely had time to register. It was huge, whatever it was—with soaring black columns and only two walls that weren't open to the air, before he was pushing her backward.

She gasped as her back met one of those stone columns. She tried to push him away, tried to catch her breath for a second, but he wasn't having it. The King of All grabbed her wrists and easily pinned them over her head with his metal gauntlet.

"Wait, I—" She never got the rest of the words out. Like he was ever going to listen to her in the first place.

His lips silenced her, devouring the rest of her complaint in a kiss that would have buckled her knees if she weren't pinned to the column. Were they still fighting? Or they had just traded out what kind of blows they were using?

Twice now, they'd fought in the sand, and twice now, she'd found herself wishing it would end with him, pinning her down, *taking* what was rightfully *his.*

A dark fantasy she knew he shared. One she felt ashamed of even having, lurking in the back of her mind. Who wanted to be eaten by the wolf? After what she had just seen? After what he'd just done?

His flesh-and-blood hand trailed down her body, pushing aside the split in her top, grasping her breast and squeezing it hard, drawing a moan out of her against his lips. He met it with a hungry growl of his own.

When he pulled away, just enough for her to fill her aching lungs, his chest was also heaving. "Tell me to stop, and I will. Tell me anything else, my starlight, and I will heed no words from you—but wish it to end, and I am gone. Do you understand?" His words were a dusky growl that sent a shiver through her that filled her with both ice and lava in equal measure.

When she hesitated, his fingers grasped her nipple and pinched it so hard she cried out, arching her back into his grasp. It was a promise and a warning. *You can stop me. But you can't slow me down or temper me. The wolf is starved, and the King will have his spoils of war.*

This would be brutal.

And God help her... that was *exactly* how she wanted it to be. It was wrong. It was twisted. It was depraved.

But deep down inside, she wanted it. Wanted him to *take*. Meeting his heated stare, she met his words with the only thing she could think of.

She pulled back a hand and slapped him as hard as she could.

The King of All moved his head with the blow, more out of momentum than with the force of the strike. He laughed. Quiet, insidious... and pleased. She had given him her answer.

"Perfect as always, my starlight." He ghosted his lips over hers. "Let us begin."

A flurry of movement followed as he twisted his hand in her hair and threw her from the column, sending her sprawling to the floor. She was already exhausted from the brawl they'd already had in the field. He'd already kicked her ass *once* today.

She didn't know how much fight she had left in her for a second round.

But that wasn't the point.

Rolling out of the way of a kick that was meant for her midsection, she stood and dodged another one of his blows, ducking under a swing of an arm and elbowing him in the ribs.

He chuckled. "You are learning."

"You're—" She was going to taunt him. But he swept her legs out, sending her landing heavily on her back with an *"unf"* instead.

The King of All loomed over her, his dark hair falling in tendrils around his pale face. A face she recognized, worn by a man she didn't know. But one she was learning she... still very much wanted. "I know you wish to lose, but that badly? Come now. Put up a real fight."

"Fuck you."

"That is where we are headed, yes, if you hadn't—" He snarled in pain as she dug an obsidian dagger into his calf.

It was a dirty move, summoning a dagger to a fist fight. But she would have to fight mean to get anywhere. Rolling away, she staggered back to her feet and took the second or two it would take him to rip the knife out and heal from the wound to catch her breath.

It didn't take him nearly as long as she'd hoped. She learned that when his forearm met her chest and sent her staggering backward, nearly knocking what little wind she had left out of her.

The world spun. And this time, when she met a column, it was as he pressed her to it face-first. He didn't slam her into it hard enough to hurt—she didn't see stars. But there was no room for argument as he pressed his arm across her shoulders, keeping her trapped there.

She growled, trying to push away, but he leaned his weight against her.

And when his hand trailed down over her ass, squeezing a globe roughly before sliding between layers of fabric to plunge a finger deep into her core, her strength suddenly fled.

A wavering gasp was all she could manage as he began to rhythmically delve that finger in and out of her, slowly, revealing just how eager she had been for this moment.

Nuzzling into her hair, he chuckled quietly. "How I've dreamed of this moment... you, surrendering to me, giving in to me." A second finger joined the first. When she moaned, he pressed his body closer to hers. "Yes, that's it—just like that. Your heart is yours. Your mind and soul—*yours*. But your body? This—this belongs to *me*."

He pulled away from her. The absence of him was as jarring as it was disappointing. But it was brief. His hand twisted in her hair as he yanked her away from the column, pulling her into the middle of the floor, before spinning her to face him.

Taking two steps back, he regarded her with that cold and impassive expression of the King of All. Of the man—no—the *demigod* who was older than recorded history. Older than mountains. Older, perhaps, than the first humans who walked the earth.

And from him came a single command.

"Kneel."

Part of her screamed not to. The part of her that reminded her that this wasn't her Aon. This wasn't the warlock she loved. But it was drowned out in a chorus of rampant need and the *hope* that maybe, just maybe, *he still was.*

And his taunting of her... wasn't wrong. She didn't love him. And she wasn't loyal to him. Not yet. But this? This attraction between them? It was inescapable. It was undeniable. And it was unavoidable.

Slowly, hesitantly, she sank to her knees.

And the look that washed over him was one of pure and total bliss. The King of All stepped up to her until he was only a few inches away. He no longer smelled of old books and dusty leather—it was of crisp summer air and the wind. He smelled of incense and spices.

His human hand reached down and stroked her hair, before crooking a finger under her chin. "Look at me."

Lifting her head, she met his gaze. The lust and hunger in his spilled-ink eyes lodged a rock in her throat. The wrath she knew he was going to unleash on her was kept on a tight leash —but he was going to drop the chain. It was just a matter of when.

His fingers trailed up along her jawline, before he paused to run his thumb along her lower lip. "I remember, quite distinctly, you having a... particular talent. One I plan to *deeply* enjoy." When he pressed his thumb into her mouth, she didn't fight him. His next words were a deep growl. "The question simply remains, will you do this of your own accord? Or will I have to force the matter?"

No. No, she didn't particularly want to know what it'd be

like to have him do *that* by force. Besides... she... wanted to do this. Damn herself to hell, she *needed* this. This dark god. This pharaoh in black.

Trembling as they were, she ran her hands up his thighs. He straightened up, letting his hand go to her hair, stroking it gently as she began to undo the many buckles that held the black fabric robes around his waist.

It took her a moment to figure out the latches, but eventually, she managed to release them, and the fabric fell to his ankles in a rush. It made him no less imposing. Especially at the sight of just how badly he needed her in his own right.

"Remove your clothes." A command, not a request.

She undid the clasp to her top, tossing it aside. He'd seen her naked a hundred times. But this felt different. Somehow, she felt more vulnerable like this. Kneeling to him on the floor of an ancient temple. *Like a slave girl. Like a possession.*

Because, in this moment, that's what she was. She was the Queen of Dreams. And she was the pet of the King of All. And it was *glorious*.

When she was fully naked, she turned her attention back to him. He grasped her hair in his human fist, clearly eager as well. Half shutting her eyes, she let her tongue roll along his length, savoring him.

The sound that he made was perfect, spurring her on. When she took the head of him into her mouth, it was as though she had given water to a man dying of thirst, the way he moaned. His hand in her hair tightened. "Yes—that's it—"

She pushed him deeper, bobbing her head on him, getting used to his girth once more, preparing herself for what was to come.

He snarled. "*More.*"

It seemed one thing this king shared with her warlock was their impatience.

She took him down farther, pressing further as she worked

to relax the muscles in her throat as he filled her. He cut off her air, sending thrills through her body. She felt him spasm and his breath hitched, turning into a sharp intake of air through his teeth like a hiss. As she took him to the hilt, he moaned again loudly.

She slid back from him, and gasped to fill her lungs with air. She looked up at him, and saw him watching her with lidded, dark eyes. His expression was one of pure hunger. His hands flexed close to her, fingers stretching and clenching, as if holding himself back. She knew what he wanted to do. But for the moment, he held on to his restraint.

"Worship your new king, Queen of Dreams..." His voice was a rumble, low and dangerous. It was a threat as much as it was a plea. He twitched in her hand as if straining for more. She knew if she didn't deliver, he would take.

She didn't know which thought thrilled her more.

She took him back into her mouth and pressed him down as far as he could go, stretching and threatening the control she had over her own body as he did.

She held him there for as long as she could before pulling back, catching her breath, and repeating the gesture. She took up a tempo that pushed her limits but kept the burning out of her lungs.

God, how much she loved doing this. It lit a fire in her she couldn't deny. Her body felt like an inferno—as if someone had poured molten iron into her veins. She slipped her eyes shut again, losing herself in the sensation of him.

He yanked her off him with a dizzying force. He tossed her to the ground, and before she could react, he was on top of her, her knees pinned to her shoulders, as he doubled her in half beneath him.

"Wait—" She'd been warned. That word wouldn't work.

The King of All took his prize. Sank into her to the hilt in one thrust that made her see stars as she wailed in both bliss and agony that mixed together into one, indistinguishable ecstasy.

The need he'd had chained away was now loose. He'd uncaged the wolf, and now it was free to feed. And she was his prey beneath him, left to gasp and mewl and let out a sharp whimper of pleasure each time he rammed into her without mercy.

His lips caught hers, swallowing her sounds of tortured joy, mixing with his own moans. Only once had Aon ever loved her like this.

And he had called me starlight that night...

It had been him.

In some small way... it had been the King of All with her in that bed that night.

That should have horrified her. But instead? It comforted her. The King of All wasn't an *invader*—he had been there, in some way, the whole time. Tension she didn't realize she had been holding onto left her. It let him burrow deeper into her, somehow pressing farther into her already straining body.

He arched his back as he used his full weight, groaning loudly. "Yes, that's it—there is the *true* defeat—" Letting her knees rest on his shoulders, he placed his human hand around her throat. "Look at me, my starlight—"

She met those spilled-ink eyes.

"Tell me you are *mine*." He pulled back almost all the way before slamming back into her.

"I am yours..." The pleasure was unreal. She wondered if she'd go insane like this.

And again. "Tell me you surrender."

"I surrender..." She was clinging to him. Her body felt like putty in his hands.

A third time, and it was too much for both of them. He roared, and she felt him twitch and surge inside of her.

She couldn't take it. Her body clenched around him, the

ecstasy too much. Her overwrought, beaten, and exhausted body was overwhelmed by pleasure.

When she became aware of herself, he was kissing her gently on the cheek, stroking her shoulder with his hand, whispering to her softly of how much he loved her.

How he would never truly hurt her. How well she had done. And how she was now home. Safe. With *him*. With her King of All.

And she knew she had a terrible path to walk ahead of her.

TWO

Lydia stared down at the King of All as he slept, images flashing through her mind of everything that had just passed between them.

The King of All had come to claim what he wanted, and he had taken the spoils of war for his own.

And damn her, she had enjoyed every moment of it. She hadn't wanted him to stop.

He had held her as they fell asleep, tangled in the thin sheets of his bed. He had whispered to her how much he loved her, about how she was the only thing in his world that had ever really mattered. He had told her that his soul, his *life*, belonged to her. She would have cried if she hadn't been so tired. And it was there that she had woken, curled up in his arms.

Really, his bed was more of a platform with a mat, feeling just as ancient as everything else in this palace of his. Two of the walls of the room were open to the world outside, framed only by the massive columns that soared overhead. It felt exceedingly exposed. But as they were up several hundred feet from the ground, she supposed she shouldn't worry too much about last night's escapades being heard or them being spied on.

Not that she suspected the man beneath her gave a flying fuck about any of that.

So here she found herself, in thin cotton nightclothes. Straddling his waist, one hand pressing against the headboard over him, the other holding one of her obsidian daggers.

It'd be so damn easy.

So simple.

Take the marks.

Take his life.

She'd have to slash the marks fast, but she could do it. He was asleep. Dark hair splayed out on the unbleached cotton pillows around him. He looked so... contented. So peaceful.

As though he had never enjoyed this kind of sleep before in his life.

Maybe he never has. Maybe he's never been happy before. Maybe he never had anyone he wanted to share his bed with.

No. He was a tyrant. He was going to kill everyone on that battlefield if she hadn't bargained herself away. Worse yet, he admitted he was more than willing to destroy everyone in Under except for the two of them—just because they were a distraction. He only let them live because their presence here made her "happy."

He was a dangerous sociopath, at best.

Actually, one swipe of her knife across his throat and he wouldn't wake up for half an hour. That'd give her time to remove the marks that decorated his face, and that'd be the end. The end of all this stupidity.

It would be so damn easy.

When she had woken up, she was tucked against him like a lover, his knees against hers, her head under his chin, arm draped over her. It was a familiar pose. She had woken up with Aon like that many, many times. But this man was a stranger in his own right.

Mostly.

One motion.

Left to right.

It wouldn't take much force—her daggers were sharper than steel razors, after all. It really would just take commitment more than anything else. Just dedication. She wouldn't even really feel it.

Just do it. Come on, it's so simple! Just commit, then it's all over!

Why couldn't she do it? Why the *hell* couldn't she kill him?

She'd been like this for ten minutes, hovering over him and screaming at herself in her mind to just kill him already. *End it all! End his miserable life and your part in it!*

But she couldn't.

No matter how hard she shouted at herself inside her own head, she couldn't make her hand move.

It wasn't hypnotism.

It wasn't the work of the Ancients.

It was her own *stupid* inability to kill him.

Whoever the King of All was, he wore the face of the man she loved. He shared shades of the man she adored. This was the body and, just maybe, the *soul* of the man she would throw her whole life away for. Maybe their minds weren't the same, but... was everything else? Was that enough?

If a portal opened to Earth this very moment, she would reject it to stand beside her warlock, this man beneath her. The man she had, for better or worse, whether or not she should, come to love. Her monster. *Her madman.*

But now, she didn't know what, or who, he was. She had no clue who wore this mask of flesh and blood. Last night he had been so similar yet so foreign to the man she knew—reverent and violent in the same breath. He had pledged himself to her, swore that he was hers, even as he broke her down and pieced her back together. She couldn't deny she had enjoyed every second of him and every inch of what he gave her.

But now?

What happened now?

Left to right. It would be so easy. *Just do it, you stupid idiot!*

Doubt gnawed at her like termites under a house. What if her Aon was still in there somewhere? What if he was really in any way the same man who lay sleeping peacefully beneath her? Could she really kill him?

She loved him.

What if his insistence that they were the same man was right?

Or was he a monstrous creature that made all others pale before him?

Tears were down her cheeks. She wasn't sure when they'd started, and she honestly didn't care. Edu and the rest were terrified of this man. They had hated the King of Shadows because some part of them could remember the King of All.

She could end it. Right now.

"If you wanted to be on top, all you had to do was ask."

She froze. She had thought he was asleep. But as his dark eyes drifted open, he turned his head to look up at her. He didn't grab her wrist and didn't force the knife away from where she was hovering it near his throat. In fact, he tipped his chin back to give her easier access. He watched her, his face free of anything but a kind of passive acceptance edged in grief.

She hung there silently, wide-eyed and unsure of what to do.

"I take this to mean you are upset with me," he said after letting her inability to answer hang in the air for a long moment. He still didn't move to stop her. "Do it, if you must. My life is yours to spend. Now, as it always has been, and ever will be, my love."

With a frustrated growl, she rammed the knife into the headboard over his head. Stuck it halfway to the hilt. She couldn't do it. Not when he had been asleep, and certainly not when he was looking up at her with sorrow in his eyes.

She pushed herself off him but couldn't find the strength to go far. She sat on the bed and buried her head in her hands, feeling the tears redouble their efforts. His weight shifted on the bed. At first, she flinched, wondering if he would be angry at her. But instead, she felt his hand slowly stroke over her hair. He knelt behind her, his knees on either side of her legs. His arms curled around her, gently urging her to lean back into him. She gave in. His bare chest was warm against her back, and it lulled away some of her turmoil, even if her issues were *about* him.

His head settled atop hers. "I braced myself for what I might see in your eyes. But I admit, it stings worse than I could have imagined."

"Which is what?" she murmured into her hands, trying to keep herself from all-out weeping.

"You look at me as you would a stranger." His voice was tight in pain. "You look at me as if you do not know me. There is mistrust in your eyes. You look at me, truly wary. Not the mix of fear and delight when I seduced you as a madman, but *real* dread..."

Suddenly, his hand fisted in her hair and yanked her down. He bent her backward and twisted her over his right thigh. She hissed in a breath of surprise and found herself with another dagger in her hand. She didn't even have to think about it before it was in her palm. She held it up against his throat once more, startled into action, thinking he was about to hurt her.

"You see? You would never have reacted in such a way to the man you knew before. You would have seen this as another game and relished my touch. Now, you think I am going to hurt you—*you!* The only thing in this world that carries value to me." His expression twisted up in agony. "You trusted me as a madman, but you do not trust me now. You would never believe that version of me would hurt you, so why do you think I would do so now?"

His power seemed to fill the room, seemed to crackle through the air like lightning and clench around her stronger than the fist that curled in her hair. Aon had been intimidating before, but not like this. Still, he didn't move her dagger from his throat. He knew as well as she did that she wasn't going to use it.

"You're more dangerous than he is."

Spilled-ink eyes narrowed as they bored into her. There was such age in those depths. The cold-hearted king who loomed over her was as sure and as cold as a stone mountainside. "That is false. Very false."

"What do you mean?"

His eyes flicked over the writing on her face as if reading them again. Only then did his gaze soften even a little. The hand in her hair did no such thing. His clawed hand drifted up to settle over her throat. Not tightening, but as if he were remembering a keen desire to do just that. "I nearly killed you so many times, Lydia. So many moments where I was on the brink of giving in to what I wanted to do to your mortal flesh. Or worse, losing myself into the insanity and tearing you to pieces as though I were a rabid animal. You walked the razor's edge every day you spent in my presence, ignorant to how close to real danger you truly were."

"But he never did it."

"We are the *same man*—and I would have. It would have only been a matter of time. Edu merely killed you before my own insanity would have done the deed. And after, you chose to reject your mask and you did not hide your marks from me, even then. How long before, in a fit of darkness, I tore them from your skin and returned you to the void?" His eyes searched hers, pleading—*desperate*—for any understanding.

"I trusted—" *him.* She stopped herself from calling him different people again, but just barely. "You."

He leaned his head down to place a kiss at the corner of her mouth. It made her shudder despite herself and the compromising position she was in. "You are naïve. You are young. You will learn." When he ghosted his lips over hers, she tightened her grip on the knife at his throat. "Now... either use that dagger or stop your hopeless grandstanding."

"I'm not grandstanding."

"Then do it. Slit my throat, take my marks, and send me to the void." He tilted his head away for her. "You could not do it a moment ago. You could not do it last night. You could not do it when we fought. Make good upon your threat now or stop. The blade is in my way, and it is irritating to be interrupted repeatedly in such a fashion."

Struggling, she pushed against him. She wanted up.

Obediently, he let her go without a fuss. Standing, she paced away from him. Threading her hands through her hair, she let out a wavering sigh. She wanted out. She wanted to quit. "What do you want from me?"

"I want you to love me."

"So why not just make me? Why not rewrite my head and make me love you? Why wait?"

"While I will love you, no matter what may remain of you... if they were to take you by force, you may end up little more than a shell. If you fight their dominion, you will break. I do not wish to see that terrible pain come to you." Hands settled on her shoulders, one metal and one warm. She jolted in surprise and shouldn't have been shocked she didn't hear him approach. "I... wish to avoid that outcome."

She squeezed her eyes shut and lowered her head, trying to hide behind her long hair as it fell alongside her face. Love him or be broken. She didn't even know if she *could* love him. It wasn't a choice she could willingly make. "My love would be a lie."

"A shattered queen whose love is a fabrication is better than an eternity alone. I have destroyed this world countless times in my need to have someone at my side. You are the answer to that hole in my very being. Whether you wish to be or not. I am sorry, my starlight. But I will not let you slip away. You belong to me, and I to you."

There had to be another way out. There had to be some talking sense into him—some way to get through to him. There had to be. Otherwise, there was only one other way out. She looked down at the knife in her palm, and she had the sudden urge to tear her own marks off with it. To simply end it all.

Death was a better fate than this.

"Kill me. Just kill me. Or I'll do it myself."

Hands whirled her around to face him. "Do not *dare* say such a thing."

She looked up at him, startled at his sudden reaction. "I'd rather be dead than—"

"No! No. Do not speak the words." His eyes were wide in panic. He snatched the knife from her hand and hurled it away. "Do not leave me alone! Do not make me drag you to them so soon. I will *not* let you harm yourself. I will chain you to the wall, bind your arms and legs if I must."

She glared at him. "I'll find a way to do it. You know I will. I'm a lot of things, one of them being stubborn."

"I—" His eyes went glassy, and his body jerked suddenly as if something had been torn out from his back. His hands slipped from her shoulders, and he collapsed to his knees. His shoulders were now hunched, his head down. He buried his hands into his hair, clenching them tightly, shoulders heaving as he pulled in sharp, painful breaths. He moaned in agony.

Lydia blinked at the abrupt change. What the hell just happened to him?

Not knowing what else to do, she knelt in front of him and put her hand on his shoulder. He flinched at her touch.

"Dragonfly...?"

Her heart wrenched so hard it may have stopped. Her breath hung in her throat, and she looked at the man in wide-eyed horror. As his face turned up to hers, there was such torment in those flickering dark eyes that she knew the image would be burned into her memory for the rest of time.

There was no coldness there. No impassive, timeless king. Just a raw, exposed fire. Emotions flashed over his face. Pain, fear, torment. *Love.*

"Aon—"

He interrupted her before she could tell him how much she loved him. How much she missed him. He reached out and cupped her head in his hands, shifting to kneel closer to her. "They let me go. Just for a moment. Just so you could see. They wanted to sway you from seeking to take your own life." His breaths were still coming fast and hard as if he might hyperventilate. As if he were fighting off the edge of panic. "It is false hope. They are liars. This is an illusion—" Face twisting in pure suffering, he doubled over again. "*I* am an illusion. That is all I have ever been."

She threw her arms around him, cradling him against her. He half collapsed into her embrace. "Aon, I love you. I love you and I'm so sorry."

"I beg you, do not end your life. Do not doom me to a reality where you are truly gone. The wrath I would pay to this world and all the others... there would be no returning from the damage that would do to my soul." His body spasmed as if someone had shoved a red-hot poker against him. He pulled in a hissing breath. "This is why they have freed me, if but for a moment. To convince you to live. For in this desire, in this common goal, all parties are agreed."

"I—I don't know what else to do."

"Do not take your life. Take mine instead. Find a way to end me. Please, my dragonfly." He lifted his head and rested his forehead against hers. His voice was tight and thick with whatever pain the Ancients were flooding him with.

"I can't—"

"There is no way to save me and there is no hope of my return." Tears rolled down his cheeks. "You are stronger than me. Stronger than the man I truly am."

"I tried to kill you. I love you. I... I can't."

"You must." He kissed her, a frantic press of lips to hers, as though they were on a sinking ship and this was their last chance. Perhaps it was. "Or I will destroy you. I will destroy this world and everyone in it, just to have you... and the man I really am will tear you to pieces to get what I want." He held her face in his hands in his frantic need for her to understand.

She understood. But knowing and doing were very different things.

"My life has been a ceaseless cycle of destruction, of yearning for what I could never have. Do you think the Great War was the first time I acted in such desperation? Your history is repeating itself and so is mine. You are on this terrible, endless circular path beside me. End it all." His eyes were turning glassy again. His hands were slipping from her cheeks. He was fighting to stay conscious, and he was losing.

"Aon, don't go." *Don't leave me alone again.* "Please, don't—"

"Do you know your eyes are now turquoise?" He smiled through the agony, a fascinated and awe-inspired expression that she knew would haunt her until she turned to dust. "Since you returned from the lake where Rxa had put you... I haven't had the chance to tell you how utterly *radiant* they are."

Her heart was cracking, and she let out a small, choked sob.

"I will always love you, my dragonfly."

And with that, his eyes rolled into his head, and he slumped down against her.

Laying her head against his shoulders, she held him. Held him and wept. For him, for her... for them both.

THREE

For a moment, Lydia could almost forget.

She could run her fingers through his hair as he slept and believe just for a second that when he woke up, everything would be back to "normal."

Normal. Right. None of this shit's been normal for months.

Normal was her home in Boston. Her job. Nick. Her apartment. Normal was far, far away from here. It was all gone to her now, either through a portal or buried under sand and blood. God, she missed Nick. But like everything else, he was dead and gone.

All that was left... was him.

And even *he* was changed, now.

After he had passed out, she had hauled him back into bed. It hadn't been graceful, but she was stronger than she used to be. She didn't feel like sleeping, but it felt wrong to leave him lying on the floor like an idiot.

And so, she stayed with him, leaning up against the headboard, with his head in her lap. She traced her hand through his long black hair, and once her tears had finally dried out, she took the time to think.

Maybe she should give in. Maybe it'd be easier that way. To just let him drag her to the Altar of the Ancients and let them rewrite her brain. Let them possess her in the same way they were doing to Lyon. Or worse, like Aon, where they were plugging holes in his head like a sinking ship.

For a moment, the Ancients had shown her they really were the same man. They had let go of their control of him so she could speak to the part of him that she recognized. And her Aon had begged her to kill him. Begged her to end his life. But she just couldn't bring herself to do it. He was still, somehow, some way, the man she loved. Even if he was just a smaller part of the whole, he was still there.

Could she love this man? Could she love the "bigger picture?" She honestly didn't know. He could be cruel, but so could the man she knew. He was egotistical—no change there. But the one thing that worried her more than anything else was his coldness, the stoic loftiness she saw in his dark eyes.

It was as though Aon really had been changed out for his older brother. There was a hardness there, an aloofness that worried her. But could she learn to love it, this dark king? Or would she always miss her madman, even if he was right in front of her? Even if those eyes that seemed so cold to her now softened—just a little—when he looked at her?

She didn't know, and there was the problem. If she knew the answer, she'd kill him, or herself, or let him drag her off into the altar and let them bash her head open like a coconut and put someone else in her place. The fact that she didn't know left her locked in indecision, stuck in the mire and unable to move.

How long the Ancients would let her linger like this, she had no idea. But she was certain it wouldn't be enough time, in her opinion. For giant, world-controlling super-monsters, they seemed damn impatient.

For all her problems, she felt for the man who was unconscious in her lap, this King of All. It seemed he was doomed to always be suffering. Even when he finally had the only thing he ever wanted—her—she didn't know if she loved him anymore.

That had to hurt worse than she could imagine. He had been alone for longer than the mountains on Earth had names. And now she was taunting him with her very presence.

That was the other reason she stayed with him—she couldn't help but sympathize with him. She couldn't fix the problem, she couldn't flick a switch and just magically love him again, but she couldn't abandon him either.

His metal hand was lying in her lap, palm up. She watched as one of his fingers twitched once and then went still. His breathing never changed, but she knew better. Aon had done this a few times before. He had just woken up but didn't want to move. He'd pretend to be asleep so he could stay where he was with her.

"Hey," she said, her voice barely above a whisper. Just in case she was wrong, even though she was damn sure she wasn't.

Nothing.

Lydia couldn't help but grin. "I know you're awake," she said, her tone still low.

Silence. Just slow, perfectly paced breathing. It was a good act. Too bad she wasn't buying it.

She thought for a moment before an evil plan came to mind. "On Earth, we invented a thing called a 'wet willy.' It's when you stick your finger in your mouth and then shove it into another person's ear." She stuck her finger into her mouth and let it make a pop noise as she withdrew it. Grinning, she lowered her hand toward his ear. This time, she was going to call *his* bluff for once.

His human hand shot up to catch hers before she could follow through. He kept his eyes shut and otherwise hadn't moved. "Do not dare."

Chuckling, she withdrew her hand. "Just proving my point."

He was fighting off a smile and losing. It caught purchase for a moment before he finally let it have its way. It hung on him for a second or two and then faded away. His eyes drifted open, but he didn't lift his head or make any other movement to get up.

She let her hand fall on his shoulder. "I'm glad my stupid antics can still make you smile, even if you don't want to let them."

"They always will, even if perhaps I do not show it as much as I used to." He curled the fingers of his metal hand in toward his palm one at a time before releasing them and repeating as if he were testing the mechanism. As if it really were foreign to him. "I know I am... less emotive than the man you knew. I know I am quieter than him. I am sorry for that. But I do not know how to change, after all this time, to better suit you."

She went back to gently stroking his hair. He was hurting. It was hard to see, but it was in his eyes, even if his face and tone were flat. "It's not your fault. And I don't expect you to change."

"But it is still my burden to bear." His eyes slipped shut again, and his brow furrowed. "I find myself jealous of my own shadow. For it is that which I cast upon the ground that you love, not me."

Wincing at his words, she leaned down and placed a kiss on his temple. "I'm not giving up hope. I don't know yet. I don't know *you*."

"You are resilient above all else. I remember the first time I laid eyes upon you in the waking world. Thrown from a horse, you were terrified, battered, and beaten. You had certain death chasing at your back. And yet you were brave enough to face down one demon with another close behind."

"You remember that?"

"I... remember a girl." He furrowed his brow as if it was a struggle to recall all the details. "A mortal, weak in body but stronger in heart than any I have ever known. One who took pity on a broken man. One who saw value in his empty heart and took his darkest needs with joy. And then she rose like a phoenix from the grave... I remember her forgiveness, her sympathy, her kindness, even as I took away her friend and her freedom."

He took her hand from his shoulder with his human one and pulled it to his lips, pressing a kiss to her fingers. His breath was hot against her skin. "I remember how she looked at me, blue eyes wide in fear and excitement. How she delighted in running from me yet how she would let me take her by the hand and lead her into the darkness. I recall how—despite all that broken *monster* had done—she loved me. I remember those who were too jealous, too afraid, to give that shell of a man the only thing he had ever wanted."

He too waffled back and forth between calling his nightmare the same man and calling his mad self "he." It must be hard for him to resolve as well. Like a fever dream.

"I think you need a new name."

"Hm?"

"It's not fair to call you Aon." She smiled faintly down at him. It hadn't felt right to call him that, anyway. "And it's not fair for you not to have a name."

"It is somewhat adding insult to injury, yes." He sighed and let his eyes slip shut. "Then name me, my Queen of Dreams."

"Hmm..." She looked off thoughtfully. Naming things was fun, even if she was terribly bad at it. "Koa? For the 'King of All?'"

"No. Sounds feminine."

"Aoff. Y'know, like A-on, but A-off." She knew it was a horrible idea.

"Absolutely not." He was fighting a smile again.

"Well, if he was the alpha and you're the omega, how about Oon?"

"Are you attempting to insult me more?"

That made her laugh, and now the man in her lap was grinning despite his best efforts. She looked down at him and thought it over for another moment. "How about Noa? 'Aon' backward. All the parts are there, but... just... different."

"He is my reflection in the glass."

"Right."

"Very well." He paused. "Noa. I accept this name, my mother of monsters. Although I worry for the species of creatures you will create as time goes on. Your sense of humor is... pervasive... if nothing else."

She laughed and leaned down to kiss his temple. "You have no idea."

"I look forward to finding out." The amusement faded from his eyes. "If the Ancients do not take that from you, first." The moment of levity was gone, as he was reminded of the position they were both in. All that she was suffering, he was going through as well.

They fell silent as she felt the weight of her looming debate over them once more. "If it were your choice, what would you do?"

"Between what options?" He seemed as though her running her fingers through his hair was lulling him back into sleep. His voice was faraway sounding. It seemed her touch still did that to him, even if as he said, it showed less on the outside.

"If you were me. I can hope that I fall in love with you—which I have no control over. I can't just *make* myself love you."

"I am aware."

"So step one is... try and hope for the best. But if that doesn't work out? I have two options—I could kill you or get dragged kicking and screaming to the Altar of the Ancients and get my mind rewritten."

"You could choose to kneel willingly at their altar. Choose to commit your heart to me, if it does not wish to be mine of its own volition." It was clear the topic was uncomfortable to him.

"I get mind-fucked either way."

He chuckled at her crass language. "Yes. Precisely. And there is a far cry difference between willing intercourse and rape."

When he had a point, he had a point. She couldn't think up a retort. "Fair. Fine, there are three choices. What would you do?"

"If our situations were reversed?"

"Yeah."

He paused for a long time. "I could not bring myself to kill you. Even thinking that there was a shadow of a woman I loved within you, I could not do the deed. Faced with the other choices? I would kneel willingly before their altar and sacrifice the sanctity of my mind."

"Bullshit."

"I would rather no longer be my true self than to be alone a moment longer. The man you knew believed the same. That is why he burned the world away to save you. I am no different. I am he. Do not forget your youth in comparison to my years. I have been alone for a very, very long time."

She paused and considered his words. She couldn't accuse him of lying, not really. He really would lay it all down to be with her. He already had. After a long pause, she finally admitted to him what she was feeling. "I'm scared."

"I know." He wove his fingers between hers and held her hand close to his chest. With a long, weary breath, he made his own admission. "Please, do not leave me."

It was clearly his own plea for her not to kill herself or try to find a more permanent way out of this mess. Tears threatened to fall. She shuffled down to lie on the bed, pulling his head onto her shoulder, holding him.

The way he nuzzled into her broke her heart. He clung to her, draping his arm over her, and she knew he was listening to her heartbeat. The tension melted out of him. The warmth of his body and her own exhaustion were starting to lure her own eyes shut.

It had been a hopeless threat, saying she wanted to kill herself. She couldn't leave him alone. Not her Aon, and not Noa. She found that she couldn't bear to look at this man and turn her back on him. She didn't know if she loved him... but she couldn't abandon him.

"I'll stay. I won't leave you." She couldn't bring herself to lie to him. "I promise. I'm sorry I was being dramatic, I just... I'm overwhelmed."

"I understand. And for my part, I am sorry I am not the man you love."

"That's also not your fault." It's true, it wasn't. Noa had no part in any of this shit-show. He was just as much of a puppet in all of the madness as she was. "And... maybe you are. I just haven't figured it out yet. Maybe I just need to get there."

"Someday."

"We're immortal, aren't we?"

"I suppose we are." He leaned his head in and kissed her collarbone, and she couldn't help but feel herself grow warm even at the innocent gesture from a half-asleep man. "Tomorrow, I must sit upon my throne and deal with the needs of my people. They squabble and bicker like children. Will you attend?"

"That sounds horrible."

"It will be. But come with me, anyway."

She chuckled quietly at his honesty. "Why?"

"It lifts my mood when you are near me."

"Wait. This has been you in a *good* mood?"

It was his turn to chuckle as he clutched her to him as though she were a stuffed animal. "I love you, starlight..."

When she couldn't say it back, her heart broke, just shattered in her chest, and she felt the tears form and run along her face into her hair. She leaned her head in to kiss his forehead. If he cared, she couldn't tell—he was already asleep.

She wrapped her arms around him and silently cried until sleep took her as well.

FOUR

Edu felt the chains biting into his flesh.

It was a memory he had long since sought to wipe from his mind. And for a very long time, he had succeeded.

But now, the nightmares he had banished to the recesses of his mind had returned. He was on his knees in a dungeon, hidden away from the blinding sunlight, save for one small window that cast a single square of light upon the floor. It never moved, for the sun did not track through the sky like it did on Earth. He could only tell the passage of time by its presence or absence as it slipped into eclipse.

His mask was gone. His arms were bound behind his back and attached to the wall behind him, and another chain was wound around his throat, tethering him to a heavy metal loop in the floor between his knees.

He knew he could not break it.

He had tried for thousands of years, after all.

The worn groove in the metal told him that yes, this was indeed the same ring of steel. He had put that dip in the metal with his constant thrashing. This was the same place.

A question occurred to him—which was the dream? This

agony, or the past five thousand years of a peace they had, if only by comparison?

He had not expected to wake. Not after Ylena had died and the King of All stood poised over him to remove his marks and send him to the void. But Lydia had intervened and seemingly spared his life and sent him to the pits of this hell instead.

He could not even straighten up, trapped as he was in this forced supplication. His arms were lashed to the wall behind him and his neck to the floor beneath him. He could not crack his aching bones or stretch his sore muscles in any way. It was meant to be an insult—it was meant to demean and degrade—and it worked. He knew that no matter how his body screamed to move, he would not be allowed such respite. The King of All knew how to break him.

The King of All knew how to destroy *anyone.* He always had. Now that he had regained the memories he had so willingly thrown away, he could see the comparisons between the man he knew as Aon and his true self. To call the King of All a sadist was to call a tree a flower. It was a gross understatement.

He was not the only one who dwelled within this dungeon suffering. While he could not lift his head well enough to see very much, he could hear the voices of those around him. Ini, and by her narration of things, Vjo, and Dtu were here as well but still unconscious. One voice hurt him more than most.

"You okay, Big Red?"

Evie.

The King of All had taken Evie. Kept her as a prisoner in the same cell as him. There was no doubt as to why he had done it and not put her in the cages with the other lesser-ranked and rebellious souls.

It's a reminder of who I still have to lose. It's a reminder that Ylena is gone, but there are others I must protect. He wants to tell me that he can still hurt me.

Edu nodded faintly. No, he was not okay. Not under any circumstances. But he did his best to lie.

"You sucked at lying b'fore I could see your cute face. Now, you're just awful."

His fib had gone about as far as he had expected it to. He huffed a laugh and lifted his head as far as he could to look at her where she sat, chained to the wall, still finding the ability to smile at him. Although it didn't quite reach her eyes.

"No wonder you all hid your faces. You're all crap at lying without them."

"Oh, wonderful child, we hid our faces for many reasons. Our desire to hide our motives is just one of them. But, yes, Edu is a miserable liar." Ini giggled.

If he turned his head as far as he could to one side, he could see her where she was chained by one wall.

It was dangerous keeping them all here in one cell—Dtu, Vjo, Ini, himself, and… Evie. Notable by her impending danger, Edu knew. But it took a great deal of power to keep their own gifts tamped down, captured and kept muted by the symbols etched upon every surface around them. There were not many cells that could hold a king or queen of Under, let alone four.

Ini battered and broken, spent beyond the point of healing her wounds, but not being allowed to die. And yet the glimmer hadn't left her unnaturally bright sapphire eyes. It never would, no matter how hard the King of All tried to remove it.

He found himself smiling faintly at the Queen of Fate, the only one the King of All could *not* break. And oh… how he had tried throughout the years. Edu could remember her screams in those years gone by.

For the King of All knew how to ply his favorite trade—torture. Never was there a creature more skilled in the art of twisting a body to his whim than him. Not in this world or any other. Even Edu had begged for mercy on more than one occasion. Even Edu's pride had fallen before knife and needle and screw. But not the Queen of Fate. She would only laugh when she had the air to do so.

Now that Edu could see Ini's face, he remembered it, with her almond-shaped sapphire eyes and stunning features. Dtu and Vjo were also stripped of their masks and their pride, lying on the ground or propped up against a wall. Neither of them had awoken from their slumber of death yet.

Dtu was going to be livid when he awoke. With the chains that bound them keeping their powers as shackled as their bodies, he couldn't take his wolf form and howl, which was some small favor. Edu did not know if his headache could withstand the noise.

The door to the chamber swung open. He turned his head and strained to see who had entered. His heart fell along with his hopes.

"Good evening, all."

"Hello, Aon!" Ini piped brightly, greeting the man in such a manner to purposefully needle him, both in her tone and her use of his false name. "A wonderful night, isn't it?"

The King of All ignored the attempt at goading him. "I see the dog and the spider have yet to wake. A shame. I wished to speak to you all at once. You will have to convey my message to them once they rise."

A whisper of fabric on the packed dirt floor was all the warning Edu had before a metal hand twisted into his hair and yanked his head backward painfully, not caring for the iron around his neck that made that position send stabbing pain through his shoulders. "I suppose you will be unable to convey any message at all, hm? How clever of my false self to take your tongue. I think I prefer you this way."

Edu glared and listed off a myriad of insults in his mind.

"I do not think you want to know what he said." Ini chimed in a sing-song, taunting tone. The psychic could hear his thoughts, and those had been particularly loud and colorful. "But know it was quite clever and unique."

The King of All laughed dryly and let go of Edu's hair, letting him drop his head back down to lessen the pain. "To think I would have expected gratitude that I allow you all to live. How foolish of me."

"I was wondering, why *do* you let us live?" Ini asked.

"If I were to kill you, the Ancients would replace you," the King replied simply.

"And what is the matter with that?" Ini tilted her head. "You have always despised us."

"That's easy," Evie said and tried to stretch her shoulders. His fiery redhead did not know when to keep her mouth shut. He loved that about her. When he had owned a tongue with which to speak, he was quite similarly matched in that trait. "'Cuz he doesn't want bunny to know we're down here. He was supposed to let us go, I'm betting."

The King of All merely turned to her and glowered dangerously. Evie, either blissfully unaware of the danger she was in, or more likely, belligerently uncaring, merely grinned back at him. "Oooh, look at that face! I'm right, I knew it. If you killed us, she'd know the jig was up when some other idiot walked around in that much red ink."

"Bunny? Ah, you mean Lydia." The King of All walked toward Evie.

Edu yanked on the chains viciously and knew what was to come by the tone in his voice. *No! Anyone but her.* Let him flay the skin from my flesh before touching her!

Hearing the racket, the King turned to look at Edu with an arched eyebrow. Sighing, he shook his head. "Old friend, always eager to think the worst of me. That is how we wind up in these *situations,* again and again." He gestured at the chains that bound him to the walls. "I was merely going to ask your lady friend two questions."

Edu growled low in his throat, sound more like Dtu than himself, he supposed.

"First." He turned to face Evie once more, folding his metal hand at his lower back. "If you believe yourself so clever, little one—then tell me, *why* are you my prisoners in the first place?"

"I—well—" Evie blinked. It was an obvious question with an obvious answer. Which meant it was an obvious trap. "Because we were trying to fight you."

"Precisely. You stood against me. When I gave you the choice to flee from this city and live your lives in peace as you see fit—*free* from my rule. From my presence. And you chose this, instead." His metal hand slowly curled into a fist. "So do tell me, *exactly,* why I would release you to allow you to do the same again?"

"Because you made a deal." Evie stood firm in her conviction. "I know Bunny, and I know she thinks we're free. She's going to be *pissed* when she finds out—"

"Yes. I am certain she will be. But by then, I will have earned her heart. Or been gifted it by the Ancients. We have all seen what she is willing to forgive for love." He shrugged dismissively. "A few politely imprisoned *traitors* should be nothing."

"Politely—" Evie cackled. "Look at what you've done to Ini! Look at how you've got poor Edu strung up like a Thanksgiving turkey—"

"I am not responsible for the pain our Queen of Fate has suffered. Those injuries were the result of her capture." The King of All glanced over his shoulder at Ini briefly.

Edu snorted in derision, though he suspected it was a true statement. The King of All had no reason to lie.

"As for this one?" The bastard gestured at Edu. "He is like an obstinate horse. He must be broken repeatedly to be reminded his place in the world, little one. Which brings me, quite neatly, to my second question." The King of All crouched down in front of Evie, tilting his head to the side slightly. "Why do you believe you are imprisoned in this room with the rest of the royals, little servant?"

Evie's haughty expression flickered for a brief second. "I—" Fear took over those yellow eyes of hers.

"Hm. You are clever. Too clever for the idiot child, but... to each their own, I suppose." The King of All straightened up. "Yes, little servant. Should he decide to be *troublesome,* each slice to your flesh will hurt him tenfold."

Edu snarled in rage and yanked on the chains again. But he could no more budge them than he could the whole of the temple itself. His futile redoubling of his efforts brought a laugh out of the other man.

"See? Even simply stating the obvious sends him into a fit of rage." The King of All chuckled as he walked back to Edu, standing near enough to the chains to taunt him. Close—but impossibly out of reach.

"Are you gonna hurt us?" Evie was no stranger to torture at the hands of the man in black. It was clear the memories of that torture were coming back to her, fast and hard.

"There was a time, long ago, when I would have amused myself with these creatures you see around you. When I would have pitted them against each other and made them bleed like puppets on strings playing out stories to pass the years." The King of All walked toward the door. "I... find myself no longer intrigued by such distractions. I have alternatives now."

"Because you have her." Ini tilted her head back, resting it against the wall. "Because of Lydia."

"I find she quiets my mind." A faint, sardonic smile twisted his expression. "How foolish of you all not to see what an opportunity for true peace you had in her existence. How you *squandered* it so."

"But now you are free. Aren't you glad for that?" Ini's smile was so saccharine it was mocking.

His jaw ticked. "If you are all obedient, none of you shall be harmed. If you are all *peaceful* in your captivity, you will be well-cared for. And your *guests* will be kept the same. Should you make matters troublesome? Then trouble shall follow. Do I make myself clear?"

Silence.

"Yes, *my King*," Ini sang back to him after the pause.

He left the room with a slam of the door.

Edu yanked against the chains one last time, uselessly, before hanging his head limp and letting out a long, ragged sigh.

"Hey—hey. It's okay, Red. We're going to be okay." Evie tried to console him. "At least he isn't torturing us."

Bless her heart. May it never fade. Yes, the King of All wasn't torturing them. Because nothing had gone wrong for him.

Yet.

FIVE

Lyon looked down at the form of his wife and felt his heart break in two. Bound in gold chains, held taut to the ground, she glared up at him with green, feline eyes burning into him like fire. There was such anger there it verged on hatred.

Oh, how he prayed that would not be so. How he begged the Ancients that this would not be how their story might end.

This cell was separate from the others. He knew that the King of All had defied Lydia's bargain and kept Edu and the rest imprisoned.

It was hard not to, hearing Edu hollering and raging against his captivity as he was in the dungeons. More grief upon the pyre that was Lyon's heart.

But it was the will of the King of All that they remain here. *They are alive.* His king had vowed not to take their lives, nor were they being tortured.

He was happy for that. When he had pressed him as to what they would do when Lydia found out—and it would be a when, he was certain—the King of All had shrugged and said it did not matter. He said her love for him would be solidified before such a thing came to pass. Dread at the statement had welled in him.

For there was nothing in this world that could make Lydia do anything she did not wish to do. And he doubted, even in their magnanimous wisdom—that even the Ancients were capable of such a task without great cost following in its wake.

But he was here for another matter. Not to reminisce on the dilemma of others. No, this was a far more personal problem he had come to solve.

Kamira hissed up at him angrily, baring her teeth but saying nothing. His wife. The love of his life. The one soul in this world who truly mattered to him above all else.

If he could not convince her to join them, he would be forced to let his creators break her as well. He knew his wife would far prefer death over such a thing.

What a horrid path lay before him. The only painless route was one that she would not walk. The other option was to drag her down it, and to do so would destroy her.

Or, as a third and far less desirable choice, he could grant her likely wish and kill her. In the process, he would destroy the only part of himself he valued.

His was not a life worth living without her.

Kamira could not shift forms, trapped and chained as she was. They were too tight for her to do much else but kneel upon the ground and glare.

Ah. And swear. The first words that left her lips toward him were a colorful stream of obscenities that spanned several languages. Damning him and painting detailed pictures of exactly what she would do to him the moment she became free.

Lyon sank to his knees in front of her and reached out to touch her, to cup her face in his hands.

"You are a lie! Do not lay your hands on me, you false-faced piece of shit!" Kamira snarled at him, baring her teeth as he came near. She hissed like a jungle cat and snapped at him, threatening to bite through his flesh should he dare go much farther.

"I am of my own mind, my tiger," Lyon urged quietly. "I am the man you know. The one you married."

"No. If that were so, you would not have betrayed us! You would not stand next to that *despot!*" Kamira yanked against the chains in a futile attempt to free herself.

"Betrayal? I am attempting to save you from your foolishness, and to kneel at the altar of our gods is the way things must be." Sadly, he shook his head. "Our king and I have the same goal—to serve the Ancients and their will."

"Which is what, exactly? What is it that they want?"

Lyon reached out, and though she jerked her head away at first, he managed to stroke his hand along her dark, braided hair without her attempting to bite him. "To see our world restored to its rightful way. What we have known has merely been a shadow, a broken semblance of what Under once was. Now that they have risen—now that our lord has taken the throne— we may work to reclaim our former glory."

"Bullshit," she snapped. "They want us all dead!"

"No, they do not wish you all dead." He frowned. "They wish you nothing but happiness."

"They want us *subservient*."

"If that is what guarantees your happiness, so be it."

"Then it is as good as the same thing! I will never bow to anyone, so kill me now. Not to Dtu, not to the Ancients, not to you, and certainly not to that cretin Aon!" Kamira yanked violently against the chains. It was as ineffective as it was during each of her previous attempts.

Lyon let out a dreary breath. "But you serve Dtu. You served the Ancients when they were captives. You were subject to their will all the same."

"Not like this. I was not a slave. I had choice."

"You only had the illusion of it."

Kamira yanked at the gold chains that bound her again. But his magic held strong. More so than his heart threatened to. "Kill me, Lyon. I will not live in this farce."

"I cannot live in this world without you. I will not let that come to pass."

"Then kill me, then end yourself. I do not care what you do once I am gone."

The words were cruel, and Lyon winced. She was angry and often said things he did not think she meant when she was in a rage. Yet they stung all the same. He remained silent.

"I will not kneel to them. I never will." Kamira spat down on the ground beside her.

"I will take you to their altar if I must. I fear for what will become of you, the moment they take your mind unwillingly. You must accept them with open arms, lest they take what parts of you they must to see you made right. Please, my love, do not make me do this."

"Let me go, Lyon. Unchain me, and you won't have to do anything." The dark twinge to her voice spoke volumes of what she meant to do if freed. "Unchain me, and you'll never have to worry about what they'll do to my mind."

"Sadly, I cannot. Our king has decreed that if I cannot turn you, I must force the matter. I cannot kill you. It is beyond my ability to do such a thing."

"You'd rather they burn out my mind? Like they did to Aon and to you?" Kamira howled in laughter. "That is no kind of love. That is selfishness. That is only you, wishing to save yourself the grief of my passing."

"That is not true."

"To rid me of myself is a fate far crueler than death! No, stupid mosquito. Hear me and hear me now. I will die before I let you take me to that forsaken altar and let them destroy my mind. My free will is sacrosanct."

"You say this now. I can only pray that I may change your mind."

"You will have a long wait."

"I am good at waiting." Lyon shifted and sat down on the ground, leaning up on the wall next to her. If she struck him, he would not defend himself. Sensing this, and not one to take an easy shot at him, Kamira grumbled and lay down with her head in his lap. He smiled and rested his hand on her shoulder.

They fell into silence for many minutes. It allowed his mind to wander and trace the steps they had taken that brought them to where they were.

"Do you remember the first time we met?" Lyon said down to his wife.

"Of course." She smiled, and her eyes drifted shut. "It was the day of your descent to Under. I stood in the crowd and watched the shrinking masses of terrified souls. All but one cowered in fear. All but you. A towering thing, sticking out from the crowd like a sore thumb. Dirty and mortal, weary and worn, but unafraid. You looked up at the figureheads of the Ancients with nothing but awe in your eyes. You were so placid, even then. Your old age has merely made it worse."

"You tripped me as I walked toward the pool."

Kamira snickered. "I wanted to see you wear an expression. I wanted to see if the tree would make a sound as he fell."

Lyon smiled. "I returned from the pool as Rxa's elder."

"And I tripped you on the way out as well." Her face was a fiendish grin, happily remembering the mischief.

"I thought you despised me."

"You have always been too sensitive. Too quick to dismiss a woman's interest."

"You do not express affection in any semblance of a normal way, my love."

"It is not my fault that I needed to resort to a more direct approach to get your attention."

Lyon chuckled. "Is that what you call what happened that fateful day?"

"Mmh, I had to get through to you somehow."

They fell into silence once more, and Lyon shut his eyes, letting his memory wander.

The Great War.

That was what the others were calling what lay out before him. It did little to encapsulate the carnage and the needless suffering and loss of life that accompanied such a trite name. For twenty years, the Houses had been at war. For twenty years, it showed no sign of slowing.

In all honesty, this was a war between two people, Aon and Edu. As it always was. Yet, here Lyon stood, clothed in white—a laughable choice for a field whose slick and muddy surface had been tinged and darkened crimson with blood—fighting for his king. Battling at the command of Rxa to lead this battalion to fight.

Lyon's boots were already covered in the substance that coated the ground, a slurry of gore, and dirt, and rain. Trudging through the already spent forces of a previous fight, his shoes sucked into the muck and mire as he walked. This was the remainder of a battle his side had already lost.

One field over was another battle, already raging on. Lyon was to approach from the flank, and to do so, he must pass through this field to the other side of a small forest that split the previously grassy areas apart. The blades of green were long since trodden away by the beasts and men who fought and died in this place. Lyon and his priests could have flown there, but their arrival was intended to be a surprise.

They were to sneak—as stealthy as a battalion could—behind the lines of those on the neighboring field. Those carrying the banner of Qta would not expect them. It was simple, risky, and would likely mean the death of many. But their hope was

*not to destroy the legions of dreamers, but merely distract them
long enough to give Aon and Vjo's forces an advantage.*

*Lyon and his fifty-or-so soldiers who walked behind him
made it to the edge of the wooded glade that separated the two
fields after weaving their way through the gore and death. The
stretch of forest was a few hundred feet wide. It was not until
they had made it halfway, surrounded by the woods on all sides,
that the trouble began.*

And it started with a howl.

Before their world knew the truth of the battle, when the
two sides waged against each other and had not recognized Aon
as the true instigator. In those early days, the Houses were split
into two factions. On one side raged the House of Moons, of
Flames, and of Dreams. On the other, Shadows, Words, and
Blood stood shoulder to shoulder. As always, the House of Fate
remained neutral.

It was then that they had stood opposite each other on the
field of battle. He had been sent with a battalion to take the
House of Dreams by surprise. But they had been betrayed
already by Aon, and his position had been given up to Dtu and
his ilk. Unbeknownst to him at the time, Kamira had readily
volunteered to be the one to hunt him down and end his life.

*Crimson dripped from his golden talons as he prepared himself
for what was likely to be his last fight. The creatures were
prowling low to the ground, circling and snarling at him, but
they did not attack. Why? The monster who had advanced
upon him was sniffing the air and let out a low, quiet growl of
discontentment.*

Ah. Their pack alpha had not yet arrived...

*A woman approached, and he knew her well. Kamira,
Regent of the House of Moons, Elder to Dtu. Lyon sighed
darkly. This would not go well for him. While he had never*

matched tooth and claw against the tigress, she was known to be a fighter fierce enough to nearly pin her own King, let alone a priest like him.

Kamira's teeth flashed white in the darkness as she grinned at him. Her canines, upper and lower both, slightly too long to be human. But who was Lyon to judge, he who could extend his fangs on command to feed upon others?

"Leave," Kamira commanded the other shifters. They snuffled and shifted uncomfortably, clearly unwilling to leave their current alpha alone with a living foe. "Go!" she said, her voice almost overcome with a roar as she did, both a human sound and one that was decidedly not, mixed together in equal parts.

The other creatures turned and left, slinking off into the darkness. That left Lyon... and Kamira.

He suspected he was about to die.

Lyon lifted his golden claws in preparation for her attack. "A fair fight. I appreciate your sense of honor, my lady."

Kamira laughed and shook her head, stepping into the clearing. "A fair fight, boy? Hardly. I merely wanted to render you to pieces myself." Kamira was barely clothed, as she always wished to be, merely wearing a loincloth and jewelry. It did not trouble him, more than being immensely distracting. Kamira was—had always been, if he admitted it—a source of interruption in his thoughts.

The shifter was barefoot, her skin covered in dirt and blood, and she was uncaring for either, it seemed. She was a force of nature. The woman was the raw, untamed wild. Lyon had always found that entrancing—hypnotizing, even. It was so far from his own cold, calculating, and reserved demeanor that it shone to him like the stars in the night sky.

It seemed he was not the only one enamored, if in a strange way. The woman grinned at him, feral and unkind. "I have long since wondered what you taste like."

With that, her form changed, grew and warped, the sound

of snapping bones and ripping flesh as her body painfully recon-figured into that of the Tigress that was so feared in battle. Some ten feet tall, muscular, and terrifying. Claws and teeth like iron daggers, and far faster than even her king might claim.

Lyon was proud to hold his own against her as the fight began. She was a fiend. Strong, unflinching, unwavering in her single-minded conviction to kill him. Lyon found himself impressed with her, even with his high expectations.

Lyon's golden claws found their way into her flesh from time to time, digging in and attempting to slow her down. But the wounds seemed only to encourage her and to inflame her will to fight. He was using every trick he owned, exploding into bats and reforming when she might land a killing blow or disappearing and reappearing as unpredictably as he could manage.

It did not last for very long. Five or ten minutes of a fight at most, which was four or nine minutes longer than Lyon expected himself to survive, to be fair. That was what ran through his mind as the paw of the massive tiger slammed his head into a tree, and his world went dark.

When he woke, he found himself sitting on the ground, back up against the tree that he believed his head had impacted so violently a moment prior. He went to move and hissed in pain. His hands were not free, and whatever held them in place was unkind. He looked up with a deep sigh as he realized his hands were pinned to the tree with a white-hilted dagger shoved through each palm.

The daggers were from the bodies of some of his own fallen comrades. How adorable. Kamira was crouched at his feet, watching him intently, her eyes narrowed as if she were trying to discern some manner of a deep secret by staring alone. There was a confusion on her face that he did not understand.

"I am a prisoner, then?" he asked.

"Yes," she confirmed. But something else seemed to be troubling her. Lyon dared not ask what it was. The side of his face felt wet underneath the mask that covered it, and he knew it was blood that traveled below the porcelain surface.

"Will you take me to Dtu or merely eat me here?" Lyon asked, again curious at her odd silence and her inexplicable expression as if she were debating something. Whatever it was she was turning over in her mind seemed to be surprising and confusing to her.

Kamira's expression shifted as her internal debate seemed to suddenly be over. She stood, and Lyon tried not to make a reaction as she stepped to straddle him and knelt to sit atop his lap. Kamira tilted her head to observe him thoughtfully like some wild beast might do. *"Neither. Not yet, anyway,"* she said with the hint of a smile.

"Do you intend to torture me?" Lyon asked as a follow-up, perplexed as to why the nearly nude woman was now sitting on him.

"Not yet, anyway," she repeated herself with a bright and playful grin. She reached up for Lyon's mask, and Lyon pulled in a startled breath. He pulled his head back from her as best he could. But pinned and nailed to the tree as he was, there was nothing he could do. She lifted the mask from his face and let out a quiet *"hmh"* in her throat. It became clear what she was after as she leaned into him.

Lyon could only gasp as he felt her hot tongue slide up his neck, trailing the line of blood that was oozing slowly down his face. She traced it up over his marks, and Lyon could not help but shudder at the sensation. He squeezed his eyes tight.

She laughed, and Lyon jolted as the shifter ran her hands along his chest, skimming up the buttons of his white shirt. She toyed with the one at his neck before unfastening it.

What was she doing?

"Just as delicious as I had hoped," Kamira murmured. A

second button was undone now, and he watched her with a slight furrowing of his brow. What meant she by doing this?

She was not looking at him, though, instead amused thoroughly with the slow, careful undoing of his shirt. Perhaps she meant to take her pound of flesh, to slice out a portion of his chest and eat it whole.

They fell into silence as she went about slowly working the third, then fourth, then the final button of his shirt. She pulled where it had been tucked away into his pants and sat back to look down at his pale skin and saw the few scars that marked him there.

Her fingers traced one along his side, and he could not help but twitch in response. That brought out another thoughtful noise from Kamira, and Lyon swore at himself silently for his instinctual reaction. The shifter chuckled at him and tutted in her throat as she slid her body closer to his on his lap, leaning up to hover her face by his, as she let her hand slowly glide over his exposed chest.

"Kamira, I—" As he began to speak, she shifted her weight on him, and the feeling of her body atop his made him pause once more. It was like the skip of a stone across the surface of a pond, his thoughts hitching for a moment. But he finally managed to force out his words. "If you are to devour my flesh or to tear me apart before delivering" —he hitched again at the feeling of her body so close to his— "me to your king, I ask that you get on with it."

"Mmh, do not be so hasty..." Kamira leaned down closer, and Lyon could not help but let his expression betray him as she slid her body down his. Her nearness was utterly surprising to him. The feeling of her hot skin on his cold chest was enough to make him jolt beneath her. He had expected pain—pain he was sure was still to come.

For would it not be fitting for her to touch him so, only to take the hand that lingered at his side and rip out a kidney?

"Well, so hasty in such a regard," she said thoughtfully. Her words were a deep purr in her throat. Lyon knew not what to do in the face of what was atop him, what was right before him.

He knew not what to do when her lips met his.

All he could do was sit in awe of the desire that suddenly raged in him like a bonfire, wild and free as the object of its source. This beautiful, untamable creature before him.

She had kissed him. As she took him as her lover, he knew that while she had not ripped it out of his chest, she had taken possession of his heart all the same.

He had loved her from that moment onward, and not once had he ever looked back.

He belonged to the woman in his lap, the one who was lounging on him like the animal she so often resembled. Peaceful, but with a crease in her brow as a reminder that all was not well. This was not a summer night beneath the moons; she was chained and shackled as his prisoner.

Lyon pulled in a long breath, held it, and slowly released it. "I am so very sorry, my love."

"I know you are. You are always sorry. I suppose I only wish to know what you will do about it. You are in charge of my fate now."

"I must convince you to surrender to the Ancients."

"You will have an easier time convincing that bench to sing opera."

"Then I suppose I will have to fetch my metronome."

When Kamira began to laugh, he joined her. As they trailed off into silence, he looked down at her and felt the weight of his years for the first time in many. "Do you wish me to leave?"

"No, stay." Kamira snuggled into him. "You know how I despise to be alone."

"I thought perhaps I was unwelcome."

"You will never be unwelcome. No matter what they may

do to you or what form you may take. You have always been my Priest, my great white bat, and not even the Ancients can change what is fact."

Lyon smiled and leaned his head back against the wall and let his eyes drift shut. This was an insuperable condition. Chaos would come, and their story would not end well, he suspected. But for this moment, for this brief time, he would take his peace where he could have it. For in the end, memories like this would be all he had left.

SIX

Lydia had seen the throne room in her dreams but seeing it in the waking world was another thing altogether. It was terrifying and awe-inspiring all in the same moment. The polished stone floor and the carved surfaces made for a dizzying array of colors and detail. It looked like an Ancient Egyptian palace—if H.R. Giger had gotten to it first.

It was also *huge.* It stretched up easily a hundred feet. She felt so very tiny at the base of the enormous stone columns.

Depictions of monsters and of people being torn to pieces were so prevalent it was almost hard to see. It was like looking at a coral reef and trying to find each individual nook and cranny.

To the left and right of the main pathway in the center were huge statues, twisting figures of the Ancients. From their mouths poured the glowing red liquid that she had grown to hate so very much. Their blood turned the statues into grotesque fountains. They poured into moats that ran along either side, framing what sat at the head of the room. There, with its back to an opening out to the blazing sky behind, was a throne at the top of the stairs carved from black onyx.

There were no fires burning to light the chamber. There

wasn't a need. Between the glow of the blood and the bright sun pouring in from where the room was open to the city outside, there was plenty of light to see. It did succeed in casting the room in stark shadows, cutting sharp lines across the floor. It was imposing. She suspected that was very much the point.

Men and women in mixes of black and white were already gathered at the edges of the room when they appeared. Noa's arm had been wrapped around her waist, pressing her up against his bare chest, the moment they arrived.

She had tried desperately not to blush and feel ashamed about how prominent a message that sent to everyone else. With his other hand, he tilted her head up to look at him. There was no expression on his face—nothing but a cold darkness. But as he looked at her, she saw the ice melt just at the edges of his eyes. "Do not mind them," he said quietly, his words meant only for her. "They do not matter."

"What'm I supposed to do?"

"Well, as you are not yet my queen, I do not have a throne for you upon this dais. Forgive me." He let out a thoughtful hum. "I suppose if I asked you to sit at my feet, you would say no."

"Fuck you."

"Later, perhaps. I do have business to attend. Although... it would put on quite a show."

Damn this man's version of humor. That almost made her laugh. Nudging away from him, she rolled her eyes.

For a moment, there was a ghost of a smile upon his face. "Such pride. Very well, you may then go stand there, with Lyon." He gestured, and she glanced over to see the Priest standing just to the side and in front of the fountains of blood. He looked as though he were a high-ranking lord of some awful medieval court. She supposed that was exactly what this was.

As she went to leave, his arm tugged her back into place. "Kiss me before you go."

"I—" She blinked. Her cheeks went warm. It was a show of fealty. But it also just... sounded like he wanted a kiss. But in front of *everyone* after everything that had just happened? It felt weird.

Her hesitation lasted just a second too long.

With a faint, disappointed breath, he nodded. "Very well. Go."

Feeling very much like she was left on the side of the tracks watching a train rush by, she swallowed the rock in her throat and went to go stand by Lyon. Even if he was mind-warped and someone she might not be able to trust... any port in a storm. A friend was a friend.

Watching her approach, Lyon bowed at the waist. "My lady."

A friend was a friend.

But they hadn't exactly left things in a great place last time they'd met.

Lydia rounded back and slapped him. Hard. The *crack* echoed loudly in the chamber. Lyon's face was snapped to the side with the blow, and it was a long moment before he turned to look back at her, stunned. "We're going to have words later, *fuck-face.*"

"I..." Lyon trailed off, confused and still in shock from her anger. Finally, he seemed to remember why she might be upset with him, and he looked down at the ground as if in shame. "I am sorry for my previous actions. I was trying to spare you further strife."

"You *think* you were." Lydia let out an angry sigh. "Is Kamira okay?"

"She is quite fine. Very angry but unharmed." Lyon furrowed his brow. "Do you think I would hurt her?"

"I don't know what to think about any of you sons of bitches right now." She took her place standing beside him. There was a column at her back, and she leaned against it and folded her arms across her chest. At least she could sulk. And she was in a sulking mood.

"That is understandable. Are you all right, Ms. Lydia?" He kept his voice low, just between the two of them.

"I'm fine."

Her shitty lie didn't fly with him. "Well…"

She cut him off before he could get any further. "How, exactly," she bit in little more than an angry whisper, "am I supposed to take that the man I love and one of my only friends in this stupid world have been brainwashed by super-monsters that want nothing more than to watch me dance on the end of their little sick puppet strings?"

Lyon was silent and watched her, his expression frozen in an utter inability to come up with anything to say. He was a deer caught in the headlights, unsure what to do with her words. "I am sorry," was all he finally managed.

"Whatever."

"We are not unwell. This is how we should be. This is all by the design of the Ancients. This is how the world was meant to exist."

"You're wrong. I hate it. And I hate them."

"You rail against the very nature of the creatures who have made you what you are. You fight against the will of existence itself."

"Don't worry, it won't last." Lydia was bitter. And when she was bitter, she got petty. "Soon, when I fail to love him, I'll have my mind raped out of my head, and I'll be left a broken husk of a woman. But I'll love them, and I'll love that man there. Don't worry your pretty little head about it. This is all by their *design,* after all."

It was as if she had struck him again, the way he cringed and turned his face away. Their conversation fell into silence, and she was happy for it. She wasn't in the mood to talk anymore.

"Let us begin." Noa's voice broke through the silence, and

court was now in session. It broke her out of her dour thoughts. She looked up at him, and she had to admit that... damn, he looked beautiful sitting on that throne. He looked like that was where he belonged. It suited him, and the black stone of the massive chair reflected his expression.

If she thought he was intimidating before, now he was terrifying. This man was older than recorded history. Older than when people *named things*. He was a force of nature, and she felt so very small, so very tiny in comparison, and she sank back against the column and wished she could just disappear.

Suddenly, she realized how gentle he had been with her so far. How the look in his eyes had been softer around her. *This* was his normal self. *This* man was a god incarnate, an avatar to the Ancients. Unflinching. Immovable.

The proceedings of court began. After the first hour and a half or so of listening to the grandstanding, the high-flying rambling and the long, pompous introductions, Lydia came to a single conclusion.

Court was boring.

It was all talks of who-lived-where and why that was a problem. A guy did a thing, and now they wanted Noa to fix it. Somebody had a fight in the market about who had the right to sell stuff at this spot. So on, and so forth.

If Noa shared in her boredom, he never once showed it.

He was their Solomon, and they needed his ruling, especially in a world that had recently been picked up and shaken like a damn Etch-A-Sketch. Nobody had a baby for him to threaten to cut in half, so at least there was that. Everyone was confused and trying to find their new way of life in a world that had been entirely rewritten.

She sympathized.

It wasn't until well into the second hour that a man was dragged into the room. His arms were shackled behind his back. He wore no mask, like everyone else, but a red mark covered about a third of his face. He was built like a gladiator, and he was fighting as best he could. Sadly, he wasn't getting very far. Several men in white were dragging him forcefully into the room. He had short, dirty-blond hair, and it was matted crimson with blood. They hadn't been gentle with him, and by the looks of things, he hadn't made it easy for them either.

Noa sat forward just slightly, intrigued by what he saw before him. He wasn't alone—everyone seemed excited by the new development of the man with red ink.

Lyon's priests dumped the man roughly onto his knees. The prisoner struggled, trying to stand back up, very clearly not wanting to kneel before the King of All. A swift kick to the back of his legs and a punch to the head and the man gave up the argument.

"A prisoner," Noa's voice carried easily throughout the room. "Why, pray tell, has he been brought before me? I exiled all those from the House of Flames to the farthest skies. To reenter my acropolis is to accept the punishment of death."

"Yes, my lord," one of the men in white responded. "We caught him sneaking back into the city this morning."

"That is plain to see. But why have you not merely killed him? Why do you waste my time?" Noa seemed both annoyed with the vampires and intrigued by the prisoner at the same time.

"We thought—perhaps—" The man in white who had spoken was suddenly very unsure of himself. "Forgive us, our King. Murder was banned from our world prior, and—"

"You hesitate to send a soul to the void. Yes, yes. Very well." Noa sighed tiredly. "Tell me, prisoner. Are you an insurrectionist? An assassin? Who has sent you here?"

"No one! I came on my own." The prisoner looked up, trying to meet Noa's eyes, and received another punch in the head for it. "I came under no orders from anyone." The man, despite his build and look, was shaking in fear.

The King of All stood from his throne and walked down the stairs toward the man on his knees, seemingly to get a closer look. The black fabric he wore around his waist whispered on the stone floor. When the warlock reached the blond prisoner, he reached out his metal gauntlet and placed a single claw against the middle of his forehead and used the point to tilt the man's head back to look up at him.

"Then you are merely a fool. It matters not, for the cost is the same. Pray to the Ancients that they may receive your soul." He lifted his claw to strike—to tear the man's face open and rip his soulmarks off his flesh. He meant to execute the man here and now.

Before Lydia even realized what she'd done, she was standing at his side, her hand clasped around his metal wrist. She had stopped his blow. He looked down at her, astonished and curious all at once. Surprisingly, there wasn't any anger in his expression—not yet, anyway.

"Wait," she said, then added as an afterthought, "please." He was still the King. She didn't know how far she could toe the line with him.

"Whatever for?"

"I have a problem with pointless death."

"His death is not a waste. He has broken my laws and therefore must suffer for it. If you would have a piteous heart for him, you will need a better reason. Try again." Still, his voice was calm. Gentle, almost. He was giving her a chance.

She paused, and he let her have some time to think up a better excuse. "You don't know why he broke into the city. It'd be worth knowing before he dies."

"In a pathetic attempt to kill me or to otherwise undermine my power. What other reason could there be?" He shrugged and pulled his wrist from her hand.

Lydia looked down at the man on his knees and saw the fear etched into his face. The worry and agony in his eyes. For someone from the House of Flames, it wasn't a normal expression. "Someone on a revenge mission wouldn't be afraid to die. It'd be a suicide run. Look at him. If he were here to try to hurt you, he'd accept death as the inevitable outcome. Does he look ready to die for a cause?"

Noa watched her for a long moment in silence before doing as she asked. Looking down at the man with the red marks across his face, his eyebrow arched. "Hm. Very well. If you wish to know why he has come back into this city and defied my law, you may ask him."

He backed away and gestured for her to take command of the situation. If she was going to impose herself into his proceedings, she was going to have to be the one to follow through. Fine. Taking a breath, holding it for a moment, she let it out in a whoosh.

Turning to the prisoner, she knelt in front of the man. He was taller than she was—it wasn't hard to be—but he was hunched over, his shoulders sagging. Everything about his posture screamed that he was afraid to die. "What's your name?"

"Waldur," he answered weakly.

"It's nice to meet you, Waldur. I wish it were under better circumstances." At her words, the man shuddered, his face contorting in momentary fear. It was clear he was trying to tamp it down and to keep his panic under control, but it was beginning to break through. The man was doing his best to be brave. But it was very clear he didn't want to die. There was something here worth staying for.

"Why'd you come back here? Why'd you try to sneak into the city?" she asked and put her hand on his shoulder. She tried to reassure him, but he flinched at her touch. *I'm the enemy in his eyes,* she reminded herself. *I'm the King's pet. Of course, he thinks I'm going to hurt him.* When Waldur didn't answer, she pressed. "Please, answer me."

"What does it matter?" He was trying to be as tough as he could muster. But he was shaking under her hand, and his eyes looked damp. It was a bad show.

Shifting closer to him, she placed her hand on the back of his neck. "I'm trying to help you. I know you don't trust me. I wouldn't trust me if I were you either. But I can't do anything if you don't talk to me."

"You are a traitor. You are here with *him*." Waldur snapped at her—lashing out at her in his panic. "Why should I speak to you?"

"Because right now, she is the only reason you still breathe air, ungrateful cur," Noa's voice came from behind her. The man looming behind her growled. "Make your point quickly, my dear. I tire of this man's existence."

Taking a breath, she tried again. "Waldur. Help me help you. Why're you here? Please, tell me."

He swallowed thickly but stayed silent.

She tried again. "You've got nothing to lose. You really don't."

"I have my dignity," he said through clenched teeth.

"I can remove that easily enough," Noa interjected.

She was running out of time. She knew she only had one more chance to get the man to talk to her. If she couldn't, he'd be dead. The House of Flames wasn't the kind to send assassins. They didn't do subterfuge or subtlety. They wouldn't send one man on his own into enemy territory. Edu would've never let someone charge into battle alone. That option was crap, and she instantly ruled it out.

The man was afraid to die. But why? He must have known coming into the city could mean death. She didn't think those who wore red felt fear for something they seemed to worship, death for a rightful cause.

She only had one theory to go on, only one option she could try. If she was wrong, Waldur would die a second later.

"What House are they from? Shadows or Blood?"

That made the man finally meet her gaze. Terror was flickering in his eyes. She was right. She had guessed correctly... he wasn't afraid for himself. She knew that look. She had seen Aon with it a moment before the Ancients had come for him.

Waldur was afraid for *someone else.* His eyes shone as he fought back tears. But with his hands bound behind his back, there was nothing he could do to stop them. They ran down his cheeks, and she reached up to brush them off gently.

"Please," he begged. "Please don't. They'll be—he'll kill them too."

She glanced up at Noa, who was now watching them both with rapt interest, an unreadable expression on his face. She looked back to Waldur. "You came back into the city because you love someone. You're risking your life to be with them. How long've you been together?"

The man's shoulders sagged as he realized his cover was blown, and it was too late. "Two hundred and twelve years," he answered, defeated. Now, he had the tone of a man at his own funeral, looking down at his own pale corpse in a casket. He accepted his inevitable death, now that his secret was revealed.

"Which House, boy? My future queen asked you a question."

Waldur cringed and hesitated.

"She has the patience to put up with your reluctant tongue. I do not."

"He hails from your House of Shadows," Waldur finally answered.

"Give me his name. He deserves to stand watch at your execution." Noa's voice was cold, detached. Empty.

Lydia got up from where she knelt and turned to the King of All. "No. You can't."

Noa canted his head back slightly as he watched her. "There is nothing I cannot do."

He had never been challenged in all his life, had he? Not *really*. Not in any way that mattered. Either no one dared, or they were the antics of children to him.

But this?

This mattered.

Taking a breath, she stepped up to him. He seemed surprised at her nearness, as she narrowed the distance between them down to a few inches. She lowered her voice. "Let him go. He's not here out of revenge. He's not here to hurt you. He's here because he loves somebody from your own House. This Armageddon ruined their lives together. He was sneaking in to be with them."

"The Houses are all but fallen. This worm was exiled. Such was my word. And my word is law." His tone was still inarguable. As he moved to walk away from her, she reached out and caught his wrist and pulled him back to her.

There was a flicker of something like anger in those cold eyes. She was about to go too far. He was being *very* patient with her, and she knew it.

This was a dangerous game. And he could gut her like a fish at any point he wanted to. But she might be the only voice of reason in this madhouse. "He did this out of love. For someone who was in your *former* House. Consider the kinds of barriers they had to cross for that to happen. You told me once that love, above all else, was sacrosanct. That everything else was pointless. You've tried to destroy this world how many times in search of it? And you're going to destroy it now because he's annoying you?"

Noa fell silent for a long moment. "You would have me grant pardon for a broken law for that he did it out of love."

She paused. "Yeah. I would."

He stepped back into her, narrowing the distance between them, daring her to retreat. Daring her to shrink away from him in fear.

She held her ground. But just barely.

He lifted his clawed hand, and she flinched, but he used the tip of his pointer finger under her chin to tip her head up to him. "Nothing in my world ever comes for free. What will you give me in exchange for his life?"

She searched those spilled-ink eyes of his for a long moment before she had her idea.

Reaching up, she took his face in her hands, resting her palms along his jawline, and going onto her tiptoes, she kissed him. His hands went to her hips, grasping her as he leaned into the embrace. She held it for a long time, for two reasons.

One, it was supposed to be a public display of her allegiance with him.

And two... hell, she didn't want to stop. Embracing Aon had always been like kissing wildfire. Dangerous, hungry, brutal, and raw. His passion more than made up for what might have been little to no experience in the act.

Kissing Noa was different. This man's touch left her chasing his lips for more and lit a spark deep inside her that was so intense it almost scared her. It taught her how dangerous Aon might have been, if he had been more practiced in the art. But hidden away under a mask, Aon hadn't kissed anyone in five thousand years. Noa, clearly, had no such problem.

When she finally broke away and went back down from her tiptoes, she was out of breath and her heart was pounding in her ears. He looked caught in a dream. His eyes were shut, and his features were smooth. The dour and angry expression he had worn a few moments ago was gone. He looked... content. Just as he still had a power over her, it looked like she did over him as well.

As he opened his eyes, the softness faded and returned to the icy visage. But he smiled down at her, and there was a faint gentleness in his eyes. "Very well," he muttered, words meant only for her. "I accept."

Noa whirled from her suddenly, turning back toward the throne. He climbed up the stairs onto the dais and sat back down. "I have decided," he began slowly and flashed a grin down at her, "to let this cretin live. That is, of course, if he swears himself to me and bows before the throne of the rightful King of All."

Waldur lowered his head, curling down over his knees until he was doubled over. He was clearly struggling with the choice before him. Die, or pledge loyalty to the King of All.

She sympathized, she really did. But she had done all she could.

"Well? What will it be, boy?" Noa was once more the force of nature.

"I am your servant, my King," Waldur said, even as tears rolled down his red-inked cheeks. He had given up his loyalty for love. Lydia cringed and looked away. No, he had *sacrificed* himself for love.

Just as Aon had for her.

Just as the Ancients threatened to do to her.

Is that all love really is, in the end? Sacrifice?

Suddenly, she realized this was probably all a show put on by the Ancients, just for her. Just to remind her the game she was playing. She had no doubt that Waldur was here on his knees in the throne room by their design. The Ancients were puppeteers, masterminding the world around her on strings and yanking her about to watch her dance.

He's from the House of Flames. He's one of Edu's own. Kneeling to either Aon or Noa is the last thing in the world anyone from that House would ever want to do. But he's here, doing just that—not for the fear of death—but for love. Lydia found a spot on the wall and stared at it, anything to keep from making eye contact with anyone.

Damn them back into that stupid blood puddle they had crawled out of. She turned her head to glare at one of the statues pouring that glowing red liquid into the inset pools on either side of the throne room. She knew they were here, flickering in the shadows. They weren't ever far away from their "Only Son," and this was their temple.

Fuck you, she swore at them silently and hoped they could hear her. *Fuck you and the bug-horses you rode in on.*

"Well," the King of All interrupted her thoughts, "then, it is settled. Welcome to my acropolis, Waldur. You may live here in peace. I will ask nothing of you but your loyalty, as is all that I ask of any who serve me. Release him."

One of the two men in white stepped forward and undid the cuffs that kept Waldur's hands shackled behind his back. He clutched his hands to his chest, afraid to stand.

"Do not waste this opportunity I have granted you," Noa continued. "Now, do get up and leave this place before I change my mind." His tone shifted to a dark growl at the end. It was enough to inspire Waldur to jump to his feet.

The man in the red ink turned to flee the throne room, but Noa raised his hand. "Ah, ah—are you not forgetting something?" Waldur froze with his back to Lydia and the throne, unsure as to what to do, as Noa finished his sentence. "You have neglected to thank my queen for sparing your life."

She gritted her teeth and resisted the urge to turn around and scream at Noa that she was not, under any circumstances, his queen—and that what he was doing right now was not acceptable. But she wasn't in any place to argue. He had just spared this man's life, as she asked him to. If she did a single thing to piss Noa off now, she knew he'd revoke the offer.

So, she swallowed it down. Fine. What did it matter if a smattering of assholes in black and white believed she was Noa's loyal queen? It was nonsense—she knew the truth, and so did he. Let him have his public persona. It seemed to matter to him.

Waldur turned his head just barely toward her. "Thank you," he muttered, half under his breath. Just loud enough to make an effort, without actually meaning it. "My—my queen." And with that, he quickly hurried out of the throne room.

Why did his words feel like such a punch to the stomach? He had said it with such fear, like she was no better than the man on the throne behind her. He believed she was just like him. It nauseated her, and she tried not to bury her head in her hands. She wished she could follow his hasty retreat, but she was very much stuck here.

"We are adjourned until tomorrow." Noa rose from the black obsidian throne. "I have heard enough for one day. Come, *my queen*." He held his hand out to her.

How many times would he do that? Hold his palm out, knowing she had no choice but to take it? The kiss she had paid him was only a gesture of what he had asked for, which was her public allegiance to him. The session in court had begun with him calling her his future queen. Now, he considered it sealed.

It was pointless to fight him right now, like this, in front of everybody. This wasn't how she was going to win. *Pick your battles*, she reminded herself as she looked up at his impassive yet somehow triumphant face. With a heavy sigh, she crossed the floor and went up the stairs to stand beside him. She placed her hand in his, and he pulled her close to his side and put an arm around her waist.

"I hate you sometimes," she muttered to him under her breath.

He burst out in a laugh and, smiling, leaned down and placed a kiss to her forehead. "I know."

In a rush of black smoke, the throne room disappeared.

SEVEN

The moment they reappeared, Lydia was slammed up against a stone column. She squeaked and pushed her hands against Noa's chest, trying to slow him down. He was going to hurt her. He must be furious that she overstepped in his court, called him out, and forced him to spare that man's life. *He's going to gut me like a fish. He's going to stitch my eyes shut or cut off my limbs and—*

Noa picked her up by the hips, sliding her up the stone. Once she was eye level with him, his human hand snapped around her throat.

"Wait, please—" She waited for his metal hand to dig into her ribs. Probably pull one out, as he had done to Ylena. "I'm sorry! I couldn't let you—I didn't—"

His lips on hers cut her off. She let out a startled *"mmh!"* against him as he crashed over her like a tidal wave. He kissed her as if he would devour her soul by doing it. Before she realized she had moved, her arms were around his neck, and her legs clasped his waist. Clinging onto him for dear life like she was drowning at sea. Only he was both her raft and her ocean, saving her and killing her, all at once.

He really is a force of nature.

When he broke the kiss, she was gasping for air, her heart beating viciously in her ears. He rested his forehead against hers and let out a low, breathy chuckle. His own chest was heaving. "That is what I wished to do to you just now in front of all those fools."

She couldn't help herself. She let her hand trace over his cheek, stroking it. His spilled-ink eyes slipped shut at her touch, and he let out a small grunt at her gesture. It inspired her to keep going, and she let her thumb trace back and forth over his face gently. When she could breathe, she finally found words. "I'm glad you didn't. That would've been awkward."

"I do not care."

"I know you don't, but I do. I don't want to look Lyon in the eyes after you fucked me up against a column in front of him."

He flashed a grin and leaned in to kiss her again. This time, it was slower. Taking his time, savoring her—far less lost in the heat of the moment than he had been a second prior. But it left her no less out of breath when he was done. When he broke the kiss, she chased his lips for a third. He chuckled at her silent admission that she wanted him.

He indulged her for a long time before breaking the embrace once more. "Perhaps he would wish to join in."

"No. No, thanks. He's a nice guy, but... I'll pass." She felt heady and a little detached. He had that effect on her. "Besides, I thought you weren't the type to share."

"I am not. But I wondered if you were, now that you have come to accept who you really are." He pressed himself against her, pulling her hips toward his. The action made her arch her back and drew a gasp out of her lips, and she swore at herself silently about how easy it was for him to play her like a goddamn harp.

"Still not my style," she said once she had the ability to speak again. "Which is a relief."

"To me as well." He drove himself up against her again, pinning her harder against the column. Even through their clothing, he made her head spin. "For I would only suffer such a request to please you. I would suffer anything to please you."

When he pulled her to him a third time, rutting himself up against her body, she moaned. She couldn't help it. He was too much. Just too goddamn much for her to handle. "Voyeurism or orgies really aren't—" She took a moment to fill her lungs with air, something she was feeling rather short of suddenly. "Really aren't my thing."

"Oh?" He stilled his attacks and leaned against her, pinning her to the column and letting his lips wander along her cheek and her jaw, kissing her torturously. "For my own knowledge, do tell... what do you enjoy?"

"You know what I like."

"I would like to hear you say it."

She tilted her head back and away from him so he could kiss his way down her throat. She felt like putty in his hands. She always had; she always would. "You."

"All of me?"

"Yeah... all of you." *Both versions of you,* she was admitting to him. She couldn't help it. She wanted him. She suspected that in the way they expressed desire, Aon and Noa were more closely aligned than with anything else. Even if one didn't feel obligated to keep the training wheels on for her and the other liked to take things one at a time.

"Good." He caught her lips with his own. He kissed her slower this time, gentler, and when he broke the kiss, she was shivering in his arms. "You were beautiful in that throne room. Standing your ground against me for the sake of your belief. For your morality."

"You aren't mad?"

He chuckled. "Do I seem mad?"

No, he didn't. He "seemed" a lot of things, but she highly doubted this was how the man expressed his anger. She shook her head silently.

"I want you to be my queen, Lydia. I want all of what you have to offer. Your compassion, your humor, your steadfast adherence to what you believe is right. I have no conscience of my own, my love. I do not... know how to be like them. I want you to be that for me. Temper me. Fix me. Make me a better king. One more to your liking."

"I..." She didn't know what to say.

"I know this is all happening too quickly for you. I know that I am not quite as you knew me. But he was cruel, egotistical, sadistic, and vainglorious."

She cut him off. "And you aren't?"

He huffed a laugh and leaned his head down, resting his forehead against hers. "You stood in my throne room and listened to me make judgment upon judgment, did you not?"

"I did."

"And were any of my decisions rash? Tyrannical? Sadistic? Self-serving?" His hand at her hip twisted in her skirt idly.

She paused. "No."

"I do all I can to be *fair*. My laws must not be broken, but they are not *cruel*. But you are my Queen of All. I will give you anything you desire. If you wish to take cord and lash to my flesh, it is yours. Whatever you can ask for, I will grant it."

I want things to be normal. But she couldn't ask for that. She knew he couldn't give it to her. That was the one thing outside his control. And what was normal in a place like this, anyway? "Why did you let that man live? Because I wished you to, or because you knew it was the fair thing to do?"

He put her down and took a step away from her, his expression one of resignation and injury. "You are disappointed with me. I did as you asked of me, and yet I have still fallen short of your expectations."

"I..." She didn't know what to say.

"I am not human, starlight. I am not *like* them. I never have been, and I never will be." His expression twisted up in one of remembered pain. She recognized it well—Aon had worn it frequently. It was gone a moment later, lost beneath the layers of hard stone that he wore instead. "Compassion such as you displayed... is... foreign to me. No matter how hard I try."

There was such pain in those words—such defeat and lone-liness, it made her heart crack. She stepped toward him and picked up his hand in hers, lacing her fingers between his. He looked surprised at the gesture.

"I'm sorry." It was the best she could do.

A metal finger crooked under her chin to tilt her head up. "I would give you all that you ask for. I will give you anything—*anything*—if you would but love me as you did before."

Tears stung her eyes. She threw her arms around him in a tight hug and buried her head against his chest. Her heart felt like it was shattering. She didn't know what to say or what to do to make it better or how to make him hurt less. For in his ice-cold eyes she had seen pure pain. Pure hurt. Pure emptiness.

And there wasn't anything she could do to fix it.

That stung her worse than anything else.

There's one thing I could do to fix it. I could make myself love him and choose to kneel at the altar for him. She tucked her head lower and wished she could hide from the thoughts. No. She couldn't go to the altar. She couldn't let them warp her mind and rewrite her like they had done to him, Lyon, and who knew how many others.

Noa was stroking her hair with his human hand, resting his head atop hers. "Tell me you will never leave me. Even if you never love me as you did before, say you will stay by my side..."

It was a plea, and it tore what was left of her heart out of her chest.

"I promise. One way or another, I'm here with you, forever."

"Thank you. For that, I will be endlessly grateful. Even if you only do it for the memory of the man you think I was." His words were a whisper as vacant as the void.

"No, it's not just that." She looked up at him. Her pain echoed his. And in that agony, she realized something. She might not love him, but she... *cared.* "It—" And there wasn't any point in lying about it. "It's for you too."

Something glistened in his eyes. His human hand cradled her jaw, and he tilted her head to look up at him as he drew her close. "Tell me that is the truth."

"I can't abandon you. I don't know if I can love you. I don't know if I can't. But what I do know is that I can't leave you. Not now, not ever."

His face smoothed, and he smiled softly down at her. There was a kindness there that shocked her—one she hadn't known that *either* of them had been capable of. "I deserve nothing. But that you think such things of me gives me hope. Such as I have never known."

He picked her up, lifting her off her feet to kiss her, wrapping his arms around her waist. She folded her arms behind his neck, meeting his embrace. It wasn't a kiss of heated passion. It was one of emotion.

One of a lonely soul seeking companionship.

One of love.

And she did her best to match it. Even if she didn't know how.

After a long moment, he placed her down on her feet. The look of peace on his features faded like a cloud passing over the moon. "Sadly, I must leave you."

"What?"

"I have more business to attend. This world is nothing if not needy." Whatever he was about to go do was not pleasant.

It worried her. "What're you going to do?"

"Attend to some loose ends."

That didn't sound foreboding or anything. He clearly didn't want to tell her. "Like what?"

His only answer was a faint smile.

Lydia took a step back from him. Aon had never shut her out of his dealings. If she had ever asked Aon what he was doing, he happily showed her. But now, Noa had proverbially shut a door on her. She hated how that felt. "Whatever you're going to do, you know I won't like."

"Precisely."

"You asked me to temper you, to be your conscience. Let me do that now."

"Not until I know for certain your heart is mine. Until then, you are my prisoner of war. Explore my home. Come to know this place that is now the rest of your eternity." His voice was a dark rumble as he took another step away from her. He placed his hand to his chest and bowed to her. "I will return to you as quickly as I am able."

"Wait—" But it was too late. He was engulfed in a swirl of black smoke and was gone.

* * *

Edu was growing quite tired of being chained as he was, doubled over with his neck lashed to the floor and his wrists to the wall behind him. Every muscle in his body had already gone through several cycles of screaming in agony and tingling numbness.

The conversations around him were drab and meaningless. None of them had a plan. None of them knew what to *do*. Their armies were scattered. Their powers restrained.

And even then, were they freed and their armies intact?

What good would it do them against the King of All?

None.

The door to their cell clicked open. He clenched his fists. There was only one visitor who would come to them at this point in the afternoon. It was not for a meal; therefore, it meant only one thing.

"And how do we fare, old friends?"

Edu jerked against the chains, trying to lunge forward at his nemesis, praying that the iron might snap this *one* time in thousands of attempts—but the loops held fast.

The King of All merely watched him with a single arched eyebrow. "And here I am doing my best to be pleasant."

Ini chuckled. "While I do appreciate not being tortured, I do wonder, for whose benefit is it really?"

The warlock shook his head. "I did not come to debate my motives with you."

"You spare us the lash not for your own amusement, but so that *if* Lydia finds out we are still your prisoners, she might not be so furious with you." Ini laughed, taunting their captor.

"She will discover nothing until she is in such a position as to forgive me." The King of All walked over to where Evie was sitting on the ground, her feet tucked close to her body, staying quietly out of the conversation.

Edu let out a shout, thrashing against the chains as he walked toward the young woman. *Get away from her! Do not dare touch her, you bastard!*

"Oh, be still, you idiot." The warlock flicked his wrist. The chain that bound Evie to the wall gave loose from the large loop attached to the stone. He picked it up from the ground and wrapped it around his hand. "I merely wish to interview the young thing."

"Why?" Vjo was the one to speak up this time. "What good is Evelyn to you?"

The King of All remained silent as he walked toward the door, dragging Evie along by the wrists. Evie was shaking, her eyes wide and terrified, as she stumbled behind, her legs clearly stiff.

Edu howled and yanked against the chains harder, feeling them bite into his flesh. Hot liquid dripped around his wrists, and he knew the cuffs were tearing up his skin. He could not care less. *Leave her be!*

"If you mean to harm the girl, take me instead." Ini stood. "You and I have not danced together in so long, King of All. You *know* I scream so very well."

But the warlock did not answer. He merely walked from the room, dragging Evie behind him. The door slammed shut in his absence.

And all Edu was allowed to do was scream in his wordless rage.

I am going to kill that man, once and for all. Or I will die trying.

EIGHT

"Can you tell Dtu to stop shouting? He's giving me a headache," Kamira complained from where she lay.

Lyon had been rarely away from her. He stayed at her side, talking of the old days, speaking of hope for the future. She had become quiet the past day, barely responding to him, instead merely crawling into his lap and staying there in his arms.

His wife was not well suited to imprisonment.

The chains and the walls were doing more to harm her spirit than the rule of the Ancients over their world, he knew. She had passed through her restless stage and now was sinking into a deep mire over her current condition. How he wished to set her free. How he wished to set her mind at peace.

"He is troubled."

"He's a great many things." Kamira let out a breath as she snuggled into him. "You're cold. You haven't fed recently."

"No, I fear I have not."

"Why not?"

"I have not had the time."

"Bullshit." She looked up at him, her green cat's eyes

narrowing. "You get like this when you are upset. What is wrong?"

He arched an eyebrow down at her and did not respond. He needn't bother. She knew as well as he why he was not in the mood to feed. She scoffed and stood from where she lay in his lap and paced as far away as she could, chained as she was. "You are fretting over me."

Lyon stood and brushed the dirt from his pants. "Of course."

"Then free me."

"You know I cannot."

She flew at him, and before he could react, she had slammed him up against the stone wall, her hands twisted in his lapel. He didn't fight it. If she wished to bring him pain, that was her right.

"Bullshit!" she snarled a second time. "These chains are yours. Let me go!"

"And then my king will hunt you down and kill you."

She flinched as though the thought had not occurred to her what might follow if he made good on her desire to be out of this cell. "He said that?"

"Yes."

"Arrogant bastard!"

"He is King. I believe that is a required state of being."

Kamira laughed weakly and sank up against him. He wrapped his arms around her and held her. "And if you free me, you die at his hand. If I have to die, I prefer you do the deed, husband."

"You would curse me with such a memory?"

"Yes. To teach you the error of your ways for kneeling like a fool to that thing that pretends to be a man."

Again, such bitter words stung him. But he understood from whence they came. They came from fear, from a hunger to taste the wind, not from any real spite toward him. He leaned down to kiss her. While she was tall, he was still far taller. But he had long since become adjusted to craning his neck down to look at everyone.

The tension in her muscles melted at his embrace, and she sighed when he broke the kiss. She needn't say that her words were not meant in sincerity; he understood. They had been together for a very long time, after all.

"Come to the altar, my love," he begged.

"No."

He was not surprised. He had hoped, but he was not at all caught off guard by her answer.

She reached up and let her lips graze over his. The sudden heat in the gesture did catch him off guard. "How I enjoyed having you as my prisoner of war, so long ago. You were so delicious. My shackled vampire. My stoic prize."

She had him by the hand now and was leading him to the cot that was by one wall. He smiled faintly. He would not refuse her. He doubted she would let him. "I had always wanted you, since the moment I laid eyes on you. I was more than happy to be your prisoner."

"Were you now? You are always so shy. It is so terribly hard to tell." She chuckled and pushed him to sit on the edge of the cot. She straddled his lap, and he pulled her closer by the hips. She let out an appreciative purr as he slid his hands along her body, feeling every familiar curve and scar. He unhooked the decorative swatches of fabric and chains that she swore and tossed them aside so he could replace them with his lips.

When she went to push his head away, he snatched her wrists and yanked them behind her back. He kept them pinned there with one hand and let his other roam over the swell of her breast. She moaned in response, arching into his touch. She struggled against his grasp, but when he tightened his grip to the point of pain, she stilled. "My, my, being a king suits you, I think." She gasped as he let his teeth graze her flesh. "It fills my needs nicely."

A sudden hunger had overtaken him. Hunger for her and hunger for something else. She had complained he had not fed recently. He knew how she hated to wake with him cold as stone beside her. Oftentimes, she would complain of sleeping next to a corpse. Far be it from him to repeat such a sin.

Feeling his fangs extend, he let his tongue roll along the soft flesh of her breast before sinking his teeth deep. Blood flooded his mouth, thick, hot, warm... glorious.

She sank against him, trusting him, her head thrown back in pleasure as she called out his name.

It would not be all he would have from her this night.

* * *

Noa had abandoned Lydia while he went off to attend to business. He had told her to explore his home, and to be honest, she had shit-all of anything else to do.

With a sigh, she decided she might as well do just that.

This massive, imposing temple in the center of the city felt older than time. She had to admit, she was beyond curious about this place. It wasn't nearly as phantasmal as Aon's estate had been, but the temple certainly was *bigger,* if nothing else. The ceilings soared a hundred feet overhead. It was monolithic. It was ancient.

And it made her feel very, very small.

Black stone columns were covered with artwork both carved and painted on. The eldritch writing that had become so familiar to her adorned every surface. She must have walked for hours amongst the enormous stone halls and columns.

One thing hadn't changed.

People were staring at her. Now, instead of people just wearing black ink, it was a mix of black and white. Vampires and warlocks. The two Houses that swore fealty to the King of All. No one was wearing masks, even though many of them had enough soulmarks that she suspected they should be. But Noa didn't allow such things, after all. She did her best to ignore the odd looks and wide berth that everyone was giving her.

I'm always the freak. Maybe someday that'd change. But that wasn't going to be today, by the look of things.

She took a moment to sit on a stone bench by a pool of water. It was a funny little depression in the stones, filled with the clear liquid that poured from a hole in the wall like a fountain. There were lily pads dotting the surface with black flowers in full bloom. It was only about three feet deep, and the bottom of the pool was decorated with the same kind of ancient and esoteric art as everything else.

Well, now she knew who inspired the Egyptians, anyway.

The water was missing something. She leaned down and touched the surface, and from the shadows of the plants came creatures she willed into existence. These looked as though someone had crossed an anglerfish with a koi. Their teeth were far too big and needle-like to be harmless oversized goldfish, and out in front of their heads dangled glowing lamps to attract prey.

"How adorable."

She screamed.

Noa.

She hadn't heard or sensed him come up from behind her. She whirled around and nearly toppled into the water. He caught her and pulled her back to standing, his features split in a wide and entertained grin. "Let's not repeat that part of our history, hm?"

"You snuck up on me on purpose!" She slapped him hard on the bare chest, and the loud crack echoed through the stone. She knew she hadn't hurt him, though. It took far more than that to bring him pain.

He laughed at that and shook his head. "Of course I did. I will never tire of stalking you in the shadows. Not today, and not in a hundred thousand years."

"That isn't fair." Now, she was pouting.

"Mm. You enjoy my little games. You just fuss when you lose." He sat on the bench and gestured to the stone next to him.

"Whatever." Yeah, okay. He was right. She just didn't have to like it. "Is your business done?" She sat next to him. No reason to be stubborn. He curled an arm around her and pulled her up against his side. Apparently, she had sat too far away for his liking.

"Yes, for the moment. I also thought perhaps you might enjoy some time to yourself."

"What were you doing?"

"Are we prying again?" He looked down at her with one eye narrowed, although she suspected it was playful. She could only suspect, as he was so stone-faced now it was hard to tell for sure.

"If I'm going to be your queen whether or I like it or not, yeah, I guess I am." She smirked, challenging his haughtiness.

"Hmf. A fair point, perhaps." He looked off, and a small smile played on his lips briefly. He was enjoying that she was admitting her fate was inevitable. She tried not to let that sour her mood. "This world has recently been made right. There is much strife and torment that comes with accepting such a thing. Yourself notwithstanding, there are many who rail against this new, and better, state. I must protect this world. I must, more importantly, protect you."

"And whatever you're doing to protect me, you think I'll disagree with?"

"Entirely."

"Like what?"

"If I told you now, that defeats the express purpose of *not* informing you in the first place." He laughed.

She shot him a glare but couldn't argue with his line of logic. Leaning her head against him, she tried to get what information she could. "Is Kamira okay?" She knew the other woman was Lyon's prisoner.

"My Priest struggles with his own ordeal. Our condition is mirrored in his. Although I do not keep you in chains." There was a rare playful glint to his eyes. "However... tempted I might be."

She felt her face go warm. No way in hell was she going to touch that one with a ten-foot pole. In her silence, he continued.

"She is unharmed, if that is what you are asking. But to keep one like her bound as she is is a deep injury in and of itself." Noa looked at her curiously. "Perhaps you should speak to Lyon. He is in need of a friend, and I am a poor excuse. Poorer now than I was before, and that is a remarkable feat."

"You're hoping he talks me into surrendering."

"It would be a happy side effect, yes. But truly, he is moping about my temple like an overgrown phantom. It is irritating at best. I need my right hand to have his wits about him, not woeful and distracted."

"Sure, I'll talk to him."

They fell into silence for a moment before he broke it. "What do you think of your new home?"

Aon had asked her that once before, if not exactly in those words. In a time that felt like years ago, he had asked her what she had thought of *his* home. Even if she was his "ward," he never once called it her home. It was odd, looking back at it, to see how strangely respectful he had been of her, even then.

This man was far more possessive. That was something she hadn't even thought was possible.

"It's certainly big," she said as she looked toward the soaring columns and up to the ceiling that made her dizzy.

"That is all? Big?"

"It's beautiful. Different, but beautiful."

"Different."

His tone brought her gaze back to him. There was pain in his eyes, and she couldn't figure out what she had said. He stood and paced a few steps away from her, turning his back to her to hide his face. "We in Under build our homes to resemble ourselves. Certainly, you have noticed."

She had. Each house seemed to have an architecture that matched the king or queen who ruled it. "Yeah, and?"

"All you see about you is a reflection of me. As that place you knew was my shadow." He turned to look at her. "Is that all I am to you? Different, but beautiful?"

"To be fair, I did also say big—"

Her bad attempt at humor didn't work at breaking the intense expression on his face. He took two steps and knelt at her feet, grasping her hands and clutching them in her lap. "Look at me, Lydia. Tell me what you see."

She was so surprised at his gesture that it took her a long moment to find anything to say at all. Swallowing down her startled reaction, she tried to take him at face value and did her best to answer him honestly. "I see someone older than I can even begin to understand. Older than the rocks that make up this place. I see someone who has spent all that time alone. I see someone who is... certain he is always right. I see a king."

"What else?" His grasp on her tightened. "Tell me the truth. What separates me from the man you loved?"

The truth. "Aon never wanted to rule the world. You do."

"I rule this world *only* because I *must*. I do not get to make my own choices, Lydia. I am a slave to the will of the Ancients. You feel swept away in the tide—trust me, I know how you feel. I am what they have made me to be. Do you think I wish to be this way? Do you not think I wish to be free? I merely accept my fate. I understand it is inescapable."

"You put them in chains once before. We could do it again."

Noa laughed—dark and low. He lowered his head and rested his forehead against where he clasped their hands together. "Oh, my love. No. That cannot be. For even if I wished it, they would see the blow before it fell."

"Even if you wished it?"

"I do not want to return to that place of madness. My weakness resulted in your death and your imprisonment. It destroyed you not only once, but twice. This is how I must be to protect you. This is how I must be to ensure that no one ever harms you again. Even if you will despise me until the end of time itself, I would rather have your hatred than see you hurt again."

That was the same reasoning Aon had given her when he had killed Nick and when he had tortured her to try to free her of the fear that kept her hiding in his shadow.

He would rather she hated him than to see her harmed.

She pulled her hands from his, and he tensed as if expecting her to reject him. Instead, she wrapped her arms around him and kissed his temple. He relaxed, sinking into her embrace.

After a pause, she spoke again. "I see a place that is too much for me to understand at first glance. I see a place so powerful, so overwhelming, that I'm left in awe of it. Unsure of what it means, unsure of what to do. I see a place so absolute, so complete in its control, that I know I'm hopeless to fight against it. I feel like a grain of sand on the dunes outside, just realizing where I am. I feel like I'm about to be drowned in a tidal wave. I feel smaller and more powerless than I did when I was a stupid mortal surrounded by demigods. And that scares me. That's what I see in this place around me. That's what I see when I look at you."

Like the flick of a switch, his demeanor changed. He reached up and pulled her down onto his lap, her legs on either side of his. Cradling her head in his hand, he devoured her lips with his before she even had the time to realize what had happened.

The stone of the bench was at her back as he leaned her against it for leverage. He bent her back until her head was resting against the surface. She was trapped. She had no advantage, and he had her pinned. Instantly, it was like hot lava had poured through her veins. Every nerve caught on fire and was alight as he slipped a hand to her hips and ground himself against her. He was going to take her—right here, right now—and she didn't know if she could stop him.

More importantly, she didn't know if she wanted to stop him.

When she slid her hands to his chest, he grasped her wrists and pinned them to the bench over her head. He easily kept them there with his metal hand as he wandered his human one over her slowly. But his touch was rough and hard, making his claim known.

"Say the word, and I will cease."

It was the same command he'd given her before. When he'd taken so much from her, when she had wanted him to take it all. He had asked her to stop him. To say the word, and he'd relent. And how she begged him to wait or slow down. How she had begged him for mercy. But never once—never *once*—had she asked him to stop.

Now was no different.

Seeing her hesitate, he tilted his head down toward her ear and whispered. "You are right. I am the rising tide. I am the consuming fire. I am the will of this world. And you belong to me." He bit down on the skin of her neck where it met her shoulder, and she arched into it with a hiss of pain. But the word "stop" still never came to her lips. As he moved against her, she wanted to ask him for something very different than that.

Right now, all she wanted was more.

"You are no speck of sand. You are no tiny creature. You are my reason, my life, my *soul*. You are my starlight. I am the sun that burns in the sky, and you are the night that answers me. I belong to you equally in return. You are my queen, and I am your slave and your master."

She wanted him so badly she could barely breathe. It was that sensation that made it so utterly jarring when he stood and abandoned her, leaving her sitting on the floor. He took a step back. The shock and agony must have been written clearly across her face, with how amused he seemed.

"I would mistake that look for one of desire," he commented dryly. "Although you could not clearly wish for me —this thing that is so very different than the man you loved. I am but a tidal wave, and clearly you could not wish to be taken. It must be my wishful thinking at work. I think I shall retreat to my rooms and daydream of what could be."

Damn him. Damn him to hell. After that, he was threatening to just walk away! This was cruel. Beyond cruel.

He turned to leave.

"Wait."

He glanced back at her with a raised eyebrow. "You have said that word frequently as of late. I have ignored it every time. What reason would I have to do differently now?"

She got up from the floor and walked over to him. He watched her approach with a hard, cold expression. But there was a hungry darkness in his eyes. It was a cold fire that burned in him, but a fire all the same. He turned to face her as she closed the distance between them, and he held still. The ball was in her court.

He wanted her to admit she wanted him.

He wanted her to admit she wanted to *be* with him.

Different, ancient, and cold as he may be, that much between the two men was the same. She remembered a night in the library when Aon had made her beg for him. Now, Noa was repeating that step. But she couldn't bring herself to care. She slid her hands up his bare chest, running her fingers over the marks that decorated him. He pulled in a slow hiss of breath through his nose, and she watched his rib cage expand as he did.

She began to kiss along a line of the marks of black ink. How she wanted to do more.

A hand twisted in her hair and yanked her head back, even as he pressed her up against him. "Do not tempt me. I have been patient and kind to you thus far."

Patient? Kind? He could do *worse?* That should have terrified her. That should have sent her screaming. Instead, her eyes slipped shut as he pinned her to his body with his other hand at her hip, pressing her against his desire for her.

His breath poured hotly against her cheek as he whispered, "Tell me you want me. Tell me you want what I can do to you. Tell me you want me to take you. The man you loved is standing before you. I may not be him, but he is me. Our desire for you is the same. Let me prove it to you. Say yes, just this once, and I will take you to depths and heights you cannot imagine. Say that you want me."

Fear coiled in her, and the ice of it was hopeless against the inferno that had her in its iron claws. Literally and figuratively. It felt like he was stealing the very air out of her lungs. She didn't know how to say no. She didn't know if she wanted to. He let her linger in the uncertainty before she couldn't take it any longer. In an exhale of breath, she let herself give in. It was futile to fight what she knew she was going to do in the end. "Yes."

A dark chuckle was what she received in response. "Good."

NINE

Lydia's heart was pounding in her throat. She was standing in the center of Noa's bedroom—*their* bedroom. A space they'd shared every night since he'd defeated her. A space they had already been intimate in several times.

But this felt different.

It didn't help that he was circling her like a shark. Like he was sizing her up. Deciding exactly how best to dismantle her.

When he stopped behind her, she broke out in goosebumps before he even touched her.

He chuckled at her reaction. His hands finally settled on her shoulders, one warm, one cold. One flesh, one metal. "Do you trust me, my starlight?"

Did she?

It was a very good question.

One that Aon had asked her, when he'd balanced her on the tips of his claws, so close to slicing her open—when she'd been mortal and such things had mattered.

"Well?"

Shutting her eyes, she let out a breath. "I trust you not to hurt me in any way that matters."

He stepped into her, and she felt him press a kiss to the top of her head. "Good."

That was the last warning she had before a cord cinched tight around her throat. Not tight enough to cut off her air—yet—but tight enough to make it very clear that it could.

Her hands shot reflexively to her neck.

"Ah-ah." He scolded her. "*Down.*"

Like she was an animal. She bristled at the notion of it. But that was the point. The surrender. The, for lack of a better term... submission. Shutting her eyes, she swallowed what was left of her pride, and lowered her hands back to her sides.

Slowly, taking his damn time, he untied her halter top and stripped her of it. Her skirt came next. He circled around her, once more like a great jungle beast circling his prey, as he stripped her naked, until she stood before him entirely exposed.

Once more he returned to stand behind her, out of her line of sight. He wanted to make her nervous. He wanted to keep her from seeing what he was doing—testing her resolve. Testing her trust.

And her point was proven when he tied a black sash around her eyes, blotting out her vision. "Magic is far more effective, but... this will do." He hummed. "You look quite lovely in it."

"I'll take your word for it," she murmured.

A chuckle was her response as he picked up the cord that he had cinched around her throat. She felt him wrap it around her neck one more time, and thread a loop in it.

Carefully, as if painting a work of art, he began winding the rope around her, between and around her breasts, around her waist—around her thighs. Cinching it tight, but not *too* tight.

Something about the meticulousness of it—the patience—the fact that he was touching her *without* touching her—it had her skin on fire. She was trembling. Waiting for him to throw her to the ground and rut her like he had before. Waiting for him to take her, like she wanted him to.

But instead, he simply wound what felt like individual pieces of cord around each wrist and each ankle, before stepping back from her completely. She could only hear the whisper of his robes on the stone floor as he moved.

"Spoiled by choice, my love... where shall we begin?"

His voice was a dark rumble that sent a shiver through her. She kept her hands clenched at her sides to keep them from shaking.

When he circled around behind her, she went tense, waiting for him to do—well—anything. But when nothing happened for what seemed like minutes, she couldn't hold her breath any longer. She let out the exhale she'd been holding in, and let her muscles go slack.

It was what he had been waiting for.

Part of her had expected whips. Or floggers. Or perhaps he was more of the spanking type. But she should have known better. If he wanted to beat her up, he'd already done that a few times.

No, he had other methods in mind.

The point of a claw dragged down her shoulder, just barely cutting her, just enough that she felt the warmth of blood coming to the surface. But it wasn't just a single slice. It wasn't a slash. It was a *line.* Followed by another. Followed by another.

He was drawing on her.

Writing on her.

With the tip of a claw.

When she hissed and went to jerk away, his human hand grabbed her by the cord tied around her throat, yanking her back to him, forcing her to stay still. "Do not move. This is delicate work."

She knew what he was putting on her. She didn't know what it would say—only one man in the world could read it, after all. And she suspected it wouldn't stay on her. The marks would fade like all wounds.

But onto her skin, he was cutting the language of the Ancients. Truth be told... it didn't even hurt that bad. Considering what he'd done to her before? Considering her pain tolerance now that she was a queen of Under? It...

Why did it feel almost... good?

He leaned down, and she moaned as he dragged a tongue over the cuts, licking up the blood, meeting the sound with one of his own, if deeper and far louder.

Power surged through her like lightning. No—like *fire*. It pooled in her, dangerous and low, begging for more. Need pounded in her veins the likes of which she'd never known, a surge of it that nearly sent her to her knees. It faded to a dull throb, but didn't leave her.

It was blood magic. What was he *doing* to her?

"What're you—" Her voice was trembling.

He chuckled darkly. "Ssh..." His human hand trailed over her, and she found herself leaning into his touch. Desperate for more. When he pulled her back against his bare chest, it was like cold water in the heat of the desert, it was such a relief.

His hand grasped one of her breasts and squeezed, and the sound that left her was almost profane.

"My, my... just a little inspiration, and look at what you become." His lips were hovering close to her ear, his breath hot as it pooled against her skin. "So beautiful..."

"What did you... what did you do to me?" She felt lightheaded.

"I am curious what you *think* I have done." He pinched her nipple. The action sent her head rolling back against his shoulder, and she struggled not to writhe in his grasp. "A simple spell. One meant to reveal the truth of your desire. Nothing more."

The truth.

Was this really how much she wanted him?

"Beyond inhibitions... beyond fear... this is how you feel for me, my starlight." The point of his claw drew a line over the swell of her other breast, just barely drawing blood once more. She knew he wouldn't dare damage any of her marks.

He wouldn't hurt her in any way that mattered.

That time, her cry caught in her throat. The sting twisted up in the pleasure of it, and became all one thing entirely. He slipped around her to stand in front of her, only so that he might bow his head and lap up the blood he had spilled, before bowing lower to sink his teeth into her tender flesh, hard enough to hurt but not hard enough to break the flesh.

Everything in her was on fire. Electric. She didn't know what to *do.* "Please…"

She didn't like how frightened she sounded. And… she was a little afraid, if she were being honest. He'd opened up a door that she'd never known existed and pushed her through it.

"I have you, my love. I am here." Suddenly, she was no longer standing. He swept her off her feet, quite literally, scooping her up into his arms. The mystery of where he was taking her didn't last long as she felt him climb onto the bed with her before placing her down. "Kneel for me."

It wasn't the haughty command of a king. It wasn't the stern voice he had used to command her to do so the first time he'd done it. It was thick with his own desire. But it was filled with a *warmth* that made her want to follow him into the darkness.

She shifted to her knees without hesitating.

He was beside her, hands stroking over her body, giving her enough to calm her down—but not enough to scratch the itch that was frightening her so very badly. "I want you to spread your knees wide and sit back on your ankles."

She did so.

Moving to kneel behind her, she felt his hands at her thighs, lashing her ankles to them. Soon, she wouldn't be able to stand. But she had no desire to. Not if it meant that he would stop this terrible *need* that he'd unleashed in her.

"Now, fold your arms behind your back."

He was going to fully restrain her and leave her helpless to him. But wasn't she already, with or without the ropes? And now, she desperately didn't want to end whatever he was going to do to her. Folding her arms behind her back, wrist-to-elbow, she held still as he lashed her arms together.

When he was finished, he stood on the bed. The mattress was thin and little more than a platform, and without springs— making it easy for him to do so without jostling her. "What a sight... how beautiful you are, like this."

A whisper of fabric, and she knew what was coming.

"Open your mouth."

She obeyed. God, she obeyed.

His hands gripped her head, and he slipped himself into her mouth, slowly at first—running his length against her tongue, filling her mouth before retreating. "Good... yes... that's it..."

She could only trust him. When he began to deepen his strokes, pressing himself deeper down her throat, she had to struggle to keep from choking. On keeping her muscles relaxed.

"Not how you usually approach the matter..." His chuckle was dark and thick with lust as he kept up his methodical pattern. "But look at you... already adapting."

Soon, he buried himself in her until her nose touched his body, only to pull out and repeat the action, never staying in one place too long, never violent—never harsh—but never slowing. Never stopping.

Still, he praised her with each stroke into her, moaning her name, telling her how much he loved her—how good she felt— how he belonged to her.

And it felt like if he even *touched* her—flicked a finger over her—she might climax from that action alone. She had never needed anything so badly like she needed the man in front of her.

Finally, it seemed even he had a limit to his patience. He

pulled away from her, leaving her gasping for air. His own breathing sounded labored as he growled. "I could spend a year like that..."

She knew he wasn't joking.

"But sadly, I think I have left you in agony long enough.

"Pl—" A cord took the place of his body as he wrapped a rope around her head, splitting her lips, cutting off her words.

"Shush."

A hand on her shoulder was next, and he tilted her forward, until she was on her knees, her ass in the air, feet still lashed to her thighs, her face on the mattress.

Utterly exposed.

His hands stroked over her ass as he knelt behind her, his claws digging into her skin hard enough to leave bloody marks, she knew, as she wailed and bit down into the ropes in her mouth.

"Scream all you like."

And as he sank himself into her, she did just that.

Relentless.

That was the word for the King of All.

Relentless.

But that was what she needed. To feel him fill her. And she surrendered to him, let him in as far as he could go, and felt her body beg him to give her more.

And he was more than eager to give.

How many times he sent her over that cliff into ecstasy, she didn't know. It was all a blur. A blur of every kind of sensation he could bring her.

It was unlike anything she'd ever experienced.

At what point he had cut her binds and taken off the blindfold, she hadn't the damnedest idea. But she was lying, cradled in his arms. He must have bathed them both, as she smelled like herbs and his hair was wet.

He was kissing her cheek, his human hand trailing gently up

and down her arm, as he whispered to her how wonderfully she had done. How much he loved her.

How safe she was with him.

She grunted.

"Welcome back, my starlight." He chuckled. "I thought I had broken you for good."

"I don't... know if I like that spell." She rolled into him. Or rather, she tried. She decided she didn't feel like moving. "Stupid... horny spell."

His quiet laugh was warm and gentle as he kissed her forehead. "It really does just remove inhibitions, my love."

"Horny spell." She shut her eyes.

"As you wish." He shuffled down to tuck in next to her, draping an arm over her body. "Sleep well, my love."

All she could do was let out a "*mmmh*" in response.

Which was probably for the best.

TEN

Lydia was dreaming.

And someone else was driving the bus.

God damn son of a bitch, she was sick of this shit.

Someday, maybe *someday*, she would be left the hell alone in her sleep. It wasn't until she really took sight of where she was that her anger caught and froze.

She was in a ballroom. A ballroom she recognized, with its soaring, Baroque-yet-twisted architecture, asymmetrical arches, and a giant circular stained-glass window, depicting a seven-pointed archaic symbol.

A point for each House. Blue, white, purple, green, red, black... But when she had last seen it, one spot had been blocked out. One spot had been left gray and shattered as if a pane had fallen from the intricate leadwork.

Now, that spot blazed turquoise. For her.

The only other time she had seen the massive room, it had been filled with throngs of people. Two hundred or more stood gathered to attend Aon's "gala," his return to the throne, all because the Ancients had rejected her from the pool as a mortal.

It all felt so long ago. It all felt like such a lie. The Ancients had been toying with everyone all along.

Now that she wasn't terrified for her life, she could appreciate the room for what it was. Its architecture was no longer horrifying to her; it was the reflection of the man she had come to love.

And there he was.

Standing with his back to her in the center of the spiral on the ground, the twisted shape made from black and white marble, he was wearing a full tuxedo, tailcoat and all. It would look ludicrous on most people, but it was cut perfectly to his frame, and he wore it flawlessly. He stood, his metal hand folded at his back, gazing up at the stained glass.

She walked up to him slowly. Her steps sounded far too loud in the empty and silent chamber. *Is this just my dream? Am I imagining this, or is this really him?* With Aon, there was no way of knowing. She stopped a few feet behind him. Afraid to reach out to touch him—afraid to get too close and have him shatter into nothingness.

He was a ghost. One she wanted to cling to as long as she could. But when he didn't speak or turn around to face her, she had to break the silence. Finally, she had to know.

"Are you real?"

He tilted his head just barely to the side. His long black hair was tied back with a silk ribbon. A few strands had fallen loose from it and lay along his metal-masked cheek. He would be the hero of some gothic novel, save for the metal mask and claw. "I have often asked myself that very same question."

She couldn't help but watch him as he moved his metal hand to raise it in front of himself, turning it over and letting the light from the moons outside the stained-glass window glint against its sharp edges. "How often I wondered if I were 'real.' I think a part of me always remembered I was not like them. Not a human soul, born of Earth, but instead a shattered, unfinished thing. I blamed my faltering mind on my years. I blamed it on my power. But the truth was always that deep inside, I am not *real*. I am only a broken toy. A cart with three wheels."

"That's not what I was asking you."

"I know."

She felt her jaw twitch and tried not to laugh at his deadpan humor. He didn't turn around, and she had no idea whether this was a dream of her making or if he had managed to manifest himself in her dreams. Or worse, if this was the King of All, using this as a cheap trick. But it didn't stop her from stepping forward and putting her hand against his back. He hissed in a breath at her touch. "You're real enough to me."

"How often I wondered the same about you."

"What do you mean?"

"I thought perhaps you were an illusion of my mind. That I had invented you from the shadows. The last vestiges of a dying mind, sinking into the throes of madness, scrabbling to clutch to a flicker of hope. I thought I had invented you."

"If you'd invented me, I don't think I'd be half as stubborn."

He laughed quietly and shook his head. "You are quite right." Finally, he turned to face her and opened his arms to her.

Without even thinking, she threw herself into his embrace. Wrapped her arms around him and hugged him as tightly as she could. He did the same, and she fought the urge to cry. She'd cried enough lately. "Aon."

"My dragonfly."

"Am I making you up?"

"If you had invented me, I do not think I would be half so irritating."

She laughed. "I mean—"

"I know what you mean. And to be frank, I am unsure. I could be myself, a part of the man I am, broken away to join you in your slumber. Or I could be a creation of your lonely mind, piecing together your memories to ease your pain."

"You don't know?"

"I am afraid I do not. I feel as though I am here. But then again, I had felt as though I was a man, just some time ago. The latter was proven to be false, so, therefore, all is now in question."

"You're so frustrating sometimes." She buried her head against the fabric of his suit. He smelled like old books and leather, and tears threatened to fall again. "I miss you *so much*."

"I have gone nowhere. I am still beside you. I am a part of the whole." He stroked her hair. "What you mean to say is that you are afraid."

"I'm terrified..."

He took a step back from her abruptly. One more pace and he folded one hand before him and the other at his back. He bowed deeply to her, the perfect picture of a gentleman and a nightmare, all at once. "My dearest lady, would you do me the honors of giving me this dance?"

She smiled. She couldn't help it. Damn him. Damn that witty, clever asshole of hers. He always knew what to do to change her mood. And right now, he was trying to—in his own stupid way—cheer her up. "Last time we did this, you mind-controlled me without warning me first."

"Tonight, I promise to do no such thing. You are free to flail about at your leisure, as there are no witnesses here in front of whom I could become embarrassed."

"Jackass."

"Always."

He straightened and held his human hand out to her, keeping the metal one tucked at his back, once more asking her to join him. She slipped her hand into his, and he pulled her toward him. He took her hands and placed one of hers on his shoulder. He put his hand against her shoulder blade and kept their other hands clasped together. "Something simple. A waltz, then."

"I don't know how to waltz."

"Then I suggest you allow me to lead."

"Letting you lead is what's gotten us into this mess."

He chuckled. "Touché. And yet, here we are. If you do not follow my lead, we will quickly wind up in a heap on the ground."

"Won't be the first time."

"Nor do I expect the last."

He lifted his hand from her shoulder blade to snap his fingers. With the click, music began, playing from nowhere, and yet it filled the space effortlessly.

"Showoff."

"Always."

She smiled up at him as he replaced his hand against her shoulder and began to try to teach her to dance. "Now, a waltz is easy. You move in beats of three. One-two-three, one-two-three," he counted, his tone that of the patient instructor. "If you would not be so very tense, I can guide you through the movements well enough."

"I'm not tense."

He silently stared down at her.

Even with a mask on, she knew exactly the kind of incredulous expression he was shooting her. "Don't raise your eyebrow at me."

He laughed. It was warm and pleasant. A sound she had heard from him a few times—real, genuine laughter. He clearly deeply enjoyed that she correctly predicted what he was doing.

"I know you pretty well by now, warlock."

"You know me better than anyone ever has. And with the immense gap between our ages, that is remarkable." He grew into his playful stern tone again as he resumed his instruction.

"Now, stop pulling back against my hand as though I am going to tear your flesh off."

"Won't be the first time." She grinned up at him.

"Nor do I expect the last," he echoed himself again. "But, sadly, now is not that time."

Lydia sighed and tried to relax. After a long moment, she forced herself to let her muscles release.

"There," he chuckled, "now, was that so hard?"

"Kinda."

"Oh, shush. Now..." He paused and pressed her backward. She took an instinctual step in time with his. "Like that. One, two, three," he counted as they moved. She tried not to freeze. She tried her damnedest to trust him. It was only a dance. Only a waltz. She'd trusted him through a lot crazier shit than this.

After a minute of him carefully guiding her across the floor in what she knew were simple, childish steps, he expanded the length of his stride. She squeaked but did her best to keep following him. "Don't be afraid." He chuckled. "You are doing so well."

Don't be afraid. You are doing so well, she echoed his words in her mind. That's what he was trying to tell her. *Follow my lead. Trust me. Don't be afraid.* That's why he was dancing with her.

He was plotting something. And this was his way of telling her.

But what? She frowned. "I don't know what I'm doing."

"You don't need to. I know where we are going."

"And where's that?" Her comment was enough to hint that she was on to his game.

He let out a quiet hum but didn't falter as he brought them across the dance floor in the slow waltz. "To the end of our dance, of course."

She broke away from him at that and stopped. He did the same, a pace away, watching her. "No," she insisted.

"What do you mean, no?"

"This isn't the end."

He sighed. "Everything has an end. Especially something as wonderful as this cannot last. It is a dance. A glorious expression of two souls coming together to create art. It cannot survive for long. The musicians must stop, and the partners must cease and go their separate ways."

"Aon, no... I won't."

"You won't, what?"

"I won't let this end. Not like this."

He stepped toward her and gently stroked his palms over her hair before cupping her face. One metal, one flesh. One warm, one cold. "You do not have a say in the matter, I am afraid. Things are already outside your control. Soon, I will die, and you will be free. Where I will go, I will not let you follow."

"Please..." She reached for him, but as she grasped onto his lapel, he slipped away from her. "No, Aon..."

"Forgive me. But know this, my love—I can die in peace. I will go and do so happily, as you will be the queen that you should be. I can pass into the void with a smile, knowing that for this one moment, we danced."

He was fading away. Slipping out of the dream like a ghost. She jumped toward him and tried to grab him before he faded away. But it was too late. He was gone.

"Aon!"

* * *

When Lydia woke up, she was lying in sheets covered in blood.

For a split second, she was terrified it was hers.

What she and Noa had done last night had been otherworldly—it had been intense—but certainly nothing like *that*.

She had to pat herself down to make sure she had all her limbs and there weren't gaping holes in her. But nothing hurt.

Nothing was missing. Everything was where it was. She shot up out of the bed so fast she nearly toppled over. She summoned clothing to herself, just in case she had to run out of the halls screaming. Best not to be naked at the time.

The blood was fresh. It was still red and damp. And it was in a trail, smeared along the stone out toward the ledge that served as a balcony with no rail that overlooked the city. Someone was slumped there on the ground up against a column.

Noa.

He was sitting there, his legs in front of him, one bent.

His chest was covered in deep and bloody gashes. Crimson trenches decorated his chest and arms as if they were put there by thick claws. They went down to the bone in several places. The wounds were too wide to be done by any normal-sized beast. They looked like they were put there by the claws of a damn T-Rex.

He was awake, gazing out at the city in front of him. The sun was eclipsed, and the moons were casting the city in a myriad of colors. Now and again he would twitch, his whole body spasming as he hissed in pain at what he must be feeling. What'd happened to him? Why wasn't he healing?

She approached slowly, stepping around the streaks of blood upon the floor. She was afraid of whatever had done this to him. Afraid of why he wasn't either healing or dying. Instead, he seemed caught in this limbo of suffering.

"Noa?"

He cringed as if embarrassed—as if her seeing him like this bothered him. He didn't respond. Aon was never ashamed of his weaker moments. This man was accustomed to being the "King of All." She had to remember that. Slowly approaching, she knelt at his feet.

He didn't look at her and kept his eyes fixed out onto the city. It would have been a beautiful night, with its warm breeze and colorful moons, if he weren't lying here, torn to shreds.

She put her hand on his leg gently. "What happened to you?"

His answer was so quiet it took her a second to process what he said. "I asked for my freedom."

Lydia blinked. "What?"

"I asked my makers to set me free. To let me be as I was, for you. So that you would love me once more." He blanched in pain as something seemed to twist in his side, and he writhed in agony. When he could breathe again, he shuddered. "They said no."

She bit down a laugh at his deadpan delivery. Another thing the two men shared, it seemed. Now wasn't the time. "The Ancients did this to you?" It explained the wounds. The size of them, the depth, the fact that they weren't healing. If they hurt as badly as it seemed, it would make sense. He should be unconscious or dead, but it seemed they wanted him to stay awake so he could feel every ounce of it.

"The Ancients have done everything to me." His expression twisted up in pain briefly. "This is nothing compared to what they have gladly dealt me in the past."

She slid up to his side, puddle of blood be damned, and took his hand in hers. She clutched it tightly, and he turned his head to look up at her.

"You called for me by that false name in your sleep. Even as I held you, even as I possessed your body, your heart still cries out for my shadow." Those spilled-ink eyes flicked between hers. "I do not know how to *win* you. I decided I would descend to that madness if it is what you want." He was flickering in and out of control. She could see the two versions warring for command— fighting to the surface. "I would do anything for you, my starlight, my dragonfly." The pain was weakening his connection to the Ancients. For the moment, he was neither man and both at the same time. "But they will not allow it to come to pass."

She reached out and wanted to pull him to her. She wanted to hold him. But he pulled away from her. "No. Please. It hurts enough as it is without you cradling and comforting the man you wish I still was."

Swallowing the lump in her throat, she found the strength to speak. "I'm trying to comfort you both."

"We are the *same man*."

She sighed and shook her head. She had to come to terms with that. They really were the same guy. Not two, not one holding the other one prisoner. Just the man she knew with all the missing puzzle pieces glued back in. "Sorry. I'll get there. I'm not the brightest bulb in the box, but I'll catch up, I promise."

He looked at her with an arched eyebrow, then chuckled. His chuckle grew into a laugh, and she joined him. As he stopped, he let out a weary sigh and lifted his human hand to her cheek. It was bloody and damp, but she didn't flinch as he placed it to her. He smiled weakly. "Then there is still hope that you may come to love me before it is too late."

"Too late?"

Spilled-ink eyes, hazy and on the edge of pain-induced delirium, met hers. "My creators gave me an ultimatum, my starlight. As punishment for my foolish request, you have one week to love me of your own accord."

One week.

Seven days to love him or be forced to love him. Or... seemingly impossibly, find a way to kill him.

As he watched her expressions flicker between emotions she couldn't even describe, he smiled faintly. His eyes slipped shut, and he smiled as if remembering something fondly. "I dreamed of the night we danced. But in my mind, we are alone on that ballroom floor. I do so love to dance. And yet I have never had another worth sharing the moment with."

He was recalling their shared dream. Noa could remember it. Of course, he could. *They're the same goddamn person*, she swore at herself in her head. Aon wasn't gone. He wasn't a prisoner. He was just... different, when the Ancients were holding him together. That was the brutal truth of it—it was both. He was both and neither, all at once. "I can't do this. I don't know how to do this."

"Your choices are simple. Love me, be broken by the Ancients, or kill me. If you cannot do the first, and I loathe to do the second, then I suggest you begin to think about how to go about taking my life. I lay it down willingly for you. Kill me. End my miserable existence. I was never meant to be. I am an unfathomable monster. You know not even half of the horrors I can perform."

"Please, I..." There was a rock in her throat at the thought of it. Trying to visualize killing him and having to live in this world without him made her heart hurt. Just trying to imagine it made her want to cry.

He looked at her, a calm look of acceptance on his features. "I have seven days to convince you I am already dead."

Anger rushed into her at his words. Lydia slapped him. Hard. She didn't know where it came from. He turned to her, wide-eyed and taken aback as she shouted at him. "Don't you dare talk like that!"

Stunned, he was silent and watched her as she fumed at him.

"Don't you fucking dare give up." She glared. "I won't allow it."

"You hit me."

"Of course, I *fucking* hit you. You deserve it. In the past seven months, I've been kidnapped, chased, threatened, kidnapped again, murdered, brought back from the fucking dead as a goddamn monster queen, threatened again, thrown into a lake to drown for eternity, and then don't even get me started on all this bullshit! I've had everything I've ever cared about taken away from me. My home, my best friend, and my life. The only thing I have left is you. I won't let you go too! I—"

Noa's stunned expression had faded to a soft smile while she had railed against him. His eyes flickered, and she saw such love burning away in him that it stopped her mid-rant.

Her anger cracked and fell to the ground like a popped balloon. She swallowed the rock in her throat and finished her rant with what was really underneath her anger—fear. "You can't leave me."

"Very well. If my queen commands, it shall be so." The glint in his eyes revealed his meaning even if his tone was dry.

"Now, you're being sarcastic. You're lying here on the floor, cut to ribbons, and you're being fucking *sarcastic*."

"Would you have it any other way?"

She laughed. It was a tired, weak laugh. Sitting on the ground next to him and, with a flick of her wrist, she summoned a bottle of alcohol to her hand. That was a nifty trick, she had to admit. It was one of the ancient glass onion bottles like she had found in the Temple of Dreams. She uncorked it, took a swig, and offered it to him.

He took it in his human hand, took a few hard gulps of it, and handed it back. "Thank you."

"Least I could do." She took another sip. "You're like this because of me."

"I am the way I am meant to be. This is my true self."

She shot him a look. "I meant you're currently bleeding on the floor, unable to die or heal, because of me."

"Ah." He reached for the bottle, and she gave it to him with another small laugh. He took a hard swig. "Yes, well."

After a long pause, she looked up at him. "We're fucked, aren't we?"

"Most likely. Either you find the will to end my life or I drag you to the altar on broken knees and return with a woman who barely resembles the creature sitting beside me now." He sniffed and hissed in pain as it wracked him for a moment before it subsided and he could pull in a shattered breath into his lungs.

"You don't think I'll go willingly? Or learn to love you?"

"No."

That was a change in tone. She looked up at him curiously. "Why?"

"It is a foolish hope. Nothing in my life ever goes as I wish it. No matter how hard I try. Why should this be any different? Besides, now, I have but seven days to convince you to love me? You are, as you noted, a stubborn creature. Perhaps in seven years, I could change your mind. But days? I think not."

She got up onto her knees for a moment and turned his head to look at her. Puzzled, he watched her, unsure what she meant to do. Leaning in, she kissed him. Gently. A kiss for a kiss's sake. Not to devour, not in passion, not in hunger. A kiss that tried to tell him she was sorry. A kiss to say she loved him—part of him—and maybe, if they had enough time in these seven days, the whole.

This poor, ancient creature. This dark king left low because he made the mistake of loving her. When she broke away, she smiled as much as she could muster. "Hope isn't ever foolish."

"I love you, my starlight."

She kissed his forehead and sat back down beside him. She wanted to snuggle up against his side, but he didn't... really have a side to speak of right now. "Are they going to let you heal?"

"Eventually. Once they decide I have suffered enough."

"And you really want me to surrender to those assholes?"

He chuckled and shook his head, then turned to look down at her. He pulled in a breath and let it go. She saw his weariness and his age play out over him for the first time.

He looked tired of it all. Of the struggle, of holding himself together as the dread King of All. She had seen him lonely and heartbroken but never *tired*. It bothered her a lot more than it should.

"You wear their marks. You belong to them, just as I do." He shut his eyes. "Your free will is an illusion. You know this, don't you?"

She could fight it as hard as she wanted, but it was a fact. This world was her home now. This place the Ancients had sculpted from nothingness. She belonged, one way or another, to the only creature they had made from scratch who was currently bleeding all over the floor. Trying to say otherwise was nothing but her trying to hold onto her stupid pride. "Yeah. I just don't have to like it."

"Then you know how I feel."

She leaned her head against his shoulder and sat there beside him in silence. He was still twitching occasionally in pain. They sat like that, both lost in thought, passing the onion bottle of alcohol back and forth between them. It was a silent under-standing.

Neither of them wanted to be like this—but here they were. Seven days.

She had seven days to decide if she would let them burn out her mind and sacrifice it all to be with Noa... or to kill him.

Or, perhaps, by some miracle, she might love him.

But was that enough time? Somehow, she knew it wasn't. Because that was the fucking game, wasn't it? *He sacrificed it all to save you. To be at your side. And you won't do the same for him?* That was the angle the Ancients were playing. That's what they wanted her to prove to them. That her love was "worthy" of him.

The Ancients loved him, as much as creatures like them were capable of such a thing. And yet, they hurt him. They tortured him, but they had engineered everything that had happened to her to bring her here to his side. They picked her. Now, they were trying to decide if she was the right choice.

She was wondering the same thing.

"Hey."

"Hm?" He looked down at her curiously.

"Take me out to the city tomorrow, if you're patched up by then."

"You wish to see my acropolis?"

"Yeah, I do." She let her eyes drift shut. She smiled faintly as he wove his fingers between hers. His thumb made slow passes back and forth along the side of her pointer finger.

"Nothing would make me happier."

"Well, not nothing." She smiled sarcastically. "If I said, 'You, me, the altar, let's do this,' you'd be happier."

He chuckled. "That is fair. But one thing at a time." He paused for a long time before speaking again. "As you said... Hope is never foolish."

ELEVEN

Edu was at the breaking point. He hadn't been allowed to stand or move in days. He had done his best to hunker into his suffering, to go to some peaceful place inside his mind and retreat from the ache that had become a searing pain in his body.

His body was meaningless, after all. It was nothing. His flesh meant nothing to him, and it never had. Perhaps that was the source of his hedonistic ways, all those years. This torture had taught him that his body was only a tool and a means to an end. Nothing else.

Indeed, he would let his mind drift away from the pain if it were not for the simple fact that Evie had been taken away. Hours stretched on, and he counted the seconds.

One.

Two.

Three.

On and on, he counted. There was nothing else to do. For hours, he counted seconds in sets of ten. For he could not move his arms, he could not lift his head, he could not kill those he wished to crush and save the woman he loved. The woman he lived for.

How many seconds he counted, he could not say, before the door swung open once more. In walked... Navaa, oddly enough. Edu had been expecting the King of All. In his hand was a chain. And walking behind him—on two, unbroken legs, was Evie.

Edu's heart soared at seeing her. She seemed, against all odds, mostly unharmed. Though there was a deep purple bruise along her left jaw that made Edu's fists clench tight.

"The King of All sends his regards. He is busy this morning." Navaa linked Evie's chain back to the wall before shoving her to the ground beside Edu. Far closer than she had been shackled before. For that, Edu supposed he owed Navaa a small bit of thanks. And with that, the Elder of Shadows left, slamming the door loudly behind him.

Evie shuffled forward. The length of chain allowed her to just reach him. Though she couldn't free him, she could at least *touch* him. Resting her head against his shoulder, she let out a rush of air. "What a *helluva* day."

"What happened, Evelyn?" Vjo was the first to speak up. "Are you all right?"

"I—I'm fine. I mean." Evie chuckled and pointed at the bruise on her jaw. "I opened my fat mouth one too many times, but what can you expect from me?" She flashed Edu a grin.

How he wished he could hold her. To kiss her. To tell her how proud he was of her to be daring enough to run her mouth to the King of All.

"He... wanted to talk. Asked me about Lydia, is all. About how she and Aon had fallen in love." Evie shook her head, clearly confused. "It was like tryin'a explain it to a space alien. I don't think he *gets* it. But he's so desperate to."

"Hm." Vjo furrowed her brow, deep in thought. "A weakness in the armor. He fears that he cannot win her heart as he did before. So he searches for a path forward by any means necessary. *Interesting.*"

"Can we use this, sister?" Ini was lying on her back on the ground but was no less engaged in what was going on. "This fear of his?"

"Perhaps. I will need to think it through." Vjo tapped her finger on her chin.

Edu cared not. She would have plenty of time to scheme. He had another matter he suddenly wished to see to.

The King of All may not understand love. But Edu very much did.

"Ini, I am in need of your assistance."

The Queen of Fate sat up, curious and bright blue eyes watching him in fascination. "What is it, my dragon?"

"I wish to ask Evie to marry me. Here and now."

Now, she was beaming in an ear-to-ear smile. "Oh! Oh! Everyone! Dtu, wake up! Wake up, you stupid dog!"

From where he had been asleep by the other wall, Dtu growled angrily in his throat, a low rumbled vibration of a dog who did not wish to be conscious. "What do you want, *elf*?"

"Oh, shush, Dtu." Ini was almost bouncing where she sat. "Vjo! Forgive me. We do not have the Priest here, so you will have to do the honors."

"Honors of what, sister?" Vjo swept her hand back through her dark hair. "You have forgotten to clue us in, once again."

"Evie! Evie, dearest—Edu wishes to ask you if you will marry him."

Her yellow eyes went wide, and she turned her head to look up at him. Edu smiled down at her, suddenly feeling somewhat sheepish. Somewhat boyish, despite all his years. Never once had he wished to marry another. Not even Ziza, all those years ago, for he had not seen the value in a ceremonial title.

Now, he did.

"You serious?" she asked.

Edu nodded. He was, and very much so.

A rattle of chains later, and she was kneeling in front of

him, straining against the reach of her own bindings to meet him face to face.

As her hands slipped through his hair, brushing back his sweat-matted curls, she leaned in and kissed him. When she broke away, she smiled, laughing in both joy and through the absurdity of it. "Of course I will, Red. I love you. You know I do."

Edu let his eyes drift shut and felt a peace he hadn't ever quite known. Too bad it was here; too bad it was like this. But he knew himself well enough to see that if all had been well, he would not have come to realize how much the girl meant to him. It is only in his darkest moments that he saw the flames that burned brightest.

"We are gathered here in witness," Vjo began, recounting the ceremony that was so rarely performed in their world. "We are gathered here, before the Ancients, to bow our heads in reverence to love. For even in this darkness and death, such roses may grow. To join together is to be above all other strife this world may paint upon you. No one shall wield your union against you. For love is eternal, and we are only ageless. Do you, Evelyn, take this man as your husband?"

"I do."

"And you, Edu, King of Flames, do you take this woman as your wife?"

He didn't look over at Vjo or the others. His eyes were only on Evie, who was gazing at him with wide, sparkling yellow eyes. They were perfect; she was perfect. This wedding was not what he would wish for, for her. With them both trapped in the dungeons and her battered and brutalized.

But it would be the only opportunity they ever had.

Edu nodded.

"Then I declare, by the Ancients themselves, for you to be joined as one. Wife and husband, husband and wife, may your roses grow. And may they grow with thorns."

That last bit was new, a bit of Vjo's dry commentary showing through. He didn't have long to think it over, for Evie was kissing him, holding his face in her hands and embracing him with all the strength she had. He returned the favor and wished more than anything that he could sweep her off her feet and carry her somewhere he could enjoy her company. Hell, if he were not chained as he was, he would do the deed here, the others be damned.

"I love you, Red," Evie said to him, her yellow eyes glistening with tears.

"And he loves you," Ini replied.

"No need in tellin' me what I already know." Evie grinned up at him, and he smiled back. "I used to be so 'fraid of you. An' here we are." She kissed him. "All things considered, could be worse."

Edu chuckled quietly. There was only one way it could be worse, and it was if she were dead. And that day was likely coming soon. But he would cherish this moment until his last days. Which, once more, were likely not far off.

Evie lay down, snuggling up onto his legs, resting her head on his thighs. He sat down on his heels as much as he could, the pain in his shoulders be damned. It was the only shelter he could give her, and he would do it at any expense.

The girl was as afraid and hopeless as the rest of them. But as she fell asleep against him, she did so with a smile.

And that, right there, was worth it all.

* * *

Lydia walked beside Noa through the streets of his acropolis. The buildings here were far better built than the ones she had seen on the outskirts. They were polished white stone, soaring high with ancient architectural details that made her stop and stare. The trim of the buildings was painted blue, purple, turquoise, black, white... all the colors of the Houses, even green and red.

He had taken her to a long stretch of water, a low canal that ran out from the temple and through the city. It was dotted with reeds, palm trees, and other grassy areas. It was stunning. Periodically, there were benches or small round platforms, made of granite and etched on nearly every surface with imagery and symbols.

She realized that instead of the hieroglyphs like in Ancient Egypt, here it was replaced with the eldritch and esoteric writing of the Ancients. The language only one man could read —the one who walked beside her with his hands clasped behind his back, a cold expression on his face that only softened when she caught his gaze.

They weren't in the city alone. For the first time, she saw people wandering around and going about their days. They wore ink of every color, save hers, naturally. "You let them stay here?"

"Those who serve may live in peace."

"Even Edu and Dtu's people?"

"In truth, the Houses are dissolved. They are but subjects of the Ancients and to myself. If they kneel to their King, they are welcome here. I am not a tyrant, Lydia, however much you wish to believe such a thing."

"I don't want to believe that."

"But it would be simpler if I were irredeemable, would it not?"

She'd thought the same thing several times since all this mess started. If she could hate him, it'd make her choice to kill him or kneel to the Ancients a lot simpler. But part of that stained-glass window of a man was the one she loved. And she was only just starting to get to know the whole. "I don't hate you."

"For that, I am glad." And with that, their conversation trailed off.

The King of All enjoyed silence.

He was so stern. So serious. Her warlock would have been quipping remarks or complaining about the sand in the air and the blazing hot sun on his black clothing. They walked in silence for a little bit longer as she debated his words.

"It's fucking bright," she complained.

"Deserts tend to be so, yes," he replied with a small chuckle.

With a flick of her wrist, she summoned from thin air a pair of sunglasses. Grinning goofily at how awesome that trick still was, she put them on. That felt so much better, not having to squint in the glare of the sun off the sand.

"What are those?"

She looked at him, surprised he didn't know. Then she realized he didn't remember much of the past five thousand years. All of human advancement was lost on him. "Sunglasses. The tinted lenses darken everything and make it easier to see."

"I assumed such by their name." He reached out with his flesh-and-blood hand and carefully plucked the glasses from her face. He turned them over as he examined them with one eyebrow crooked.

Then he put them on.

Lydia snickered loudly.

"I see their purpose. But I do not like how they dull my sight of the shadows," he observed dryly as he looked around the area with them.

Lydia cackled in laughter.

"What?" He turned back to her. "What is so very funny?"

"You look ridiculous."

"No more so than you." He pulled them off his face and watched her, utterly confused as to why she was laughing. He handed them back to her, and she put them back on. "You are an odd creature."

"You just look seriously out of place dressed like an evil pharaoh and wearing a pair of Ray-Bans."

"I thought they were sunglasses."

"It's a brand name."

"Brand name?"

Lydia laughed again and took his hand in hers and squeezed it. "Never mind. Silly human stuff."

As they resumed walking, she kept her hand in his. He looked down at her after a moment. "Tell me of Earth. It has been a long time since I have visited it."

How the hell do you sum up five thousand years of human history? "It's... smaller than when you were last there."

"Has the void struck Earth as well?"

"No. No, I mean... there are a lot more people. A *lot* more. Eight billion of us and counting. We're slowly destroying the planet and each other. But technology's advancing, and while we still have a long way to go, I have hope it'll all work out. Honestly, I don't think people are any different than when you knew them. For all our advancements, all our technology and spreading civilizations, we're still the same."

"What do you mean?"

"Well," she gathered her thoughts, "I read an article once about a bunch of Ancient Egyptian craftsman who wrote on pottery about how their wife snores like a donkey and how they hate it when the in-laws come to visit. That kind of stuff— that's what I mean. We'll climb a mountain just because it's there. We'll hate, we'll love, we'll form our tribes. People are still people."

"We."

"Huh?"

"You said 'we.' You think of yourself still as a human, as a mortal and belonging on Earth?"

"No, I guess—" She paused. Did she? "It's hard to come to terms with everything that's happened. I know I'm not human.

I know I don't belong there anymore. But it's recent history for me."

"How long has it been since you came to Under? I fear my sense of time is... disjointed at best." He looked off, a dark expression crossing his already dour features. Disjointed was a nice way of saying "broken." He clearly blamed his mad self for the issue.

"Seven months now, I think, give or take."

He chuckled and shut his eyes. The hardness smoothed. "Forgive me. Of *course*, you still think of yourself as one of them. You are so very young. It is easy for me to forget. Not even a single year has passed."

Shrugging, she smiled at him. "Apology accepted." They kept walking and once more fell into silence. He really wasn't a tyrant, was he?

She jumped up onto a long row of stones that ringed the water and decided to walk on that instead, for no real reason other than she could.

He watched her, fondness softening the coldness in his eyes. "As the eons stretch on, I hope you never lose your sense of playfulness."

"I can't make promises. I can't even wrap my head around living that long."

"It changes us all. Slowly, perhaps, but like mountains whittled down by the wind, it is inevitable."

"What about you?"

"Hm?"

"What were you like, all those thousands of years ago?"

"Violent."

That made her laugh.

He looked at her, confused for a moment, before understanding flashed over his features. "Ah. You think I am violent now. My love, you cannot fathom the creature I was when I was first born. My creators are entities of blood, death, and pain. I had no one else to learn from, no other examples to follow. I would gather unmarked humans from Earth in the thousands —tens of thousands at a time—only to slaughter them and bask in their destruction."

That made her stop walking. He turned to face her. For the first time, he had to look up at her a few inches, since she was still standing on the granite stone that ringed the aqueduct.

It was a dumb question, but she asked it, anyway. "Why?"

He pondered it for a moment as if struggling to remember. "Merely because I wanted to. I wished to taste their flesh. I built this world out of the deaths of mortals."

"Your undead army." She finally put it together. "That's where they came from."

"From where else did you think they hailed?"

"I guess I never thought about it, or I thought you were making a fashion statement." She shook her head, feeling like an idiot. "I guess I thought the answer was 'magic' like everything else."

His fingers twined with hers, and he lifted her hand to his lips and kissed her fingers. "Those days are gone. I mistook the void I felt for bloodlust. I grew tired of the slaughter. It took me so very long to realize that what I desired was a companion... a soulmate. Now that I have that, perhaps I will finally know peace."

If only it were that simple. But somehow, she really doubted it. *People don't change. Love doesn't make them different.* She always knew Aon was a "bad man." She always knew he was violent, dangerous, cruel, and sadistic. She had loved him, anyway. And maybe, just maybe, a sick part of her loved him because of those things.

If she could look past those parts of her warlock and love him, could she do the same with the man who stood before her? She still didn't know.

Without warning, he reached up his clawed hand and

poked her on the end of her nose. She jumped, startled, and he smiled dryly at her reaction. "You look so morose. I find I do not enjoy your serious expression. It hurts my heart. Do change it."

"Is that an order, *my King*?" she teased.

"Yes, in fact, it is."

Laughing, she shut her eyes for a moment and let her laugh trail off in a beleaguered sigh. When his hands went to her hips, she felt him step into her. Even with her standing on the row of stones, he was only an inch or two shorter than she was. For once, he had to tip his head up to kiss her. She let her hands fall on his shoulders and felt the warmth of his skin beneath her palms.

Even if he was being possessed by the Ancients—or made whole, or whatever—being around him was like fighting an addiction. She traced her fingers up his neck and across his cheek, and he moaned quietly against her lips at the sensation.

But he ran the show. He called the shots. He was kissing *her*, not the other way around. He took his time, languorous and slow, exploring her.

She knew she shouldn't be enjoying this as much as she was.

He broke the kiss, pulling his head away just barely. He was teasing her, making her chase his embrace. He was tempting her to follow him down this path. As he always did, and always would, he was luring her into him.

Catching one of her hands in his, he slipped it down between their bodies. Before she could react, Noa palmed her hand against him, cupping his arousal. She gasped at the sensation and froze. He broke the kiss to move his lips to her ear, whispering, "Do you see what you do to me, with just a single kiss? No one in all my years has ever done this to me. No one but you."

Her mouth went dry. Even through the clothing that separated them, she felt as though her body had been lit on fire.

Damn him to hell. Damn herself for how much she enjoyed him and how much she never wanted him to stop.

"I would throw you over that bench and rut you like an animal in this city square if you would let me," he murmured into her ear before placing a hot, wet kiss against the hollow of her neck. "But I think you would refuse me. You are so terribly bashful."

"You're the worst." She tried to sound firm, even as her already questionable restraint was fading.

"That was not a denial," he teased and let his teeth graze her jaw, nipping at her. "You should not have let me discover I was your weakness. You must have known I would use such an admission against you."

His clawed hand went down and grabbed her ass and squeezed it *hard*. It made her yelp and move in the opposite direction, which was to press herself up against his chest instead. She glared at him angrily, and he chuckled at her expression.

"I hate you sometimes," she complained in a growl. It only made his grin bloom wider. "Wipe that stupid—"

There was the sound of water moving from behind her as if something huge was rising from the deep. There was a deafening roar. She turned her head to see a massive, forty-foot crocodile breaching the surface. Its maw was open and streaming water, rows upon rows of deadly teeth like a shark shining in the sun.

And coming straight for her.

TWELVE

Lydia screamed.

Suddenly, the ground was rushing up toward her. Noa had thrown her there, chucking her behind him as the creature reared up to snatch her from the shoreline like a wayward goat.

She hit the sand and rolled on her back. He had literally put himself between her and the monster.

With a raise of his clawed hand, the monster burst into black flame.

The crocodile shrieked, pulled a full reverse, and fell backward, landing in the water with a loud splash and a sizzle. It slunk away beneath the waves, injured but not dead.

Noa turned to look down at her and grinned. "You look delicious to more than just me, it seems. A shame it felt the need to interrupt and ruin the mood."

"Hah hah." Pushing to her feet, she brushed herself off. "That one certainly wasn't one of mine."

"No. The Broken Ones have only one master. I do not think it knew I was here, or else it would have known better than to attack."

"Broken Ones?"

"So very much of the understanding of our world has been lost." He sighed drearily and clasped his hands behind his back as he watched the wave of water move up the aqueduct with the swish of the monster's tail. "So much that they have all chosen to forget."

She walked up beside him, and he looked down at her with a faint smile. He wrapped one arm around her and, with the other, traced his fingers down the lines of ink on her cheek. "The Broken Ones are those who enter the blood of the Ancients but whose minds cannot withstand the change. They are shattered in the process, left barren of anything but bestial, primal needs. And so, their bodies change to reflect such."

Oh.

That was why they were like that... that made so much more sense than what she had assumed, which was "because the Ancients and reasons."

Seeing the proverbial lightbulb go off in her head, he chuckled and leaned down to press a kiss to her forehead. "I would ask what you believed had happened to them, but I think your answer would be 'magic' and 'you didn't think about it.'"

"Pretty much." She turned to watch as the last of the creature disappeared beneath the level of the water. Fear suddenly ran through her, as cold as ice, and it made her shiver despite the heat of the sun. "Is that what'll happen to me, if I refuse to surrender?"

His hand cupped her cheek and turned her to face him. "No. Never will you become like they are. You are too strong to fall in such a fashion. Even if they decide to remake your mind, you will persist."

"How do you know? Have you ever done this before?" She tried to find shelter in her cynicism. "How many other potential brides have you had?"

He chuckled. "None, I assure you."

"How're you so sure I *won't* turn into a Broken One, then?"

"For you are the strongest soul to ever grace this world, my love. If you were to challenge the Ancients themselves, I am not so certain you would lose. I know you will persevere and continue to resemble yourself."

Resemble myself. That's all I might be, in the end. Someone who resembles who I should be. That was why he wouldn't drag her to the altar kicking and screaming. Because what might end up coming out the other side might not be the same.

She didn't want to confirm her theory, so she only stepped into him and hugged him. Really, she wanted to hug Aon. Her warlock. This man would have to do, even if he was the reason she was in this predicament to begin with.

He folded his arms around her. "You needn't be afraid."

She was terrified. No need to tell him that. He knew. She stayed silent, which was as much of a confirmation as he needed.

"Today was meant to lighten your mood, not ruin it." He squeezed her tighter against him briefly. "I have an idea on what might distract you."

She shot him an incredulous glance. She could guess.

He laughed at her expression and shook his head. "No, no... not that. Later, perhaps."

"What, then?"

"I would like to teach you to fight."

"Don't I already know how to fight?" She thought she had been doing damn good, all things considered. "Ouch."

Noa chuckled and looked down at her with a haughty but playful smile. "I did not mean it as an insult. Besides, it may cheer you to knock me around for a while."

"You'll let me hit you?"

"I'll let you do a great many things," he said with an arrogant twist of his lips. "If it brings you joy." The insinuation dripped from his voice like hot wax, and it made her shiver again. Some things about him hadn't changed; that much was clear.

The world around them warped as he teleported them away. When they reappeared, they were standing in what looked like the middle of a large coliseum. She didn't want to ask why he had a building like this. She was pretty sure she had seen enough movies about the Roman empire to get the gist of it.

The stands were empty. She wouldn't have any witnesses for her getting her ass handed to her. His expression was just a little too eager. Narrowing an eye at him, she had to ask. "Is this just an excuse to beat me up and battle-hump me like the last time?"

Noa's face was caught in surprise at her words, and then he laughed, loudly and sincerely, at her choice of words. Unexpectedly, he caught her face in his hands and kissed her. It was a gesture of pure affection. Of love. The look on his face when he pulled away was happiness. "Once more, I hope you do not lose your sense of playfulness. Or your odd humor. While I have never heard the phrase 'battle-hump' before, I find I am instantly fond of it."

"That wasn't a 'no,'" she teased, parroting back his words from earlier.

"This isn't about conquest, I assure you." He took a few steps back. "Although a lovely side effect, I suppose. I wish to teach you to better defend yourself. You hold your own well enough, but you have the potential to be so much more."

Lydia shrugged. "All right. Why not?" It'd get her mind off things, that was for sure.

"Good." He flicked his hands, and a pair of wooden rods appeared, one in each, meant to look like practice swords. "First, a spear is the wrong weapon for you. Qta had a foot of height on you and a hundred pounds of muscle. You need something faster and something that reflects the passion you fight with. He had strength, whereas you have speed. Fight with these instead." He tossed her the weapons, and she caught them. Clumsily.

He summoned another pair of his own. "Now, defend yourself."

That was all the warning she had.

If she thought he was going to go easy on her, she was dead wrong. He was fast. He seemed to come out of nowhere. She had to stop thinking and just focus on trying to keep him from pummeling her silly. She jumped backward, deflecting his blows with her practice swords. It wasn't until a minute in, of her simply trying to avoid getting her skull smacked open, that she realized that was his point. He was trying to distract her. And it was working.

"Move on instinct," he instructed.

She deflected another blow, and this time took a swing back at him for the first time. She hadn't intended to; it just happened. He jumped back, the wood stick narrowly missing him. He grinned, proud and fiendish all at the same time.

"Don't *think*. Move."

The loud cracks of their weapons impacting each other were almost deafening. He seemed to take her attempt at hitting him as a sign to dial up the pressure and the speed. Just when she thought she was catching her footing, he changed the name of the game.

Wasn't that the story of her life here in Under?

Every time she tried to adjust, the world turned up the dial. And the King of All was nothing but a perfect representation of this world. In all its fucked-up glory.

"Feel where you need to be. Feel where you need to go."

Her arms stung from the impact of weapon-on-weapon. Taking the blow with her sticks was about half as bad as taking them to the flesh. But half was just that—half. She ducked under one of his swings and cracked a wooden sword into his ribs. He let out a grunt and knocked her back with a knee to the chest, nearly sending her sprawling to the sand. She had to stagger to catch herself. But he didn't give her a chance to recover, and he was on top of her, never relenting, never easing off.

"Be in the moment, my starlight."

He caught her in the arm with one of his swords. It was a glance, but it stung, and she could feel the welt already forming. Snarling in anger, she swung for his head, and he barely managed to pull himself out of the path of her swing. Noa laughed. When he started to speak, she swung again, and this time he needed to jump back again.

Something surged in her.

It was anger.

She was *furious*.

Not at him, not really. Because despite it all, she knew that none of this was really Noa's fault.

She was angry at the world. At the Ancients. At all the fucked-up bullshit she'd had to go through.

She went at him like a wild animal, not caring anymore if he hit her back. She needed to hurt someone as much as she'd been hurt. She was sick of being a punching bag.

And he was the one swinging wooden swords at her head right now, so he was a perfect target.

She let out a shout of rage and went at him with everything she had. She let go. Let go of it all. The urge to beat the ever-loving hell out of him overpowered her.

"That's it," he praised, grinning from ear to ear. He held his own against her rally. She didn't really pose a threat to him, she knew. All the talk about training was a sham. He wanted her to get all her anger out and did it the only way he knew how.

It worked. She'd give him that.

She ducked under one of his swings, avoided his knee to her chest, and cracked her stick across his back. That one caught him by surprise, and he hissed a breath in through his teeth as the wood left a red welt across him, painting crimson across pale skin and black ink.

When he went to strike her with his elbow, she dodged again and rammed the hilt of her other sword against his ribs. He grunted and staggered, and he barely blocked her next strike. He locked weapons with her, and for the first time since they had started, she stopped to breathe.

It was a mistake.

As she looked into his spilled-ink eyes, something in her couldn't take it anymore. In the vacuum left behind by anger, her grief was all she had left. Tears stung her eyes, and she felt her grip on her weapons loosen.

When the tears began to fall, she couldn't do it anymore. Her hands went slack, and her wood swords fell to the dust. She collapsed to her knees a moment later. She just couldn't do it anymore.

He said she was strong.

Strength only went so far.

She was sick of this. Sick of fighting. Sick of the unfairness. Sick of having to stand her ground against the world itself.

The Ancients asked too much of her.

They wanted to break her?

They might just get their way.

Before she really knew what was happening, she felt him sit in the sand next to her, and his hands were gently lifting her, pulling her into his lap to hold her. She let him and sank into his embrace. She couldn't deny there was comfort in it.

"It will be all right. It will all be all right." His voice was a quiet murmur close to her ear.

"Don't lie to me."

"I will do many things. But in this, I am sincere." Lips pressed against her forehead. "I will never lie to you. Not now, not ever."

Her heart felt like a gaping black hole, because she

knew... just somehow *knew*... that was false. Resting her head against her shoulder, she shut her eyes and let herself cry, because she so desperately wanted to believe him.

* * *

Evie was finally asleep, curled up by Edu's side. How he wished he could have spent a proper wedding night with his bride. But this would have to do.

Somehow—*someway*—he would ensure that the world she lived in would be free.

Whatever the cost.

"Do not think like that, my dragon," Ini scolded from where she sat. "Do not rush to death so blindly."

"I am not blind, Ini. I am mute."

Ini giggled at his bad joke. "Regardless. There is hope."

"All I can hope is that my demise is worth something in the end," Edu thought as he looked down at his new bride. His only hope was that his end might set her free.

"I will not repeat that," Ini grumbled. "I will not accept your death-march as inevitable. You seek this because you *wish* it, Edu. A noble suicide is still a waste."

"Then tell me how else this goes, Ini."

Ini sighed heavily and looked to Vjo. "Edu wants to know our plan."

"Plan? Who said I had a plan?" The Queen of Words chuckled.

"Because you *always* have a plan." Ini rolled her sapphire eyes. "And I have already heard it in your head."

Vjo looked over at her fellow royal and then up to the window and the moons beyond. "I have no plan. Merely a hope. Our hope lies in the heart of our young miracle."

"Riddles, spider." Dtu grunted.

Vjo stared at Dtu blankly. "Lydia."

"She is no miracle." Dtu shuffled, scratching his back against the stone wall like a bear might do to a tree. "The Ancients made her. They planned all this bullshit from the start, and you know it."

"I am glad to hear you no longer blame her." Ini smiled over at the wolf. "That is progress."

Dtu sniffed. "Progress is worthless if we all wind up dead." He scratched at the stubble at his chin and nicked a scab that was healing from their war. He winced but made no noise as he reopened the wound carelessly and it began to ooze. "So, what does the mare have to do with us?"

"She does not know we are prisoners. She believes the King has kept to his word and set us free. When she learns, and it is a when, old boy—" Vjo smiled. "She will come."

"You think she will choose us over the man she loves? Pah!" Dtu laughed. "You're a fool. Love isn't logical. Love is stupid, Vjo. It is as foolish as it gets. She will never betray him, no matter what he does. Look what he did to the boy, her friend, and still she forgave him."

"She does not love him. Not yet. And even still, I do not believe you are right." Vjo leaned back and shut her eyes tiredly. "For in the end, she *trusted* Aon's intentions. This King of All cannot be trusted, and she is about to learn that. The play is already in motion. Actions are already being taken."

"How do you know what's going to happen?" Dtu shook his head. "You aren't the psychic. That's baby blue's domain."

Baby blue. Edu smiled. He hadn't heard Dtu call Ini that in a very, very long time. He forgot how much it amused him. Judging by the matching beaming expression on Ini, he was not the only one. Even though Dtu was technically the youngest of them, Ini was doted upon by all—save Aon—as the prized youngest sister.

It reminded him that these were his siblings. His family. His wife was lying asleep at his side. He would have been overjoyed if it were anywhere but here.

No, he didn't want to die for the sake of it. He did not want to throw himself to the flames for that he did not wish to live.

But he *would* die to protect them; it was as simple as that.

"I know what is going to happen, for I have been told what will come to pass." Vjo yawned and lay down on her meager pile of straw, matted in blood.

"By whom?" Ini asked eagerly.

"By someone who wants the downfall of the King even more than Edu. Someone who hates him even more than all the rest of us, combined."

"Riddles, spider. Riddles," Dtu growled.

Vjo smiled. "All I can tell you is this—I have been visited by an old friend who has come to me in my dreams. It is by his hand the King shall fall in the end."

* * *

Lyon sat and watched his wife sleep on the cot at his side. He had spent the day and night with her, only venturing out of the cell to fetch her food when she hungered.

She was not well.

Kamira was not made for captivity. In the few times she had been forced to spend a few days inside the Cathedral of the Ancients due to war or severely inclement weather—in the days they were together before the mountains crumbled and the skies were no longer capable of producing such things—she would grow weary, weak, and a malaise would overcome her.

It was the only time she would not speak her mind or grin and snap playful insults at those around her. She would sink into a deep mood from which it was impossible to rouse her. Not until the open air touched her face again.

Over the past few days, he had watched her begin to wither like an Earthen plant denied sun.

He traced his fingers over the marks that decorated Kamira's face. Evergreen, beautiful, running down both her temples, and a swatch in the center of her forehead. It looked like Gaelic warpaint.

Lifting one of her braids in his fingers, careful not to wake her, he toyed with a bead that sat at the end of it. It was an act he did frequently and from the very start. He had sworn to stay here at her side, and he would do so until the very end.

Kamira had defeated him. The ambush she had laid upon his ill-fated battalion had been perfectly successful. She had taken him as her prisoner of war... after making love to him in the woods.

If Lyon had been told such things would come to pass the day prior, he would have expected his life to be forfeit. He would have expected he would not wake the next day, instead devoured and torn asunder by the wrathful woman and left to rot in a field.

Lyon would have expected, if he woke at all, to smell the scent of drying and stale blood where it lay cool and coagulating upon the ground. Instead, it was the aroma of the woman that greeted him as he awoke with her head resting against his chest. She smelled thickly of incense, of cloves, of fresh grass, and the woods.

They were in a tent, and judging by the thick leather and the crude red symbols painted upon it, it was in Edu's war camp. There were shackles clasped around his wrists, upon which were markings, inked in red. Edu's kind was not known for their spell casting, but they knew how to keep a prisoner. Even one whose body could change shape, like his. He was a prisoner. It was not a surprise.

The pile of furs stacked by one post on which they were lying was surprisingly comfortable, and Lyon decided the image of the woman with a fur blanket pulled over her was awe-inspiringly beautiful. Indeed, Lyon admitted to himself, there was little about her that did not take his lifeless breath away.

He knew why, then, he had accepted her seduction so quickly, why she had so easily scaled the walls to his self-control. Lyon had always found her alluring and mysterious. He had always wanted her. But what, he could not fathom, led to her change toward him?

Lyon reached a hand up to gently examine one of the beads sewn into her hair. It looked as though it was made of bronze, and he found himself fascinated by how it caught the light.

Kamira stretched, suddenly reminding him entirely of the felines with whom she shared so many traits. She arched, stretching out her arm across him, and yawned broadly. Her incisor teeth were also slightly too pointed for normal, he observed idly, as she let her arm fall back across him. She shifted into him, let out a small "hmnh" sound, and seemed content not to move. As if right here was precisely where she wished to be.

The tigress was now lounged against him. Lyon could not complain. He did not fight his impulse to gently wrap his arm around her. "What will happen now?"

"I do not know," Kamira answered. Her next words surprised him. "But I have decided that I will not leave your side."

She never had. Not even now, after she viewed his allegiance to the Ancients and to the King of All as a betrayal, did she send him away. Even as he kept her prisoner, a state so very far against her nature. The thought that his wife may never again roam the mountains as the beautiful and deadly predator that she was brought him deep sorrow.

He could not let this come to pass. He had to convince her to surrender to the Ancients, as he had done and as they all must do. For if she met the void, he would follow shortly after by his own hand.

Kamira shifted and let out a snarl in her throat. Her brow furrowed in her sleep. She was having a nightmare.

He shifted to roll her onto her back and sat up to gently shake her shoulder. "Wake up, my love."

She never suffered such things, not in all the time he had known her. To see her like this now worried him deeply. She did not rouse. Instead, she bared her teeth at whatever was troubling her so in her dreams and let out another growl.

Lyon shifted to sit up more fully so he could hold her shoulders with both hands and give her a stiffer shake. "Kamira."

Her eyes flew open.

Her fist met his face.

With a grunt of pain, he turned his head to the side and sighed. It had hardly been the first time. He prayed it would not be the last, all things considered.

Before he could speak, her arms flew around his neck, and she hugged him tightly. He returned the favor. "You were having a nightmare, my love," he said quietly.

She nuzzled into his neck, the feeling of her hot against his tepid skin. "It was not a nightmare. It was a vision." She sighed and leaned up to kiss him on the cheek where she had punched him. It was as close to an apology as she would give.

"A vision? Of what?"

"Of my death."

Lyon pulled back to look down at her and ran the backs of his fingers across her cheek. She leaned into his touch, and he rolled his hand to instead cup her face gently in his palm. "It was only a dream, my love. Nothing more."

"I saw how I will die, husband. I know how it will come to pass if you do not free me from this room."

Lyon shook his head. "I cannot. You know that. I serve the King, and it is by his will that you are imprisoned."

"It is by his hand I will die, lover. Mark me."

Lyon winced and wished he could argue that such a thing was outside the realm of possibility, but that would have been a bold-faced lie. If his king decided to execute Kamira for treason, it was his right. What he may do in such a case, he could not say. He dreaded to think about it, and so, in a rare act of avoidance, he did not. "He has said nothing to me to such an effect. Merely that if you cannot surrender, he would see it done. I requested mine be the hand to do the deed."

"In five days' time, I will be committed to dust, Lyon. Mark my words."

"Five days?"

"The Ancients have given the bastard that long to convince Lydia that she loves him. He won't. That means her mind shall be forfeit, like yours. Then I, Dtu, all the rest will die, since we will no longer serve a purpose. Even you and his loyal servants, maybe." She huffed a laugh. "And I thought the warlock was a madman."

"I... you were dreaming. This is a fanciful nightmare." Lyon felt a creeping cold run up his spine at her words. He wished he did not believe her. But some deep part of him was welling with a sense of dread. What if she were telling the truth? What if her spurious nightmare was indeed a vision of the future?

From where did this vision come, if so?

"Ask him yourself, then." Kamira jabbed a finger into his chest. "If you will not believe your wife, you will believe your idiot King."

As he did not know which of her errant beliefs he wished to correct—that his king was an idiot or that he was, in fact, her king as well—he decided to correct neither. Even as she issued the claim that he would not listen to the counsel of his wife, he knew such words would be wasted on her. He leaned down and kissed her forehead gently. "Very well. I will ask him what he intends and set these fears to rest."

"You will set something to rest before long if you do not release my chains, my love. And it will be me." Kamira lay back down and sighed. "Now, I have a migraine." She murmured something that could have been *"shadowy bastard,"* but he was not quite sure.

Leaning down, he kissed her, and she met the embrace with a small smile. "Sleep. I will return."

With a stretch and a heavy yawn, his wife was already half-asleep once more. Of that ability, he was heavily envious. She could fall asleep anywhere and on a moment's notice. It took him hours of lying awake to quiet his mind long enough that he might finally drift away. One disturbance and he was a lost cause until the next opportunity arose.

But not her.

She was out like the proverbial light, lying on her side now, her hand curled into the fabric by her face. She was untroubled by whatever nightmare—or vision—had just graced her.

It had not been a lie, he knew. Kamira was many things, but a spinner of falsehoods she was not. They caved in seconds, and she could never bring herself to waste her time with them. She was, in all ways, brutally honest. And he treasured that about her. She believed this vision to have been real.

With a heavy sigh, he stood from the bed and summoned his clothing. The dread in him returned, as he was slowly coming to terms with the simple and unavoidable fact that he may no longer be able to avoid the question of which master he truly served, the King of All, or his love for his wife.

Before long, he feared he may need to choose.

And in the process, one way or another, it would mean his destruction.

THIRTEEN

Another day had come and gone. The sun had slipped into its eclipse, and it marked that in the morning, she'd have four days left to decide if she was going to kill Noa or let the Ancients make her love him.

Or hope, by some miracle, she might love him. But since she had no control over that option, she really could only focus on the other two and pray that lightning struck twice.

And she wasn't even one step closer to deciding. She'd made no progress in the argument that was going on inside her head. That day Noa had taken her around his acropolis, it was as beautiful as it was intimidating, just like him. Then, he had "sparred" with her.

It'd been a cheap excuse to get her to let down her guard and vent her frustrations, but it had worked. There was no question that the King of All loved her deeply. He had wanted to help her in the only way he knew how.

In a lot of ways, letting her vent had helped. Tears didn't last forever, and soon they wound down. He had picked her up and taken her back inside. She hoped he would stay with her, but he had to go take care of more "business" and left her to her own ends, exploring his home.

Their home.

Whatever.

And as always, when she had time to herself, she thought and debated in her head and tried to convince herself that everything was going to be all right in the end. That in a day she'd realize she loved the King of All, and that'd make everything that had happened all okay, if it meant they could be together.

Noa. He was so much more serious, so much more ancient in how he felt and conducted himself. He was hard at times, but there was a deep, sincere kindness in him that she could see snippets of, now and again. The seriousness made his humor difficult to see for what it was, but she was learning. There were definite reflections of the warlock in the King.

They really were the same man. But did she love the whole or only the shadow?

And even if she had the answer to that question, she had a harder one that followed in its footsteps. If she did love him, *would she accept this new world for him?*

That was the rub. That was the thought that she kept skipping over in her head all day.

Did it matter if she loved him of her own volition, if she couldn't accept what this new Under was like? This world of sand, of sun, of *service*. It was far more orderly than the Under she had been thrown into, that was damn sure.

But did that make it better?

The seven Houses with their seven Kings and Queens, with their plots and wars and fighting and schemes... with their *drama*. It had cost her her life once. And cost thousands of lives over the centuries as they bickered and fought for supremacy.

But it'd been vibrant. Colorful. *Unique* and wild. Each city felt like its own place, its own strange magical world. This Under?

It was a desert. A beautiful desert with a city that took her breath away. But for all its scale, all its magnitude, all its *grandiosity?*

There was a smallness to it that she realized had been haunting her. In all her torment with Noa, in all her distraction with him, it'd been hard to get a spare second to think about. But now? Left to her own devices, wandering *their* home?

She just kept bumping up against the thought like a needle skipping over a scratch on a record.

Even if she loved him—was this okay?

Even if she loved him—could she accept this world?

Even if she loved him—where were the others? Were they okay?

She didn't know the answer to any of the questions. They all just jumbled around in a tangled mess. After a while, she came to one conclusion. There was one thing she could do to help her decide. Lydia did the first thing that came to her mind whenever she felt hysterically out of her league. She drank.

She didn't want any of her summoned shit, though. She wanted something different. Something real. And for the life of her, she couldn't figure out why it mattered.

Finding someone to fetch her a bottle of alcohol wasn't hard. Everyone in this place was terrified of her and seemed more than happy to do her bidding. Requesting that they bring her the strongest thing they had, what she received in return was a nondescript brown glass container, around the size of a wine bottle. She thanked them, they muttered something while bowing to her, and she went to find somewhere quiet to wedge herself and get drunk.

The reason why she needed to get drunk was obvious to her. She already knew the answer to her first problem. It was staring at her, in all the artwork on the black soaring stone columns and in the downturned faces of the cowering servants.

Even if she did love Noa...

She couldn't accept this new world.

Not of her own free will.

She missed the Under she knew. For all its fucked-up-wrongness, for all its *chaos,* it felt more alive. Vibrant.

Full of laughter and life. And love. And fine, a lot of murder, but there had been joy in that too. Even when they'd walked the streets of the acropolis, it had felt... too quiet. Too calm. Too *peaceful.*

There was a time she would have begged for just a second of that kind of order and peace and lawfulness to have visited her when she had just become a Queen of Under. And now? She wanted to give it all away, if it meant she could be sitting at the Festival of the Moons again.

But that wasn't going to happen. And that meant she really only had two choices.

Kneel to the Ancients and make them *make* it all okay.

Or kill Noa.

There now was no longer a third, pray-for-happiness choice.

Question one—could she kneel to the Ancients?

It just felt wrong, to give every last bit of herself up to them. Even if they were inescapable, even if she did serve them in some stupid way as the Queen of Dreams. She wore their marks, and it was their power that kept her alive. And she was grateful for that. She could finally see the beauty and terrible grace in this world of monsters and death.

But to give up her free will?

To let them into her mind to rewrite her to their whim?

It made her skin crawl. She knew it was stupid. She was a toddler fighting against bedtime. It was going to happen, one way or the other; it was only about how much crying and kicking she did before it happened.

Maybe she was just a child refusing medicine in the end.

Maybe this was something that was honestly going to help her, and she was too stubborn and foolish to accept what was best.

Then why did it feel so very wrong?

This had to get resolved, one way or another. She knew she was bound to be at Noa's side, no matter what. She knew she couldn't run from him. One, there was nowhere to hide, and two, she didn't want to. She still felt drawn to him, even now. The two of them were linked, bound together, from here on out.

Until death did them part.

What was she fussing about, really?

Why not go kneel at the altar and accept the role they wanted her to play? To be the obedient Queen of All, a partner to their only living creation? It'd be so easy to say "fine" and drop to her knees and let all her strife and worry be wiped away. To let them fill her mind with their "peace" and their will.

But this indignity was all she had left.

Everything else had been taken away from her at this point. Her home, her life, her friend, her freedom. Every shred of what she used to be, they'd ripped away. She wouldn't give up her soul to them too. That was reserved for either herself or *her* Aon.

Around and around she went.

Hence, the booze.

She pulled the cork on the bottle and sniffed it, and her eyes watered. It smelled like vodka. Strong-ass vodka. Taking a sip, she was glad to find it tasted sweeter than it smelled. But holy hell, her request for the strongest thing they had was certainly met. Idly, she wondered how much alcohol she'd have to drink to get black-out drunk now that she wasn't a human anymore.

Here's to finding out.

She made her way through the palace, sticking to the outer corridors, not wanting to be stared at or gawked at by the terrified servants. Someday, maybe, people wouldn't shrink away from her like she was anathema itself. Lydia doubted her life was going to last that long. So far, she'd been right about that on both counts.

Finding a balcony, she walked out onto it to look up at the stars. The balcony was large and as beautiful as the rest of the Ancient Egyptian or Babylonian palace in which she had become a "willing" prisoner. Two of their colorful moons were high in the sky. As she was looking up, she nearly tripped over something unexpected lying on the ground in front of her.

A figure was lying there, looking up at the sky, his hands folded across his stomach. One metal, one flesh.

Drawing up short, she looked down at him, wide-eyed and startled. She hadn't expected anyone to be here, let alone him.

Noa glanced at her, then looked back up at the stars. "Good evening, Lydia."

He was lying on the floor of the balcony and stargazing. His expression was stony and unreadable. She remembered him doing something like this in his library, staring up at his painted starry ceiling, the night he told her about the Great War and his part in it. Finding someone like him lying on the ground was odd, and now it was even odder than it'd been with the warlock. That man had been nuts. This guy had no excuse.

"What're you doing?" she asked.

"Thinking."

"On the floor?" had been what she had replied that night in his library. He had answered, *"Apparently,"* and she found herself smiling at the memory. She knew he was baiting her, and she debated taking the lure just for fun.

That night, she had also been wandering in thought, with the topic of him heavily on her mind. She had also offered him a drink, and he reminded her that he couldn't drink in her presence, wearing a mask. This guy, once more, didn't have that excuse.

She offered him the bottle. "I think it's paint thinner."

He chuckled and took it. Tilting his head up, he took a hard swig of it, then another, and went for a third when his eyes began to water, and he had to stop. He wiped the back of his flesh-and-blood hand across his face to clear them and handed her back the bottle. "Upon inspection, I think you may be right."

She laughed. His dry sense of humor was starting to grow on her.

"Will you stay?" he asked, breaking her out of her thoughts.

It kind of blew up her plans to get smashed and let unconsciousness wipe away her problems, but the look he was giving her was so soft for his usually hard features that it melted her resolve. "Yeah." She sat down next to him and took a sip of the alcohol. That she didn't cough made her proud of herself.

After a moment, she glanced over to see him holding his metal claw up, turning it over, watching the moonlight glint off the surface. He was looking at it as though it were foreign to him.

"You don't remember why you have it, do you?"

"The Priest told me."

"Why do you still have it? I'm putting bets on the fact that you can regrow your hand without breaking Edu's curse." She took another sip of the alcohol. It was already starting to kick in a little bit. Good.

"That is true."

"Why not ditch it, then? Do you like having it?"

He clenched the metal gauntlet into a fist and then slowly relaxed his fingers. "I despise this atrocity."

"Want me to ask a third time, or do you want to admit you're dodging the question?" She nudged him playfully in the arm.

He sighed and reached for the bottle. After a swig of alcohol and passing it back, he dropped his hand on his chest. "You know why I keep it."

Yeah. She knew. He wore it because it reminded her of *her* version of him. Because it was a little bit of the man he wanted her to love, left over.

He had given up the world and his mind for her sake. And now, this. Just more proof of what he was willing to sacrifice for her.

And what she wasn't willing to sacrifice in return.

They fell into silence, trading the bottle back and forth. After a while, she started to feel a little cozy. "This shit's effective."

"It seems I can only get you to spend time with me if you have a bottle in your hand. I am not sure how to feel about this. You like to drink, don't you?"

Snickering, she shook her head. "Only lately. Besides, it won't kill me now. Might as well enjoy it."

"I despise being drunk. I dislike surrendering control of the situation." And yet, he took another sip and returned it. Although she suspected he had a far higher tolerance than she did.

"No shit." She laughed and grinned at him. "This is my shocked face. I don't see you ever giving up power if you can help it."

He moved his arm to pull her up against his side and rest his human hand idly on her leg. "There is one way I would give up control."

"Oh?"

"If you wished to take it from me."

"What?"

"I would give you my throne if you desired it. Be your slave, if it would please you. I would let you strip me naked and parade me through the streets wearing nothing but your chains, if it would convince you to love me."

"You're lying."

"I am sincere. If my slavery would convince you to surrender to our makers and kneel at their altar, then I would be your loyal pet until this world turned to dust."

She tried to look away, but his fingers gently turned her face back to him. Dark eyes captured hers, and she saw in them a desperate pain, a loneliness, and a frantic kind of hope. He knew their clock was ticking, just as much as she did.

He thinks I won't do it. He thinks he'll have to force me and watch me be ripped to shreds.

Then it hit her. All at once.

He's afraid.

"You don't know what'll come out the other side if you have to force me at the end of the week, do you?"

"No... I will love you, regardless."

"But I might be broken if I go kicking and screaming."

He went silent, but his jaw twitched, and he looked back up at the stars, his hand falling away from her face. "I do not want this to come to pass. But I find myself helpless to change the fate I see before us."

"I don't want your throne."

"I know." He shut his eyes, his brow furrowed in pain. "I do not know what else to give you. I would lay it all at your feet. But I know it is not the same. That this is not how love 'works,' as you say. But I know not what else to do. I would have let you linger like this for ten thousand years, but the Ancients will not have it."

"Why?"

"I do not know why they act the way they do."

"No, I mean, you said you'd let me linger like this for ten thousand years. Why? Just because you don't want to see what kind of fucked-up mess I come out the other side?"

His dark, spilled-ink eyes met hers and captured her gaze easily. "Because with you, I am happy. This is *enough* for me.

With you, I have felt a void in me filled for the first time in all my years."

"That might be the alcohol. Or you put something somewhere weird by accident."

He laughed. "No. I mean my words." Before she could react, he pushed himself to his feet and took her by the arms and lifted her to her own. He was so damn strong, and she was just starting to feel the alcohol, so her reaction time was a tiny bit slower than it should have been. "And you are avoiding them."

Yeah, she was. She was trying to dodge his words like bullets. But they hit their marks. He was afraid; he was desperate. He was trying his best to make everything right for her. He loved her. She was more important to him than anything else had ever been.

And she was being selfish.

She was clinging to a world that wasn't ever really hers.

And the man she loved was still right there in front of her. Just a piece of a bigger whole.

The more she looked up at him, at the fear in his jet eyes, the more she needed that desperation to go away. It hurt her, straight to her soul. She didn't know if she loved the "big picture," but she knew she cared about him, and she just learned how deeply.

Maybe that was enough.

She looked down at the bottle of alcohol, took one last swig, and put it down on the ground. She took him by the hand and gently led him over to the railing-less edge of the balcony. She looked out over the acropolis. The city that Under had become or, rather, returned to.

The world she decided wasn't enough for her. Somehow. Despite its beauty.

Selfishness. He had laid everything at her feet. And she still wanted more. Not even—she wanted *something else.*

Taking a deep breath, she held it for a moment and then let it out.

Fuck it.

Fuck it all.

She was done fighting. What was she worth, in the face of all this? In the face of an entire world, of a man who had lived maybe a *hundred* thousand years alone, what did it matter? She'd be with him... one way or another. It was just about how much of her mind was still hers when it was all over.

This man had given up everything for her. Both versions were still willing to give up everything. But she was belligerently clinging onto the shred of hope that there might be some secret way out that would appear from thin air at the last possible second.

Shutting her eyes for a moment, she steeled herself. Maybe it wouldn't be so bad. Finally, she was ready to break the silence. "Four days."

He turned her to look at him, his brow knitted in confusion. He didn't speak, but his expression was one of utter disbelief.

"I'll go with you to the altar. I just want the four days. Once it's up, I'll go willingly. I'll kneel at your side. And I'll become your Queen. And I'll welcome them in."

Suddenly, Noa fell to his knees in front of her. The look on his face was one of pure joy, disbelief, and shock. A man who had just won the lottery. No, a man who had terminal cancer and was told he was going to live. He wrapped his arms around her waist and rested his head against her midsection.

Reaching down, she ran her hands through his hair. It took her a long moment to realize he was crying. She tilted his head back, and he tried to turn away from her. He looked embarrassed. He only stopped trying to turn away when she cupped his face in her palms and stooped down to kiss him. When she broke the kiss, she wiped his tears away gently with her thumbs.

"Forgive me. I have not cried in five thousand years. Not since I cast my creators into the pit in my despair."

"You have. You just don't remember."

He growled playfully and rose from his knees. But still, the wavering hope and happiness hadn't left him. "You are a contemptuous little imp when you are drunk."

"One, I'm not drunk. I'm buzzed. And two, I'm always a contemptuous little imp." She squeaked as he scooped her up, and she found herself taller than him again as he held her off the ground and looked up at her as if she was the world and the stars to him.

He called her his starlight, after all.

Damn him.

Damn him for what that did to her heart. This was inescapable. *He* was inescapable. Madman or king, he always would be. She kissed him again and knew she meant her words. She'd let him take her by the hand.

She'd become his queen.

* * *

Lyon knelt at the foot of the throne. It was mid-morning, and the king had been late to rise. Judging by the mild smile upon the man's normally dour features, it had been for pleasant reasons. Indeed, his lord seemed distracted, gazing off into the dark shadows of the throne room as if thinking of something else.

Perhaps that would bode well for him, for the conversation he was unsure as to how to begin with his king was a deeply unpleasant one. If he did not tread carefully, he would be placing his own life into grave danger. He was more than aware he lived at the pleasure, and at the leisure, of the man who sat on the onyx throne above him.

"Speak, Priest."

Dread welled in his chest and took away his voice for a moment. He had sat all the rest of the night and morning debating how to begin this conversation with his king, and now that he was here, it seemed like a foolish, deadly endeavor, no matter which way he approached it.

His reluctance to speak did not go unnoticed. The King of All watched him with his whole attention. "You are troubled. Come, now. I find myself in a good mood this morning. There is little you could do to dampen it."

Oh, but he was certainly bound to try. Lifting his head, Lyon looked up at the other man. "May I begin with a question?"

"I do not see why not."

"How fares Lydia?"

He smiled. "She has agreed to be my queen. In four days, when the sun eclipses, she will come to the altar with me and kneel of her own accord." The man was *beaming*.

Lyon could not say he blamed him, although he was deeply surprised.

Then the realization of his words sank in a half second later. Four days. Lyon rarely felt a chill, and yet he felt as though his lifeless blood ran cold as ice. His wife's words, speaking of a vision that promised her death in now four days' time, echoed through his mind.

"Does she know you still hold the others prisoner?" he asked quietly, schooling his tone to be even and stoic. Perhaps that would be a careful enough transition to the topic at hand. He could not believe Lydia would not be currently screaming and railing against their king if she knew she had been deceived by him. Let alone agree to... surrender.

"No. But soon enough, it will not matter. For then she will serve the Ancients without question, and their imprisonment will no longer be of consequence to her."

"What do you plan to do with them once she kneels?" He

dreaded to ask, but it was the only reason he had come. He needed to know.

"Execution." The King of All let out a breath. "Which, some part of me shall mourn those idiots I have known for so long. But they cannot be trusted to leave well enough be. They will forever seek to overthrow my rule. I shall make it quick and painless, I assure you."

Lyon bowed his head. He did not bother to ask for his wife's freedom, for he knew her vision had been true. Whoever had granted it to her, however it had come to pass, it did not matter. In four days, death would come for her. Be it by his hand, or by the King of All, he did not know. It did not much matter.

The King chuckled. "Do not be so glum, Priest. You have a wedding celebration to plan, do you not? Let us make this an occasion that all of Under will remember for thousands of years to come." When Lyon did not lift his head, the King of All let out a small grunt upon seeing his expression, one that was surely painted with the grief and angst that threatened to hollow out his heart. "Ah. Your wife."

"Yes, my Master."

"Convince her to kneel, Priest. Convince her to join us. Or I fear I do not know a way to spare her from the fate of the others. I cannot suffer a traitor to live, no matter the cost. You know this." To his slight credit, the King of All held some remorse in his voice.

Lyon stood slowly, bowed, and turned to leave. He needn't hear any more.

"Was that all, Priest?"

"Yes, my King. Thank you for your time."

Halfway from the room, the King of All spoke again, arresting Lyon's steps. "For what it is worth, Lyon, I have faith you will succeed. Yours and Kamira's love is the strongest this cursed world has ever known. I remember little of those years I spent in madness, but I remember how I sought to destroy all love where I could in a jealous rage. But yours—yours was too sacred for even me to sour with my violent covetousness."

Lyon bowed his head in silent thanks and, with that, exited. He hoped he had successfully hidden the dark cloud that consumed his thoughts. He prayed his years of keeping all emotion from his face kept his anger from leaking through.

It was not his sadness and grief he hoped the King of All had not seen. For that, he did not care. It was what else burned beneath the surface, like a raging river beneath a frozen surface, that he needed to keep tamped down.

For the first time in as long as he could remember... he felt *rage*.

A dozen steps away from the door, and he wavered. He balled his fist and drove it into the wall next to him, cracking the stone surface for feet in all directions.

He made no noise of anger. It was not terribly effective at calming the fury inside of him, although, perhaps, it did enough. Reluctantly, he admitted to himself that the outbursts of his compatriots like Edu made a small bit more sense now that he understood the context.

The servants around him scattered in fear. None of them had ever witnessed him in such an outburst. Before anyone else could come investigate, he disappeared into a rush of white bats. He had only one place he needed to be, which was with his wife.

His fury was not at his king, for it was his right to do as he saw fit. Nor was it at the Ancients, whose rule was absolute and whose will would always be his to serve.

No, his anger was pointed far more squarely at himself and at the horrendous choice he had before him.

Now, he must decide between his fealty to his king and the Ancients he served... or his love for his wife.

Either way he may decide, he knew one thing for certain. It would cost him his life.

For either the King of All would take his head for his betrayal or he would take his own in grief when she lay dead upon the sand.

FOURTEEN

Lyon stood over the sleeping form of his wife. She had not roused, despite it being well past midday. She was often one to sleep in and nap, and honestly, she enjoyed lounging about as much as she enjoyed a fight.

But still, it was odd she did not wake upon him entering the room. Even if he had done so silently, he had never once in his life ever succeeded on sneaking up on her, even if she was asleep. It spoke once more to how she was sinking into the bog caused by her captivity. She did not wake, for she did not have the strength to do so.

Their roles had reversed indeed. He was now the keeper of chains. She, here in this cell. It was far more dismal than the conditions she had kept him in as a prisoner of war so long ago. But, sadly, he did not have much say in the matter.

He sat down beside her on the cot, and the shift of his weight stirred but did not rouse her. Her brow was furrowed in an unpleasant dream, although not a nightmare as he had seen before He ran his hand slowly along her hair, stroking it back from her face. Leaning down, he kissed her forehead gently, and the press of his tepid lips against her warm skin soothed whatever she could see within her mind's eye. Snuggling into the pillow, she let out a small grumble and sank back into sleep.

She could not take this place much longer. She would not have to, one way or another. Lyon gave up the feeble hope that he might convince her to surrender. It had been a childish wish of a naïve heart to ever think otherwise. It was the only path he saw before them where they would both survive.

Truly, he had taken to imprisonment far better than her. His conditions had been considerably more amenable, if confusing, he had to admit.

A few days had passed with Lyon as a prisoner of war within Edu's camp after Kamira had captured him. The tent they kept him chained within was comfortable, and they treated him well. He was an Elder, after all. They fed him and did not torture him. He could not complain.

Kamira had even fetched him some books she managed to scrounge up and borrow from others. Mostly the dreamers, she admitted. Few else in the camp kept such things, especially not on a campaign. But the dreamers were never found without their works of fiction in their bags.

And he was never found without the tigress at his side, it seemed. She returned to his tent every night to sleep. Between them, conversation—and physical affection—flowed easily and freely. It did not feel like he was a prisoner at all. It was boring when she had matters to attend to, such as today, and he was left alone.

The tent flap flew open, and in stormed Kamira. She looked none too pleased. Lyon closed the book and stood quickly. "Brace yourself." She sounded irritated at best.

Lyon did not have the opportunity to open his mouth before he saw the reason, and they were hard to miss. One of the two men was a sizable creature, let alone both.

Edu and Dtu strode into the tent, one after the other as they would not fit abreast through the gap. The leather flap closed behind them. Dtu was in human form. A rare occasion, but his wolven form would barely fit inside the enclosure.

Lyon suspected he may be about to die. Or, at the very best, to be set free in a bargain with Rxa. Interesting that each carried a similar weight of dread in his heart.

A matter to debate if he survived the night. He dropped to a knee. "King Dtu, King Edu," Lyon greeted them formally. They were still kings, even if they were his enemy through no actions of his own.

The direction the conversation took was quick and unexpected. Perhaps Lyon had spent too much time sitting through lengthy discussions of politics. What followed was not what he would have predicted.

Edu laughed.

"What is funny?" Kamira asked, sounding indignant already.

"If you wished for a pet rock, Kamira," Edu teased, "you only needed to ask for one."

Dtu nudged Edu in the arm with his elbow. "What she's been using him for far exceeds what a rock might deliver."

"That depends entirely upon the size and shape of the rock," Edu quipped back.

Dtu let out a loud guffaw and slapped Edu on the back, a motion that barely budged the bigger man. Lyon could only watch the exchange with thinly veiled mortification. He looked down at the ground between his knees, and he heard the two kings laughing at his reaction.

"I think the bloodsucker is blushing," Dtu observed.

"How can you tell?" Edu shot back.

"I think you both have had enough fun already at our expense," Kamira snapped at them, stepping forward from the edge of the tent to challenge them in their goading.

Edu raised his hands, shoulders still shaking in laughter. "Very well, very well. We mean no offense, kitten."

"Of course you do. You always mean offense." Kamira's hands released from their fists at her side, all the same. "You come with news, do you not? Of Rxa's answer for your offer of trading for him?"

Edu sighed heavily and shook his head. "Rxa will not trade."

"What?" Kamira and Lyon said in unison.

Lyon stood quickly from the ground in his shock, and Dtu took a step forward as if to strike him back down to his knees. But Kamira stepped in between the two, an action that both confused and amazed Lyon. He was not the only one, judging by Dtu's posture. The wolf pulled himself back in shock.

"You would protect him?" Dtu asked. "Why, Kamira?"

"Why has Rxa refused the trade?" Kamira asked, intent upon ignoring her king's question. "For what reason has he left Lyon lying here to rot?"

"If Lyon has been lying down, it has not been to rot," Edu quipped again, unable to help himself from making the joke.

Kamira growled at him, her hands tightening into fists once more.

"Dtu, look how defensive she is!" Edu stepped toward Kamira, calling her bluff. The tigress took a step back, forcing Lyon to retreat as well, lest she back into his chest. "Tell me what your intentions are with the prisoner, and I will tell you Rxa's words."

Lyon knew best to keep his mouth shut.

Truth be told, he was eager to hear the shifter woman's answer. While he had entirely different reasons for wishing to know the reasoning behind her protectiveness of him and her insistence to stay near to him, the desire was the same.

Kamira swore and began shouting at Dtu and Edu in the shifter language Lyon did not understand. They were the only

House to have their own dialect, one utterly foreign to any of the others. The style of speech was raw, primal, and unrefined.

As Kamira finished her rant, Dtu drew back in surprise at whatever meaning she had conveyed. He asked her a question, clearly second-guessing her words.

Kamira shouted one word in response.

Dtu clicked his tongue, sighed, and then shrugged. "You have odd taste, Kamira. But... very well. I accept your choice."

"What in the name of the Ancients did you two just say to each other?" Edu asked, sounding disgruntled to be left out.

"She has chosen him as her mate," Dtu explained. "She says she defeated him in battle, and now she is claiming him. It is her right."

Edu paused for a long time and then howled in laughter. Kamira growled and opened her mouth to yell at the big man but didn't have the chance. Edu scooped her in a hug, pulling the tall woman up off her feet. "You are quite something, little tiger!"

"Put me down, you oaf!" Kamira snapped. But the warrior would not be convinced and kept her in the one-armed bear hug up against his chest.

"As far as I can tell, that is how you idiot animals express that you are enamored of another. You have fallen for the High Priest!" Edu roared again in laughter. "How astonishing. Finally, Kamira, perhaps you have someone on which you can cut your teeth. Or maybe you intend to use his tall arse as a scratching post. I, for one, will be eager to see you calmer. Perhaps your pet will be good to eke out some frustrations, hm?"

Kamira growled deep in her throat and narrowed her eyes angrily at Edu's masked face. "Put me down, old man."

Edu dropped her back to her feet and chuckled at her anger. "Very well. He is yours to do with as you see fit. It is clear Rxa has no interest in rescuing him."

Lyon's thoughts were reeling, tangling over each other. Was

she saying she... no. That was impossible. He cleared his throat. "May I..." He paused as the three of them turned to look at him. When nobody punched him or shouted at him to shut up, he continued carefully. "Ask why, precisely, my king has abandoned me?"

"So polite," Edu replied gruffly. It was not a compliment. "For someone who has been betrayed for the warlock. Rxa has abandoned you for Aon's benefit. The specifics are unimportant and are lies I do not care to repeat. That is the fact of the matter." Edu turned and began walking for the exit. "Come, wolf. Leave your kitten to her new scratching post."

Dtu chuckled and walked after the bigger man. "Ah. Kamira. You may release him from his restraints."

"Why?" Kamira asked warily.

"Mh, it's simple," Dtu said and turned his wooden wolf mask back toward the two of them. "If he were to leave here and return to his own forces, they would kill him as a traitor and a spy. You are one of us now, High Priest. Whether you want to be or not."

Dtu and Edu left without another word, and the tent flap closed behind them. Kamira let out a long, heavy sigh and clasped her hands on the back of her neck, tilting her head down and using the weight of her arms to stretch.

Lyon knew not what to say. He had many things to ask, many questions he did not know how to put into words, let alone phrases graceful enough to convey such rocky topics. Kamira's moment of melancholy faded as quickly as it had come, and she turned to look up at him with a smile. "I suppose you are stuck with me now, Priest."

When Kamira had awoken, he could not say. He was lost too deep within his thoughts and memories. But when he rose from his thoughts upon the past, she was looking up at him, green eyes fixed upon his. She had not shaken him from his reverie; she was quite accustomed to his long bouts of living within his mind. Oft, he would be accused of brooding. But after spending any length of time in the presence of the King of Shadows, he could not lay claim to any such state of being. No, Lyon was merely thinking.

Daydreaming of better times.

When he could not meet her gaze and he looked away, she sat up beside him on the cot. "You spoke to him."

He could not muster the words to speak and instead merely nodded his head once, weakly. That was all his tigress needed to confirm her vision, and she let out a rush of air from her lungs. "Then do it, already."

"Do what?"

"Kill me. Keeping me here in this cage any longer when that is my inevitable fate is meaningless cruelty."

No.

No.

He could not do it. He had to free her—

Sudden pain wracked him. Flooded his mind. It doubled him over. Sinking his head into his hands, he rested his elbows upon his knees and wished the world away. Wished everything might simply cease this torment. "Do not ask of me this thing…"

Arms circled around him, and she shifted her weight beside him to kneel and lean her body against his frame. The chains that bound her wrists and ankles rattled as she did, a horrid reminder of her current state of being. "I love you, my foolish mosquito. I would far rather to die by your hand than his in cold blood."

His grief, which might have once consumed him into tears, turned hot in rage once more. He stood, needing to express himself in such a way that he could not do with her against him. Stepping toward the wall, he balled his fist and rammed it into the stone surface. Once, twice, the stone fractured around him.

A third time and chips fell to the ground. A fourth and his knuckles were bleeding, but he did not care.

A fifth and he might have been screaming in fury. He did not know. A sixth and someone was now in the way. Kamira had stepped between him and the wall and grabbed his fist within her palm.

"Enough."

He felt his fangs against his lower lip. They had extended in his bloodlust and abandon. His eyes would be ringed in red, he knew. It was rare that he let this kind of mood consume him... very rare.

His kind's heart did not beat. Only under three circumstances would it lurch to motion within his chest and find the means to warm the ichor that was his blood and move it through his veins. The first, and most common, was when he hungered to feed. Second, in anger. Third, in passion.

Only once or twice before had he allowed himself to feed the anger that would cause his dead heart to beat once more. It was not something that came naturally to him.

As Kamira ran her tongue along the blood that oozed from the wound upon his knuckles, he did not know which of the three reasons drowned his hearing with the *thud* of his heart as it came to life. He did not particularly care.

For she was to blame for all of them.

Before he knew what he had done, he had pushed her up the wall and stepped into her body, pinning her there with her feet off the ground to even their heights. She wrapped her legs around his waist and arched her chest against him, pressing her breasts against the fabric of his clothes. How he wished it was his bare skin instead.

Tilting her head away, she signaled to him that she knew what he wanted. What he *needed.* This was not the first time a moment between them had gone this way.

Digging his fangs deep into her neck, she moaned in pleasure. As her blood, hot as liquid iron, rushed into his mouth... so did he.

The better part of a week drifted by with Lyon as—well, he supposed he was no longer Kamira's prisoner. The shackles around his wrists had been removed, and he had been allowed out of the tent to walk the grounds and catch some fresh air. The Elder of Moons hated being indoors and preferred to be on the edges of the camp.

With little else to do and finding himself unable to be split from her for any length of time, which was a matter that was as wonderful as it was unsettling, he followed her.

Kamira was sitting on a branch, some twenty feet up, lounging on the tree limb like a jungle cat. Indeed, she was even resplendent with a tail that swished idly where it drooped from the branch, curling hypnotically back and forth.

Lyon blinked as something bounced off his shoulder. He looked down at the ground and saw a pebble roll away. Furrowing his brow in confusion, another tiny rock bounced off the book he was reading and fell to the grass.

He looked up at Kamira. She was lying there on the branch on her side and propped on her elbow with one knee bent and the other straight. Full lips cracked in a playful and impish grin. One hand was cupped, palm up, and the other was picking at a pile of small stones she kept there.

"What are you doing?"

"Seeing how many."

She flicked another pebble at him, and he flinched as it bounced off his face. He wiped at his cheek with his hand. What an odd creature he had found himself suddenly both besotted with and imprisoned by. "'How many' what?" he dared ask, not knowing for sure if he wished to hear the answer.

"Until you lose your temper. I have wondered for over a

hundred years if it could be done. No one has managed it yet, as far as I can tell. Not even that wretch Aon."

Ah. It was not the first time someone took sport in prodding at him. "You will have a long wait." Lyon looked back down to his book and did not react as another small rock pegged him in the shoulder.

"We shall see."

Tap. *Another pebble.*

"I am impossibly stubborn, you know," Kamira said.

Tap. *Another pebble.*

"I surmised," Lyon responded as he turned the page of his book.

Tap. *Another pebble.*

"How many rocks do you have?" Lyon asked and glanced up at her narrowly from the book.

She looked down at the pile in her hand, shuffled them, and sniffed dismissively. "Enough."

It was a challenge, and Lyon found himself bristling unexpectedly. Was that not her goal? He tucked his anger back down and resumed reading. "We shall see," he repeated her words.

And so... it went on.

It was not long before she began to count. "Forty-seven."

Tap. "Sixty-two."

And on.

Tap. "Ninety-one."

Lyon was under siege.

History's tiniest siege, perhaps, but a siege, nonetheless. If an ancient city could feel, he knew this would be what they experienced, beset by such relentless annoyance.

"One hundred and sixty-two," Kamira counted.

Tap. *Another pebble.*

Oh, for the love of the Ancients, summon lightning from the clouds above to please strike him dead! Lyon screamed in his mind but kept his countenance still. He had been unable to turn a page in his book for over an hour.

"One hundred and sixty-three..."

Tap.

Lyon would—

Tap.

—endure this.

Tap.

He had suffered worse in his days.

Tap.

Far worse, after all.

Tap.

He had not known he had snapped until he was mid-air and mid-strike. The battle between them had ended in a tryst of passion that had resulted in much shed blood and sweat.

When they had both met their end, he let out a loud groan against her as he spent himself into her. He was releasing far more tension than just physical desire. Lyon's shoulders went slack with some great weight removed from him.

"The answer," he muttered faintly against her skin, "was two hundred and thirty-three..."

Once more, he found himself in her arms upon the cot, spent and exhausted. His heart was pounding in his ears. It was funny how deafening it was when he had it. It was one of those ever-present sounds that one did not miss until it was gone, like the birds in the skies after the death of Qta.

Kamira did not mind his violent expression of love and desire for her. If there was ever a single soul in this world he would not have to explain his actions to, it would be her. She lay beneath him, the wound upon her neck from his bite already healed. She was utterly radiant. She enjoyed the moments when he let himself free of the restraints he placed on his urges. No, she did not enjoy them; she basked in them. Now was no different.

"When did you decide you loved me?" Lyon asked Kamira gently, his voice sounding dry and scratched. He felt weak and empty in the void left behind by his anger. As it had calmed, what was left was the inevitable decision that lay before him.

"The first time we fought in that glade, I knew I was yours." Her eyes sparkled at the mischievous memory. "That first bloody dance of ours will always be my favorite. And you?"

"The same. But I do not think I admitted it to myself until the night in Edu's camp near the woods," he replied. Kamira laughed at the memory, knowing quite well the evening to which he was referring. "With those damn pebbles of yours."

"One of my prouder moments," she boasted and ran her hand along his cheek. "If I do say so myself."

Lyon laughed, as much as he could muster, and sighed, shutting his eyes. He pushed himself reluctantly from the cot and stood. Summoning his clothes back to himself, he let out a long, wavering breath. "Come what may, my tigress. I am in your hands, now and forever."

"My Priest?"

He looked back at her and raised his hand, palm down, and pulled his fingers into a fist. With a flex of his power that should feel foreign to him, and yet was second nature, he released the chains that bound her. They fell to the ground with a clatter.

In the duel between his loyalty to the Ancients and his wife... there never truly was a contest to be had.

The path before him had been set long before this moment. There was never any other way this could transpire.

Kamira rose from the cot and moved to stand in front of him, a look of confusion on her face. She did not need to voice her question; he saw it plainly.

"You will never surrender. If I keep you here, you will die in four days as you said with all the rest. I would take my life in that moment to be at your side in the ever-after. If I release you now, he will execute me rightfully for my treason. Run for the horizon, and you may yet live for a time before he hunts you down. Either way... my life is forfeit. It has always belonged to you. My heart is yours. Do as you will, my love. The choice is yours."

She reached up and cupped his face in her hands and kissed him. Tears ran down her cheeks, and he knew this was goodbye. He shut his eyes and let himself enjoy the embrace for what it was.

The tragedy in it was beautiful, in its own way. Death always was.

"Come with me." She sighed as she broke the kiss and hovered her lips over his. Her breath was like a fire against his skin, so in contrast with his own body temperature.

"I cannot. I serve my king and the Ancients. But I belong to you. The two facts are indelible and yet cannot be true at the same time. I must stay and serve my king, even if it means my death. But you... you must run."

"Oh, my love, I do not have any intention of running."

His eyes flew open at that. "What?"

"I was warned about my death. With it, I was also given strict instructions." Her lips curled into a sick smile. "I have work to do."

He had to stop her. That was madness, even for her. He would not lay down his life only to have her throw hers away. "No, you—" His voice choked off in his throat. Pain lanced through him without warning.

Kamira yanked her hand free of where she had buried it into his chest. She had ripped up under his rib cage and, upon exiting, took his heart with it. He had, to be fair, said it was hers. His wife had a sick sense of humor, indeed.

Lyon coughed and tasted blood in his mouth.

"I know you would try to stop me. I am sorry." Kamira

sighed and dropped his heart to the ground and licked some of the blood from her hand. "As much as I loathe taking instructions from *that* bastard, there is no other way forward."

He tried to beg her to rethink. But his mouth flooded, and air would not come to his lungs. She caught him as he fell and lowered him to the stones and knelt at his side. The world was fading to black as she left him to the peace of a death he would return from soon enough. He heard the door to the cell creak open.

"I love you, my statue, my Priest, my angel. More than life itself. I will do all I can to see this made right. For all of us... but most of all for you."

* * *

Edu must have slipped into unconsciousness.

It was starting to happen more frequently now, fading in and out of the waking world. He could not call it sleep, nor was it restful, per se. It was merely that his body and his mind could no longer stand the pain of being chained as he was.

But he woke to the sound of humming. Fingers were gently brushing through his matted hair. How he wished to bathe. How he wished to *move.* To stretch his legs. To put his left shoulder back in its socket.

Blinking his eyes open, he realized his head was not drooped forward, painfully pulling on his shoulders. The chains that kept him shackled were not causing him the familiar stinging pain. His head was resting on something soft. Someone soft, more accurately.

Evie was sitting in front of him, his head resting on her shoulder. She was petting his hair and humming to him quietly. Trying to soothe him. Why?

"You were having a nightmare," she muttered quietly and

kissed his cheek as if she had heard his silent question, but he knew she had not. It had merely been a good guess.

He let out a huff of air, feeling indignant that he had been having a bad dream. He couldn't remember it now, whatever it had been.

"Oh, now. Even big lugs like you get t'have nightmares. I think especially big lugs like you." Evie giggled and kissed his cheek again. "I wish I could just figure out a way to break these gosh-darn chains," she whined.

Edu nodded weakly and rested his head back against her shoulder. It felt nice to take the weight off, even if only briefly. He would have scolded her for whining, but honestly, right now he could not care much less.

"Only a royal has the power to break these chains," Vjo provided, not realizing Evie was just making conversation. Vjo had a bad habit of giving insight into situations that did not require it. It was irritating far more times than it was useful. But the spider was always the smartest person in the room—which Aon had hated to no end—and she felt the need to conduct herself accordingly.

"I wanna go home," Evie whined again.

Edu chuckled and this time could not find the ability to be annoyed at her whine. He agreed wholeheartedly. As did everyone else in the room, he knew.

The door swung open with a heavy creak on the wood frame.

For a long moment, he did not dare lift his head. He did not wish to see whoever had come to taunt them.

"Look alive, *shit-heels*."

Edu cranked his head up so fast that he pinched a nerve in his neck, and he growled in pain. The voice he heard was one he had not expected in a thousand years.

Kamira!

His statement was echoed in tandem by Ini, who tried to

leap to her feet but was dragged right back down by the chains holding her against the wall.

The shifter woman was grinning wildly, a hand planted on her hip. Blood stained her hands, and he knew she had fought hard to reach them. Luckily, it seemed most of the crimson stains upon her were not her own. Kamira looked around the room and laughed once. "*This* is what you all look like without your masks? What a disappointment. You all look... normal. Especially you, dog. You're scruffier than I would have imagined."

"Now is not the time, cat," Dtu shot back to her.

"What took you so long?" Vjo was the only one who did not respond in surprise. "You were meant to arrive yesterday."

"Lyon, of course. I love him dearly, but he could spend a solid year staring off and thinking his way through one conversation." Kamira let out a weary sigh. She walked over to Dtu and picked up the chain binding him to the wall in her hand.

What was going on? Edu would tilt his head or demand an answer, but he was helpless as he was.

Luckily, Evie shared his question. "Whaddaya mean? What're you two talkin' about?" she piped.

"I have instructions, as does Kamira." Vjo leaned back against the wall, settling back in to where she had been asleep. "Can you break the chain binding him?"

"Mmh." Kamira tilted her head thoughtfully as she looked at the metal in her palm. "I think I remember the symbols he showed me."

"Who? Who showed you what?" Evie asked.

"What's happening, sister?" Ini interjected.

"I hate riddles," Dtu complained.

Vjo and Kamira ignored the lot of them. "Let us hope you can, Kamira." The spider queen cut through the rabble of commentary that would have all been drowned out if Edu had a tongue with which to speak. "Or else we are all lost."

"Yes, yes. I get it." Kamira stooped down on the dirt and, using her nail, began to scratch the eldritch language of their Ancients into the packed sand floor of the prison cell.

"Only a royal can break the chains," Dtu grumbled at Kamira. "Whatever you're doing is appreciated but useless."

"You're half right." Kamira sniffed as she looked down at her work and tilted her head from one side to the other, examining her work and seemingly trying to decide if it was correct. "Only a royal knows how."

"I don't get—"

"Shush, Dtu." The spider and the wolf were now embroiled in an argument. Edu shared Dtu's confusion but could not voice his own. Ini was merely watching with a broad, bright-eyed smile. She enjoyed the motion of fate, regardless of what side of it she was on.

"Free Edu, not me. That asshole hasn't been able to stand up in a week."

Vjo answered him. "No. It has to be you, wolf. And only you."

"But you still aren't telling me *why*, you eight-legged—"

"There is no time to explain." Vjo cut the man off. "If we took the hours that might be required for you to comprehend what was happening, we will all be dead and dust by then."

The shifter king rolled his eyes and slumped back against the wall irritably. "I still *fucking* hate riddles."

"This is not a riddle but a mystery," the spider queen replied matter-of-factly. "Get it straight."

Now, Edu understood that Dtu was often making faces at them behind that wooden mask of his, judging by the one he shot Vjo. He couldn't help but laugh.

Kamira dug one of her nails into her palm, and blood welled around the wound. Clenching her fist, she turned her hand sideways and let the crimson liquid fall to the sand and onto the writing with a wet *tap, tap, tap.*

It sizzled and crackled with power. The tigress snarled in pain and bared her teeth as the power of the marks she etched upon the floor were tapping into her strength. She fell heavily onto one of her hands, and Edu furrowed his brow worriedly. The woman may not have the stamina to do this.

With a furious growl, she pushed herself back up straight. Reaching for the chain that bound Dtu, she thrust it down onto the blazing marks in the sand. The chain cracked, fractured, and then fell to the ground as shrapnel.

By the void.

Dtu was free.

Kamira coughed and spat blood onto the ground. She slumped onto her side and lay there, staring up at the ceiling, her features creased in pain. The woman had done a number on herself, casting magic she was never intended to command.

"Fuck" was all Kamira managed to muster.

Who had given her such knowledge?

Regardless, Dtu stood from where he had been chained and arched his back, cracking his spine loudly. Edu was deeply jealous but knew he would follow shortly when Dtu used his own strength to snap his bindings.

As Dtu walked forward to do just that, Vjo spoke up. "No, Dtu. You and Kamira must go."

What! Edu yanked angrily on the chains, feeling them bite freshly into his skin and reopen the scabbed wounds, but he did not care.

"Sister, but why?" Ini asked in his stead.

"We have strict instructions," Vjo answered, "from an old friend. That is all I can say. But Dtu must take Kamira and go. Her freeing him will be seen as an act of cowardice, of animals running to higher ground. If we are all free, the King of All will bring his wrath down upon us all. We would be dead before we made it to the edge of the city."

"Then, you have a plan?" the Queen of Fate piped curiously.

"I have been *told* the plan." Vjo shrugged. "And I see it as the only way forward, dangerous and risky as it may be. All other paths lead to our end. In this, some of us may survive before the Ancients end our world in their wrath."

Dtu growled low, clearly hating the idea. He bared his teeth at Vjo, then let out a long, disgruntled sigh. "I hate this. No, more than that. I despise it."

"No more so than Edu," Vjo reminded him dutifully. "You can stand of your own free will. He must remain as he is, if for just a little bit longer. You must go, Dtu."

"And do what?"

"I know." Kamira coughed again, clearing blood from her lungs. She struggled to stand. Dtu knew better than to offer her a hand. He would have just been clawed and hissed at for his trouble. But, weaving slightly and unsteady as she may be, the tigress remained on her feet. "I know where we need to go. If the doctor has done his part, we won't have to wait long to get our chance at revenge."

"Who?" Dtu wrinkled his nose.

"Maverick." Kamira sighed, remembering that Dtu was not familiar with the Regent of Words. "By the Ancients, you have been asleep too long, dog. Come. We should go before the guards I killed to get here wake from their slumber. Or, for that matter, my husband."

Dtu shook his head. "Politics are stupid."

"In that, we are all agreed." Vjo laid her head back against the stone wall and shut her eyes. "Now go, both of you. If we meet again, it will be before the sun may come and go once more."

"If we meet again," Dtu repeated.

"Nothing in this world is known. Nothing is immutable. Not the King of All, and certainly not us."

Sighing, Dtu shook his head and walked toward the door.

Edu could only watch as the wolf left, followed in tow by Kamira.

She paused at the door, turned to look back at him, and smiled faintly. As if she knew something he did not. Crossing back into the room, she knelt in front of him and placed a kiss on his cheek. She tilted her head to whisper, "Finish this once and for all, old man."

And with that, they were gone. And the rest of them were left, chained as they were. Evie sat there, blinking, stunned at what she had seen transpire. "Anybody wanna tell me what'n the hell just happened?"

Edu wished he knew. But he could surmise one thing from Vjo's cryptic riddles and what Kamira had said.

He would have his chance at revenge, and it would come soon.

And for that, he smiled.

FIFTEEN

"Tell me, precisely, *how* this has come to pass, Priest?"

Lydia winced at the sound of Noa's shouting.

He was furious, siting on his black stone throne. Lyon was firmly on his knees at the base of the stairs. And she was standing halfway in between, watching the scene unfold, feeling very much out of place in the whole ordeal.

Lyon's white clothing was stained crimson from the mid-chest down. There was a huge hole in the center of the fabric. About fist-sized.

As someone who had also had her heart torn out—literally and figuratively—also by the person she loved, she understood personally how much that seriously hurt.

But the thought that Kamira was free made her want to smile. She tucked it deep down and hid it as best she could. The last thing she wanted was for the King of All to point his rage at her instead.

"I can only beg your forgiveness, my Master." Lyon's voice was quiet and tired. He knew he was in deep shit, by the sound of it. He wasn't even trying to make a case for himself.

Noa slammed his hand down on the arm of his throne. "That is not an answer!"

"I am sorry."

"It does not matter if you are 'sorry,' you fool!" Noa stood from the throne and glowered at the kneeling man who did not even look up, his shoulders slumped and head lowered. A man with his head upon the chopping block. "Let us start at the beginning, then, and see if you can answer one of my questions! How is it that your wife come to be freed, Priest?"

Lyon paused for a very long moment. Finally, he let out a wavering sigh, and only then did he turn his ice-blue eyes to face the rage of the man atop the dais. "I released her."

Before she could stop him—before she could try to get in between the two men—Noa had flown down the stairs and kicked Lyon so hard in the chest it sent him sprawling onto his back. He groaned in pain and went to roll over to clutch at what was likely a shattered solar plexus. He never got the chance.

Instead, Noa bent one knee, kneeling right into Lyon's shoulder, pinning him painfully back to the stone. Noa's jaw was twitching in fury, metal claw burning in black flame. "I will ask once, and only once! *Why?*"

It felt as though the room itself was shaking with his fury. And, honestly, it might have been. Now that she knew how intrinsically tied to the Ancients, and therefore to the world itself, the man really was, she was surprised thunder didn't boom outside the building every time he had a fit.

"I could not convince her to surrender. I knew it would mean her death. I released her, so she may find a life upon the horizon."

"I will hunt her down and kill her slowly. Your folly has only ensured you *both* die!"

Ice-blue eyes flickered and... oh, hell, Lyon was crying. Tears of blood ran from the corners of his eyes into his nearly white hair. Something about the sight of it made her want to join him.

Seeing the stoic vampire in pain hit her harder than she ever thought it could.

When he spoke, his voice was calm but echoed the agony he clearly felt. "My life was forfeit either way, my King. I cannot live without her. Perhaps, though, she can live without me. If for a few days longer."

"You accept your death, then."

"Yes."

"Good."

But Lydia sure as hell didn't. She went to step forward to stop him, but it seemed the King of All wasn't done. He leaned in and snarled viciously. "Then if this world no longer matters to you, *tell me why Dtu walks free!*"

"What?" Lyon was taken aback.

And so was she.

"*What?*" Lydia stepped toward Noa. "What the *fuck* do you mean?"

He rose from where he had been pinning Lyon and turned to her, blazing wrath and ice-cold imperiousness etched onto his features both at once. "It does not concern you."

"No, no, it really does," Lydia shot back, successfully fighting the urge to take a step back. Barely. "You've been holding Dtu prisoner? Since when?"

"He attempted to sneak back into the city to free Kamira a few days past. I did not tell you, for fear of your heedless concern for a worthless cretin who has only ever wished you dead." He lifted his chin in defiance.

Something horrible ran through her. Something that felt worse than every ounce of fear she had ever felt toward him. Every bit of dread Aon, or the King of All, had ever caused her.

It felt like a poison, like acid had been poured into her veins.

It crawled through her like a living thing.

Because the one thing she never thought would happen... just did.

When she finally managed to form words, she felt as small as she sounded. As hopeless. As betrayed. "You're lying to me..."

Noa took another step toward her, calling her bluff. "And what if I am? What does it matter? Soon, you shall be my queen, and all this strife you feel shall be washed away."

Dumbly, she shook her head and took a step back from him. All she could do was repeat his question over and over in her head. *What does it matter?* She struggled to remember a time when Aon had ever lied to her. Had he? Had he ever once? He'd toyed with her—played games, sure. And sick games. But *lied?* Her betrayal turned to something like ice. "Where are all the others?"

"In the cells below. Kamira came for her mongrel king and left the others chained like the cowards her kind are." He huffed a laugh. "Animals."

"You've been keeping them all prisoner this whole time?"

"Yes."

"You were supposed to let them go!"

"I have not harmed them." He shook his head. "I did not kill them."

"Am I supposed to be grateful for that?"

He shut his eyes as if the argument was painful for him. "They seek to undo this world—to undo *my* rule. The only thing that is keeping you safe. I kept them locked away to ensure you were protected."

It was like having an argument with a wall. She could yell as much as she wanted, but it wouldn't do any good. Walls didn't budge. "You said you'd free them. That was the deal!"

"And they would never have stayed away, even if I had! Don't you understand? This was all for *you, you foolish child!*"

She put her head in her hands for a moment, and let out a wavering breath. "And what were you going to do exactly when

I finally had all this 'strife wiped away,' huh?" She went back to glaring at him. "Why did Lyon suddenly feel so inspired to let Kamira go, knowing you'd murder him for it?"

Noa simply glared at her in silence, but there was such rage in those black eyes that she wondered why she didn't burst into flames.

"You're going to kill them all." She laughed in disbelief. "Once I'm *incapable of caring,* you'll execute them. None of this matters to you, does it? None of them matter."

"Of course not." He turned from her abruptly and walked back to Lyon, who had gone back to kneeling on the floor, waiting for his fate. He clearly accepted the fact that he was going to quickly be the corpse he pretty much already resembled. The King of All glanced at her over his shoulder. "We will speak of this once matters here are done."

She felt sick. She wondered idly if the Ancients would be pissed if she threw up into the blood that ran down either side of the throne room like moats. It was the sardonic hilarity of that mental image that brought her out of her misery and back to the moment.

The King of All was back to shouting at Lyon.

"How is it that Dtu is free?"

"I do not know, my King. I did not know he had escaped until now."

"She could not have had the power to free him. Only one with the power of a king or queen could do such a thing. If you do not answer me truthfully, I will ensure Kamira suffers for a thousand years. Do you understand me?"

"Yes, my Master."

"Then how is it that Dtu has been set loose?"

Lyon shook his head. "I had nothing to do with it. I was dead on the floor in the cell where Kamira left me. I cannot fathom how she has done it. I am guilty of treason by the first count but not the second."

"Why did you betray me, Priest? For *love?*"

It was the way he said the word.

It sent a chill down her spine.

And it seemed it was not lost on the vampire either. Sadness creased Lyon's eyes as he looked up at the other man. It was an expression of pity. "If you do not understand, I fear you never will."

The meaning was painfully clear. It was a warning to Lydia as much as anything else. She thought she couldn't feel more heartbroken than she had a moment prior, and Lyon had gone and shown her she had no clue what she was talking about.

"I tire of your prattling advice. Now, you will greet the Ancients. Soon, your wife will come to follow you." Noa raised his black, blazing gauntlet, and she knew he was going to burn Lyon's face clean off.

Just as he had done to Nick.

"No!" She grabbed Noa's wrist, just below where it blazed.

He snarled at her in rage. "Enough with your interruptions!"

There was no way in hell she was going to watch Lyon die a second time in front of her face. "I'll go to the altar tonight. Just spare his life. Please."

That made him pause. His features smoothed into confusion and curiosity. He turned from Lyon to face her. "You would sacrifice your precious freedom for him? How do you know I would not merely lie to you once more and kill him the moment you turn your back?"

"You probably will. But I don't have anything else to bargain with. It's all you've left me. You've taken away everything else." She leaned in closer to him, and made sure her words lingered. "Don't worry about it, though. I'm just a *foolish child*, after all."

That hurt him. He flinched and looked off at the blazing sunlight streaming into the grand chamber from the gap behind his throne. "You would surrender your free will on the chance that I might spare his life?"

"I'm surrendering three days of suffering."

He shut his eyes and bowed his head. With a heavy sigh, he looked back to her. His expression was softer this time. There was sadness in his eyes, almost bordering on regret. "Very well. I accept your bargain. Tonight, when the sun slips into its eclipse, you and I will go to the altar, and you will emerge my queen."

"And Lyon?"

The King of All looked down at the man on his knees. "I need someone to arrange the celebrations. He will live." When she shot him an incredulous look, he replied with a faint smile. "I have no doubt that, somehow, your inexplicable adherence to this man would survive past your surrender to the Ancients. I mean my word."

"This time."

"This time."

She paused and wearily ran a hand over her face, shutting her eyes. She didn't want to know the answer, but she still had to ask. "What're you going to do with everyone else?"

"Do not press your luck, my love." He caught her by surprise with how close he was. A hand underneath her chin tipped her face up to his. "I will give you his life as a wedding present. The others are forfeit. They were the moment this world was once more made right. Your efforts were kind, compassionate, and empathetic. Those traits have no home here. I wished to make your transition as painless as possible. I see that was ultimately futile and harsher in the end. I love you, Lydia. This has always all been for you, as unkind as it may seem."

She skipped over his heartfelt admission. Right now, she was feeling vindictive, and she knew how to hurt him. And brushing him off in return was the easiest way to needle him. "What're you going to do about Dtu and Kamira?"

He flinched again as if she had slapped him. "I will let the mongrels run for now. I have other matters to attend to. I have a wedding celebration to see to, after all. The cretins down below may live until that is done. Then you will stand at my side and rejoice as I burn their marks from their flesh. Soon, you will understand that this is how it must be."

She pulled away from him, stepping out of his grasp. "You're a monster. You really are."

His eyes were dead as a frozen lake as he watched her. All warmth left him. "It seems you have finally learned the lesson all the others have been screaming to you since the moment you arrived, and you would not heed. Fear me. Hate me. Loathe me." He snatched her wrist and yanked her back to him, holding it up over her head and forcing her close to him. "But now you understand too late, my dear. Because I love you. And you *belong to me*."

He hurled her from him then, and she fell to the floor near Lyon, skidding to a stop on the smooth stone surface. There was no desire in her to get up. Not because he hurt her. He'd done far worse to her than that. But because she felt... completely beaten.

He was right.

She had finally met the man they had all told her about.

And it really was too late.

"Forgive me, my starlight..." There was pain in his voice. When she looked up at him, the regret that poured from him was nearly palpable. The line of his jaw was twitching. "I do not mean these words I say in anger. I... I am sorry for what I am. But I cannot change. I have been this thing before you for too long."

"It won't matter, will it?" She felt desolate. She sounded the same.

Noa sighed heavily and ended it with a tired laugh. "No. It

will not. Soon enough, all this will be a bad dream, and you will know peace. When the sun reaches the eclipse, you—"

A sound from outside broke him off. The sound of—Lydia didn't even know what. An explosion? She had only heard anything close to it in the movies, never in real life. She had lived a lucky life in that regard.

The building shook around them.

SIXTEEN

All three of them, Lyon, Lydia, and Noa, now stood at the edge of the opening in the throne room to look out at the city.

Their fight had been forgotten the moment the resounding *boom* had shaken the building around them. Whatever could make a building that big tremble, it had to be huge.

Lydia's hands went to cover her mouth.

It had been explosion. It was hard to see what had happened in the smoke and debris that was rising from a third of the city in a cloud, but it looked like part of the city had entirely *collapsed*.

She had seen photos and videos of earthquakes, the way the ground and freeways would crack and let go when everything underneath it moved in an unpredictable and unwelcome way.

All those people... She hoped a lot of them would be fine, picking themselves out of the rubble. If their marks survived. But without the masks to provide a semblance of armor for them? That was a crapshoot.

People in Under wore the masks to keep the King of All from seeing through to their very soul. But they also wore them for protection too. In instances like this, they were vulnerable.

But why had the city given way like that?

"What happened?" she asked, needing to voice the question even though she knew neither man had an answer.

"The tunnels," Noa snarled under his breath. His hands were tight fists at his side. "The fools detonated the tunnels beneath the city."

"Kamira and Dtu did that?"

"No. They do not have the means. It was someone else. The timing is conspicuous. There is a conspiracy at work." When Noa rounded on Lyon, the taller man took a step away from him. But he couldn't make it far before the King twisted a hand into the other man's shirt and yanked him back toward him. "Who is masterminding this scheme? What do you know, Priest?"

"Nothing, my King, I swear it. I released Kamira of her bonds. That is all. For Dtu's escape and now this, I must plead my ignorance."

"If I learn you are lying to me, you will beg for more than that."

Lyon bowed his head. "I serve you, my Master. I serve the Ancients that made me."

"We shall see." The King of All let out a long breath. "I must go. If these traitors wish to make a stand, then I will deal with it personally. Stay with Lydia. Do not leave her side. Do not let her leave the Temple grounds. Detain her if you must."

"Yes, my lord."

"Wait. There are probably people hurt down there!" Lydia grabbed Noa's elbow. "I can come help. I can—"

"No. Whatever has happened is an attack against us. I will not have you in harm's way." He jerked his arm out of her grasp. "You would distract me at best, or at worst, be hurt."

"But I—"

It was too late. Noa disappeared in a swirl of black smoke.

"Damn it!" She wanted to kick something, but everything

around her was either stone or Lyon. She imagined either option was going to wind up hurting her foot. "Lyon, what the hell is going on?"

"I meant what I said. I do not know." He reached out and put his hand on her shoulder. "You saved me a second time, my friend. I fear your efforts will be futile in the end."

She threw up her hands. "Everything I do is futile in the end. Every choice I've made has been fucking pointless." With all her soul, she wished she could just crawl into a corner and let everything blow over without her. But since day one, since setting foot in Under—since the moment she woke up with that mark on her arm—that'd been a dream and nothing else. "But it won't matter soon."

Arms circled her, and she shut her eyes and let her hands fall as Lyon pulled her into a gentle hug. "I am so very sorry. But do not view this as death. View this as acceptance. You will know peace once this is done."

"He lied to me. He *lied*. He said he let them go."

"I know."

"You knew?" She glared up at him. "And you didn't say anything?"

Sad features became even more doleful, if it were possible. He looked down at her, pleading for forgiveness in his eyes. He looked so much like a cemetery angel in that moment. "I cannot defy the will of my king."

"But you did. For Kamira."

"Yes. I love her more than I value my own life. It is for that reason I defied him." He looked out at the rubble of the acropolis. His brow creased in worry as he likely thought of the pain of those who were trapped in the blast. Dust and smoke still rose from the destruction.

"I want to go help."

Lyon sighed. "While I sympathize and share your concern for those caught in the blast, we have our orders."

"I don't take orders from him," she grumbled half-heartedly.

His hand settled on her shoulder again, but he didn't respond. Probably because he didn't want to get into an argument with her.

With a sigh, she let herself lean into her friend. Let herself accept the comfort where she could. "If you don't know what's going on, what do you think is happening?" Lyon was very particular about questions, she had learned.

"There is only one House who has the means to cause destruction on that level. Only one who would be clever enough to pile its explosives in the tunnels where it would do the most damage."

He was leaving it to her to put the pieces together. She looked out at the city and furrowed her brow for a minute. The House of Words were the keepers of technology and science. So, it had to be them. "But Vjo is in the prisons below, isn't she?"

"Then it was not Vjo."

Lydia groaned and put her head in her hands. "Fucking *Maverick*."

"Most assuredly, yes."

"He's going to get himself *fucking* killed! Noa is going to tear him to shreds! We have to stop him."

"Either the death of his wife has driven him to the point where he does not care or he has a plan. Likely both." Lyon shook his head. "There is nothing we can do to help him. Both of us have nothing left with which to bargain."

"We could fight him."

"I will not further defy my king. And even if I would, even with the two of us, he would best us in a fight." Lyon looked out over the city and heaved a quiet breath. "But I share your desire that the doctor may live. He is a good man."

"And between the two of you, I can't tell who emotes more."

"Decidedly him. Although he is a fraction of my age. He may yet catch up with me."

She laughed despite herself. "I hope when I come out the other side of this, the Ancients leave me as much intact as they've left you."

"I am certain they will." Lyon reached his hand up and stroked her hair gently. "Open your heart and mind to them, and you will remain yourself. They merely wish to take your pain away."

"No, what they want is for me to surrender to prove to them I really love that man."

"What?"

Lydia glanced up at him. Oh, right. He didn't know. "This is all just a sick game for them. They want to make sure I'm 'worthy' of their only son. They're a bunch of perverted over-protective parents from hell. They think since Aon was willing to throw it all away because he loved me, I should have to do the same to be with him."

"How do you know this?"

That made her laugh again, though this time it was sardonic and purely pointed at her own suffering. "They told me through Ziza. Or what's left of her, anyway."

His brow creased. "I did not even consider what had become of the Oracle." He shook his head. "I fear I forgot of her entirely... the poor woman. And poor you. I am sorry for what you have suffered. Since the moment they chose you to Fall, it appears they had all this planned from the very beginning."

"Yup! They left me mortal so Aon and I could have a chance to fall in love. They killed me to make me a Queen. I bet they only took Nick so Aon would kill him and inspire me to stand on my own. They probably pushed Rxa into going insane and trying to imprison me in that goddamn lake. Now, all this." She gestured out at the city in front of her.

"I suppose the bright side might be that this is all coming to an end?"

Lyon. Always trying to find the best in the situation. An ages-old vampire trying to convince her to be optimistic.

She laughed wearily and leaned on him again. "Yeah."

Tonight, she'd go and willingly kneel at the altar and give up her soul to the Ancients in exchange for Lyon's life. Because, one way or another, she wanted this to be over.

The question was whether she was going to go down without a fight. With or without a last show of defiance. A double-middle-finger to the Ancients and their only son. The King of All had lied to her, used her, manipulated her. Kept everyone a prisoner despite promising otherwise.

She gritted her teeth.

Yeah. Fuck him.

She was going to go down swinging.

"I have to go." She pushed away from Lyon and began to walk out of the throne room.

"I have been instructed to stop you."

"He told you to keep me in the building. I'm not leaving the building," she called back without looking over her shoulder.

A swarm of bats cut her off as he appeared standing in front of her. He was looking down at her sternly. "You are going to go free the others."

"Good guess."

"I cannot allow this to happen."

Lydia cracked her neck to one side and then the other. "Lyon. Get out of my way."

"No."

"M'okay, then." She shifted her form, just took a step to the left and let herself change into the shape of Q. She loomed over him, some thirty feet tall and a hundred feet long, and she snapped her wings open wide. The throne room looked a lot smaller to her now.

Lyon staggered backward, his eyes wide. He hadn't seen her pull off this trick before, and he was now backing away from her. "Lydia. I do not wish to fight you."

"Sure, *now* you don't. Now that you know you're going to lose." She flapped her wings and knocked him flat to his ass with the gust. She had other things to deal with than tangling with the vampire again. He would only stall her, and she didn't know how much time she had before Noa came back.

Taking off, she flew over Lyon, shrinking so she could weave her way through the building, covering ground much faster than if she had been on foot. She dove down stairwells, sending startled people cowering in all directions.

Down and down she went, following stairs to the bottom until there was no hint of the sunlight from outside. She didn't know where they were, but she had to assume "dungeon," and "dungeons" were usually "down."

So, down she went.

She flew down a long stone hallway until she came to a large, wooden door. It had a heavy lock on it, one she wouldn't be able to break down in her current form. She changed herself back to human. Before she could pick up the lock and shatter it with her power, she heard a voice from behind her.

"Lydia, enough. Go no further."

"You're stubborn, Priest." She turned around to face him and summoned a pair of black obsidian swords to her hands. For all the bullshit Noa had spewed at her, he had been right about one thing. She fought better with them than she did a spear.

Standing some twenty feet away was Lyon. He must have followed her as a swarm of bats.

"I have been told."

"I'm letting them go."

"You will have to kill me to do so. You and I are equally matched. By the time you fell me in battle, if you can, our king will likely have returned."

"Let's make this quick, then."

"I—"

A loud sound in the small space made her jump. A deafening *blam* followed by several more. Lyon stood, stunned, and slowly turned to look down at his chest. Circles of red began to form in the white fabric of his shirt and vest. The circles began to expand and grow as blood oozed from him.

Lyon fell to his knees and then face down onto the floor with a thud. He was dead. For now, anyway. As he fell, he revealed the source of what had attacked him.

Maverick.

Standing behind Lyon, still holding a gun aloft. Smoke curled up from the muzzle. He ejected the magazine from the turn-of-the-century-looking Luger and began to refill it with bullets he pulled from his pocket.

"Truly," he commented dryly, "while I appreciate and respect the nobility of the society of Under for rejecting the nature of firearms and their inherent gift to ignore the imbalance of skill and power between combatants, I must say, they are terribly efficient, if nothing else." He clicked the magazine back into the gun and looked up at her with a small smile. "Hello, Lydia."

Vanishing the two swords she had summoned, she ran to her friend and hugged him. He laughed and hugged her back with one arm, since in the other he was holding a pistol. "I am glad to see you as well."

"I thought you caused the explosion."

"Oh, I did. I placed it on a timer, of course." Maverick let go of her to walk to the locked door. He fished around in his pocket and pulled out a key, likely having snagged it from a guard on the way down. "It would have been foolish to stand next to it, don't you think?"

She had to laugh. He had a good point. "Noa is going to show up, not find anybody, and head right back here. We don't have much time."

"Noa?"

"I named him that."

"Ah." He narrowed a visible yellow eye at her, his brow furrowed, before it dawned on him. "Hm. Clever. Well, 'Noa' is going to find Kamira and Dtu, and they will give us as much time as they are able so we may do what must be done." He swung the door open and walked through it into another hallway, except this one was lined with locked doors. A jail. "Come. I will need your power to break their chains."

"Wait—" Lydia called after him and jogged to catch up. "How did you know Kamira and Dtu got free?"

"We have all been given strict instructions. They are playing their part, as am I. As are we all."

"Instructions from who?" Damn, Maverick could walk fast when he wanted to. She was next to him now as he stormed down the hall, searching for Edu and the others.

Maverick smiled thinly as if at a very dry joke that she was missing. "Aon."

"Wait, what? That doesn't make any sense! Why would Noa set you all up for—"

"No. Not the King. *Aon.*"

Lydia stammered and stopped in her tracks. Maverick didn't, until he had made it some twenty more feet and realized she was standing there, staring at him agog. He sighed. "We do not have time for this, Lydia."

"But—"

"You are not the only one he has come to visit in dreams."

SEVENTEEN

Lydia was left standing there, staring at Maverick, unsure what to think about what he said.

Aon.

Her Aon was masterminding this whole thing. Giving everyone instructions from the shadows... but to what end? She could guess. If she knew the warlock at all, he would be trying to do what he could to make sure he died. By whose hand, she didn't know.

"Kamira knew. That's why she took Dtu and left. She knew what you were going to do."

"Yes."

"Who else is in on this?"

"Only Vjo and myself. Now come, please. I cannot free them without you. And we are running short on time." Maverick turned and left her standing there dumbly without any more explanation than that.

Without any other option, she followed him. "Why? What's his plan?"

"You know what he's after as well as I." As a guard rounded

the corner, Maverick dispatched him with a bullet to the chest. "An end to this madness, once and for all."

A few hours ago, and she wouldn't have known whose side she was on. A few hours ago, and she would have begged them not to go forward with their plan to destroy Noa.

But he had lied to her. Betrayed her trust.

Who knew what else he had done or would do, as soon as she was too mind-warped to care?

He would kill them all the moment she was obedient to him. Not just the traitors. She was taking a solid bet that he would murder literally *everyone* in Under once she was finally and fully his. Gritting her teeth, she knew this had to happen.

Noa had to die.

And with him, Aon.

It was the only way the rest of them would stand a chance. The Ancients might destroy the world in a fit of rage, but... they were all dead either way. One was a sure thing, the other was a gamble.

Letting out a long, wavering breath, she bit back the tears that stung her eyes. "Okay."

Maverick paused in his speed-walking to look at her. Pain crossed his face for a moment as he realized as if for the first time what he was asking her to do. He put his hand on her cheek, and there was a sincere expression on his features. "You must be strong."

She knew he really did understand. Everyone had, or was going to, lose someone they cared about—Maverick was very solidly on that list. "I'll do my best."

"That is all I can ask." He lowered his hand and resumed walking. And just like that, the moment was done. "Come."

For a second time in two minutes, she chased to catch up with him. They came to the end of the hall, and there was another locked door at the end. Maverick peered through the bars and stepped aside. He gestured to the lock on the door. "I fear I do not have a key for this one."

Picking up the lock, she focused. She simply willed it to go away. A split second later, it fell to the ground, dissolved into turquoise sand. That really was a neat trick, she had to admit. She pulled the door open and stepped in.

At least everyone looked *mostly* okay. Except for Edu.

Edu was chained on his knees. His neck was lashed to a ring in the floor, keeping his head a foot and a half from the stone surface. His arms were behind his back, chained to the wall behind him. He was strung up like a turkey, unable to move at all.

And he had been like this for a solid week. His arms and hands were a hideous shade of blue purple from the lack of circulation. Blood was clotted around his wrists and his neck where he must have struggled. Lines of dried crimson dotted his arms and his back. The marks of a whip whose wounds had healed, but he couldn't even wipe off the proof of them.

"Edu is the priority." Vjo cut into her stunned silence. "Free him."

Lydia nodded. She was grateful that the others hadn't been tortured. But if there was anything in her heart that could still break for the big man, left to suffer like that, it would have.

"Bunny!" Evie smiled up at her. She had been sitting next to Edu. She pushed herself up to sitting but couldn't make it any farther than that because of the chains.

Stepping forward, she knelt in front of Edu. "I'm so sorry... I'm so sorry. I didn't know." She put her hands on the chain that bound his neck to the floor, and with all her rage, her frustration, and her hurt—she willed it to go away. The marks on the chains flared to life and fought back.

No.

No more.

No more lies, no more suffering, no more of this bullshit. She was done. This was done. All of it.

The marks popped and exploded, and with them went the chain. It fell to the ground at his knees, and Edu straightened with a pained snarl. She went behind him and did the same to his arms. He went to stand and staggered, nearly falling back to the ground. Evie and Lydia helped him up, and he leaned back on the wall behind him for support. He nodded down at her and then jerked his head in the direction of the others. Evie stayed at his side, hugging in close to him.

Lydia went to Ini and Vjo and did the same, snapped their chains as quickly as she could. Ini threw her arms around her and hugged her tightly. "Sister! Oh, sister, you came for us. Thank you! Thank you so very much!"

"I'm so sorry. I didn't know…"

"He lied to you. It is not your fault." Vjo was picking herself up and doing her best to brush herself off.

"It's still not okay. I should have known better. I should have known he wasn't—wasn't…"

"Wasn't the man you loved. But you tried to love him, anyway. Of course, you did. Anyone would! You had to have hope there was something still there." Ini was still hugging her, and she hugged the woman back. It was her first time seeing Ini and Vjo without their masks. Ini looked vaguely Asian, if she had been crossed with an elf along the way, stunningly and immensely beautiful.

Vjo was no less gorgeous, if somewhat older-looking and more refined. She bore strong resemblance to someone from India, maybe.

She wanted to know more about them. To hear more about their lives. But in a few hours… they would all probably be dead.

Or she'd have no soul of her own to care.

"I realized that even if I loved him, this world—it's too

dead. Too silent, even for me. And now? Now that I learned he lied? Not even Aon ever went that far."

"And so, it shall be the King of All's downfall. For he cannot be trusted, and therefore, he trusts no one." Vjo summoned her mask to her hand, looked down at it idly, and then sighed. "There is little point to these at the moment, is there?" She let it vanish once more, then walked over to Maverick. She reached out a hand, and he took it, kissing the back of her fingers. "You did well, my elder."

"I did as I was instructed."

"As shall we all."

Edu slammed his fist into the wall behind him, and everyone jumped. Looking over at the big man, he was glowering at Vjo and Maverick furiously. His long, curly hair was matted with sweat and slicked back from his face. She had seen Edu without his mask on the battlefield, but now she could take a moment to really get a look at him. He was handsome, in a rugged lumberjack kind of way. Painted across his face, like the mark of a Viking warlord, was one large symbol made up of dozens of smaller ones. His features were broad and bold and currently twisted into the expression of somebody who was in a great deal of pain and was incredibly pissed about it.

"You want to know what is happening?" Vjo guessed.

Edu nodded.

"We do not have the time to discuss it." Vjo looked back to Maverick. "Did you bring her?"

The doctor nodded. "She is hidden away in the temple upstairs. Somewhere no one will find her for some time."

"Good. Ini—"

Edu slammed his fist into the wall again. He wouldn't take no for an answer, apparently.

Vjo sighed heavily and shook her head, looking over at the King of Flames. "Aon—yes, *the King of Shadows*—is working to undermine *the King of All*. He has come to me in my dreams, as he has Kamira and Maverick. He knows how we can be given the opportunity to end his life. He does not wish to live on as he does now. He does not wish to see her"—Vjo pointed at Lydia —"be overruled by the will of the Ancients. He will lay down his life to spare her that fate. And *you* will be the one to kill him. That was his wish."

Edu's brow creased for a moment as he considered what the spider queen said. He sighed wearily and pushed off the wall to straighten. His arms were normal colored now, and he cracked his shoulders loudly. He was healing, although it looked like it was taking a while.

Lydia walked up to him and summoned to her hand a plastic water bottle and handed it to him. He eyed it warily for a moment as if unsure what to do with it, before she unscrewed the cap for him. He took a drink from it and sighed in relief, thanking her with a nod.

After the brief moment, Edu straightened up, and with a flick of his hand, he was wearing his leather armor once more. He looked down to Evie, and a fond smile softened his features. He cradled her head gently in his palms and stooped down to kiss the redhead.

Evie was a lot of things, but she wasn't stupid. As the kiss ended, she looked up at him tearfully. She knew this could be a death sentence for him. "Don't go, please. Let's run."

He shook his head and kissed her forehead. He patted his hand over his heart, then placed it against hers, saying either that his heart was hers or that he would live on within her. Either way, the sentiment made Lydia want to cry. It successfully made Evie. The little spitfire threw her arms around his trunk of a neck and hugged him while she wept.

They really were in love.

And this was probably goodbye.

Lydia would feel a lot worse if she weren't about to go through the same thing. Either she'd fail, and her mind would be erased of everything that made her who she was, or Aon would be dead, and she'd be stuck in this world without the man she had come to love so very deeply.

Because of that, she had to look away. Not that their affection for each other was at all shameful, but because it hurt too much to watch.

Ini was suddenly holding both of her hands. "I understand."

"You're psychic. That's cheating."

She giggled and leaned up to kiss her on the cheek. "No, silly. I would understand even if I didn't peek inside to be certain. You really must get better at guarding your thoughts."

"If we live, I'd love you to teach me."

"Deal!"

"We have no time for this," Vjo cut in loudly. "Ini. You and I must go find—"

"None of you are going anywhere."

The sudden unexpected voice made them all turn. Standing in the doorway was Lyon. He wore the gold armor along his arms and hands that she had seen him fight with once before. He was outnumbered—but Edu, Vjo, and Ini were likely weak from being restrained for so long.

Maverick had a gun, but she expected that only worked on the vampire because he was caught off guard.

And it was too small in here for Lydia to really fight full-on.

But still. It was four royals and Maverick against Lyon. Their odds were damn good. "Lyon, you're going to lose if you pick a fight."

Lyon nodded once, accepting that this was a doomed scenario for him. "I must do my duty."

"Oh, you poor thing, look at you!" Ini disappeared in a blink and reappeared behind Lyon. Without any pomp or circumstance, she put her hands on either side of his face. He jerked in surprise, but as he went to whirl around, his eyes suddenly glazed over.

Right.

Ini and the "magic hands" trick that Q had hated so damn much.

The vampire struggled again, grasping at her, trying to rally against the control of the floating elven woman behind him, but Ini worked fast. His arms went limp at his sides, and his eyes drifted close. His legs gave out as he slumped to the ground, and Ini followed him, until she was kneeling over his prone form.

"There, there," she soothed him, stroking his face gently. "Now... let's take a look, shall we?"

"What're you doing?" Lydia asked.

"It is quite like pulling weeds from a garden," Ini replied, her voice sounding even more wistful and far away than usual.

"You're... weeding his mind?" She wrinkled her nose. That had to hurt.

"Oh, you young ones are always so literal!" Ini giggled. "The Ancients are like a poison in his head. Their claws have woven their way through him like the roots of a tree might do in the earth. But they are still separate and still discrete. I am merely... untangling the two. I cannot free Lyon of their influence. He must do that himself. But I can let him see their corruption plainly. I can take the roots of that tree and show them to the Priest for what they are."

"Huh," Lydia said. "Why not do this to the King of All, then, and solve our problems?"

"For Lyon, the Ancients are an invading force. He came into this world a whole man with a whole soul of his own. For the King of All, for your *Noa*," Ini giggled, revealing she had in fact been fishing around in Lydia's head, "this is his real self. What we knew was a man whose fabric had been torn to shreds in their absence. His madness was the result of their removal. He was left on his own to hold himself together. Aon is now whole, where Lyon is… diseased." Ini was clearly distracted and focusing mostly on what she was doing as she rummaged around inside his mind.

Lydia walked up to the two and knelt at Lyon's other side. "You said it's still his choice to make?"

"Of course." Ini's eyes were shut now as well, but they reopened to meet her gaze, her focus shifting to Lydia briefly. "What good is free will if you cannot choose to give it away?"

That hit hard. Lydia cringed and looked away. She had nothing to say to that. Ini had clearly figured everything out between fishing in her head or Lyon's. Or the King of All's, for that matter. She didn't know where the Queen of Fate learned what was going to happen to her, and she didn't suppose it mattered anymore.

Doing her best to dodge, she changed the subject. "Try not to break anything in his head while you're in there. Kamira'll be pissed."

"How would she know?" Maverick teased. "He has such minimal personality to start with."

Edu chuckled.

"You shouldn't talk, doc." Lydia grinned at Maverick.

"Oh, tut, all of you," Ini scolded. "Shame on you. Picking on a man when he is down. Worry not, I know what I am doing. Now, would all of you shush, and let me work?"

"Work quicker, sister." Vjo was right to urge them to hurry.

They all obediently fell silent. Lydia reached down and picked up Lyon's hand and held it. She knew it was pointless, and the gesture was probably meaningless, but she didn't care. He was her friend, one way or another. They all sat in silence for a long period before Ini slowly drew her hands away from the Priest's face.

Lyon gasped, his eyes flying wide. Fear etched across his features, and he thrashed, trying to find solid ground on anything around him. Lydia had to let go of him as she and Ini both jumped back from his sudden reaction.

He sat up slowly and looked around at the lot of them, his normally placid features crossed with dozens of emotions all at once. Fear, confusion, anger, betrayal, happiness, sadness... they all flashed across him until he finally seemed to get control and tamped them all back down under whatever rock he usually stored them.

Finally, he spoke. "How may I help?"

Lydia let out a sigh of relief. She punched Lyon hard in the arm, and he looked at her with one thin, pale eyebrow arched. "Don't ever fucking do that again!"

"I promise I will do my best to avoid having my mind over-ruled by our creators in the future," he quipped to her dryly.

Vjo walked forward. "As charming as this is, we do not have time for any of it. Lyon, are you willing to fight the King of All?"

"Yes, but I don't understand how—"

"The black king's rook has taken the white king's bishop, it seems." The Queen of Words cut him off.

Lyon's brow creased in confusion. "If you are not the mastermind behind all this, then who is?"

Her answer was succinct. "The King of Shadows plays the King of All."

Lyon groaned in abject dismay. Out of anybody, he seemed to question the reality of that the least. He really must have known Aon as a friend, all things considered.

Vjo chuckled at his response. "I hope your acting skills are passable, Priest. You too have a part to play in tonight's ordeal."

Lyon stood, and Ini and Lydia followed. Looking at the others, he bowed his head. "I will do what I must."

"Good. Edu, Lydia, and I will go to the throne room and wait. Ini and Maverick will go find Ziza. You two must take her to the Altar of the Ancients." Seeing the odd look on everyone's faces, she sighed, clearly agitated that she had to stop and waste time explaining the details to everyone. "We cannot defeat the King of All with the power of the Ancients backing him. The Oracle was once their conduit. Like a lightning rod, she may draw their power into herself long enough to give Edu the time to finish him. That is why Aon had Maverick bring her here."

"It will burn her out. It will kill her!" Ini squeaked.

"Yes. It will. But she is not long for this world, regardless. Trust me, sister. I do not wish to see her pass any more than you. But it must be done. It is the only way."

"And who will lure the King of All back to his throne room?" Lyon asked, and at the look that Vjo shot him, he put his palm over his face. "Hence the acting skills you reference."

"Yes, my dear boy." Vjo walked past them and headed down the hallway toward the exit. "Now, enough talk, all of you. It is time to see this to the end, one way or another."

EIGHTEEN

If she died here, Kamira would be proud.

A steeply mismatched fight was no less honorable. In fact, that they were so sorely outclassed by the King of All made her feel even more righteous at how she would die. Planting her feet here atop the few surviving buildings of the doctor's explosion would be a worthy last stand. Here, under the blazing sun in this foreign and strange land, she could die with her head held high.

Her heart wept for her husband. Lyon would be forced to deal with the grief of her passing. She had no doubt he would take his own life shortly after she met the void. She wondered, for the first time, what became of them after they died. Would she simply know oblivion, as her power rejoined the Ancients from whence it came? Or would her soul pass on to the equivalent of a mortal afterlife?

If so, she hoped he would find her there.

Kamira loved him. More than the moons themselves, she loved that statue of a man. And it was for him she stood in finality against the King of All. For this world had taken her angel hostage, robbed him of his most precious gift—his morality. And for that, she would see it all burn.

Even if it was all just a funeral pyre.

Dtu stood on a building a hundred feet away, in his far more suitable wolven form. The humanoid flesh he wore was an insult to the man, and she was glad to see him now wearing the mottled fur that was so much better suited for her king.

Split up like this, the King of All would have to choose who to strike first. He would have to decide which of them was the bigger threat, and it would allow the other to flank the man and attack.

"Kamira."

She was flattered! Turning to face the man in the swath of black fabric, she sneered at him. "Hello, Aon. Wonderful to see you."

"I am not the man you knew."

"Oh, I know. I was saying hello to your other half."

The King laughed cruelly. "My other half? He was a shard. A fragment, a paltry, broken, pathetic, squandering of power. Do not insult me, mongrel."

"Suit yourself."

"Before we begin, I have a question for you. Something is troubling me."

Kamira grinned and bowed sarcastically to the man. "Oh, *please,* my liege, let me be of assistance."

"Why are you here? You took Dtu to flee to the mountains. You are here, why? The idiot Elder of Words is acting in spite due to his wife's execution. Yet you stand here in his stead."

Kamira laughed, ensuring it was just mocking enough to bother him. She was so good at ruffling feathers. Especially his. "He was right. You *are* too egotistical to predict any of this. Your hubris is going to be your downfall."

The man's black eyes narrowed in rage at her continued insults. Good. Let him get angry. Anger made people sloppy.

Those who knew how to harness such anger tended to be shifters or served in the House of Flames. He very much was neither. "Who? Who said this?"

"You did."

"What?"

Oh, this was fun. No wonder Aon loved to lord over people with wordplay. Being able to control someone like this was entertaining. She would have to give the man credit for that at some point in the afterlife when they were all dead. "I'm sorry. Your fragment, your paltry, broken, pathetic, squandering of another side. He is the one who told me this of you."

"How is that even—" The King of All snarled in rage, his metal hand clenching tight into a fist as he arrived at the conclusion on his own. "My dreams."

"Your own subconscious is trying to kill you!" She cackled in laughter again. "Your *own mind* has been conspiring against you, working behind the scenes to plan this all. If that is not a sign that you are not a worthy ruler, I do not know what is!" Kamira laughed again proudly at the furious expression on his face.

"Then there is only but one solution to my insolvent mind." His hand burst into black flame. Dtu howled from the building nearby, and the King of All grinned. "I must kill you all."

"You will try."

* * *

Lyon arrived into mayhem.

Dtu and Kamira were fighting the King of All. He was bleeding, but they were worse. They fought "dirty," dodging and weaving around him, using their speed to their advantage, never standing on open ground for long. They were going to lose, but they knew that from the beginning. This wasn't about victory; it was about stalling for time.

Vjo's words rang through his head, asking him about his acting abilities. Now, he understood. Sighing, he knew what he would have to do.

Kamira was in the form of the tigress she preferred. She was in mid-leap as he darted at her, summoning all his power to slam into her at full force. It changed her trajectory and sent her crashing into—and through—a nearby building.

The King of All looked at him with narrowed eyes. "I told you to stay by Lydia's side. I told you to guard her!"

"The others came for her. They have—" Kamira struck him back, sending him crashing into a building. Pain lanced through him, but he had expected it. In fact, he was glad she had done it. Not only had she knocked him far away from the King of All, she had interrupted a lie he wasn't excited to tell.

Kamira loomed over him, snarling and growling. Lyon looked up at her and smiled faintly. "Hello, my love."

Her form shifted. The sound of snapping bone was no longer so horrifying to him after all these years. The process of going from one shape to another was immensely painful for her, as it was for all shifters. But it was their burden to bear, as they each had their own. She looked down at him now, her tail swishing angrily behind her legs. "Have you come to your senses?"

"I have."

"Good. Ini did her job." She offered him a hand up. He took it and stood with her help, brushing some of the rubble off his chest. "You're nothing if not predictable."

"Aon foresaw this as well?"

"He did. He knows us all *frighteningly* too well." Kamira shook her head. "Including himself. I am a bit insulted."

"What are we to do?"

"You will fight me, and you will make it look as though it is in earnest. Then, when Dtu and I fall, you might try your best to keep him from killing us both." Kamira rolled her shoulder. "Are you ready, husband?"

"No. But I suppose that does not factor into this equation."

"Sadly. Come. Let us tangle one last time. I think I will enjoy this. A fitting end to our life together. Remember, make this convincing. He will know if it is not."

Lyon nodded.

"No going soft on me, love." Kamira wagged a finger, scolding him. "I know you will not wish to hurt me, but you must. I will show you no such leniency."

Lyon laughed and looked up at the sky and squinted. He was better fed than the last time he was out in the glare, so it hurt him less. But still, it made him itch, and he felt depleted, regardless. He had bested Kamira in a brawl when last they fought on the field of war, but that had been with the sun eclipsed. Now, it was a far more even fight. She may even win. He would not have to try hard to look as though he were trying to hold his own. He knew she would not give him an inch of mercy.

As she shifted forms, she roared loudly at him, a joyful and violent challenge. If this was their last moment together, yes... it would be fitting.

Lyon summoned his golden claws to his hands, and with that, the dance began.

* * *

Lydia stood in the throne room, not sure of what to do with herself. Her skin was crawling, she was so nervous. She wasn't usually a fidgety person, but now she wished she knew what to do with her hands. So she did what she always did and shoved her hands in her pockets and wished she could hide.

Edu was sitting on the stairs that led up to the throne, in

full armor, his giant broadsword in his hands, the tip resting on the ground, his head bowed. Whether he was thinking, meditating, preparing for battle—for death—she didn't know.

Vjo had returned to being a giant-ass spider and was looming up in the ceiling. It was vaulted and painted with a depiction of the night sky in Under. She had seen something like it before, in Aon's home. The warlock had spent his life faintly remembering who he had really been. Everything he had done had reflected a time he had chosen to forget.

It was poetic and tragic, at best.

Now, he was going to die. Or they were all going to die. Or both.

"Explain to me how this is supposed to work again?" she said up to the spider. Mostly because she needed something to occupy her mind before she went crazy from anxiety.

"Ziza is a conduit for the Ancients. She always has been. She keeps that connection to them, even if they are absent from her. You know this. You saw it happen, did you not?"

Lydia nodded. The Ancients had taken over Ziza to talk to her once before.

"Therefore, if we can force them into her for a time, they will be forced to abandon their link to the King of All, drawing down lightning from the clouds and forcing it to the ground, as it were. That will give us a few bare moments where he will be vulnerable."

"Where he'll be Aon."

"Yes."

Lydia groaned and lowered her head. Working together to kill Noa was one thing. She could probably stick a knife in his smug, lying face if she had to. But Aon? To have to watch the warlock she loved die was something she didn't know if she'd survive in more ways than one. "He really planned all of this?"

It was still so weird to have a giant talking spider up in the corner. "Yes. He came to me, to Maverick, and to Kamira to orchestrate this. It is our only chance to stop him and to stop what he will do to us all once he breaks you before the altar."

There was nothing she could bargain away with Noa that would spare everyone. Nothing she could ask for, beg for, plead for that he'd grant her. Oh, he might say as much, but he was a liar. He'd say anything to get her to surrender to the Ancients. Then it wouldn't matter anymore.

Either way, for all of them, it ended now.

"If we succeed—and that's a big if—then what happens?"

"The Ancients will likely destroy us all in their wrath. We will all die. But sometimes a noble death with one's head held high is all that you can ask."

Lydia understood that sentiment. More than once in Under she had faced down what she had believed to be certain death and tried to do so with as much dignity as she was capable. With a heavy sigh, she walked over to the stairs and sat down next to Edu. He didn't move as she did, his head still lowered, the huge horns of his armor arching up over and behind him.

It wasn't so very long ago that she would have been terrified to be anywhere near him. How quickly things could change. "I'm sorry, Edu. I'm sorry for all of this. It's my fault."

He lifted his head and looked to her. After a pause, he shook his head and pointed back at the throne behind him, indicating that the fault wasn't hers but that it belonged to the King of All and the Ancients who made him.

"Yeah, well," she leaned back on her elbows, "if I had just let you screw me, then kill me the night I tried to run, none of us would be in this mess. I'd be a blood splatter on the floor, Aon wouldn't have cared, and you all would have gotten to live your merry lives."

He huffed a laugh under his breath.

"Until the void swallowed us whole," Vjo interjected from overhead. "No, my sister. Your coming was necessary."

"Which is worse? The void, or this?"

Vio paused, and her giant legs shifted idly as she thought it over. "A fair point. I do not know."

Lydia tried not to squeak in surprise as Edu wrapped an arm around her and hugged her to his side. It was a gesture of friendship. "Is this you trying to say you're glad you didn't successfully kill me? Well, I guess you did, but you know what I mean."

Edu chuckled. He let her go and planting his hand on her head rocked it from side to side. He was playful, for a giant, terrifying, bus-sized warrior.

"I'm sorry we never got a chance to be friends, Edu. I think I would have liked that. I think we really would have gotten along." She chuckled. "Christ, also, can you imagine how much that would *piss Aon off*?"

That made him laugh harder. He nodded, before tilting his head to the side for a moment. Thumping his fist into his chest over his heart, he reached out his hand to her, telling her in his own, limited way that they were already friends.

She shooed his hand away and instead hugged him, being careful not to impale herself on his armor. He chuckled again and patted her back.

When she pulled away, she sat back down on the steps and tried not to think about what was going to happen. But it was hard to keep the fear at bay. She was standing between hot lava and a buzz saw, and both were creeping closer.

All she might be able to do was pick how it ended.

* * *

The fight lasted longer than Lyon had expected. Either Kamira was, despite her instance to the contrary, being soft on him, or he was still growing into his powers as a king of Under.

That was to say that the fight lasted more than a matter of seconds.

Dtu was only holding his own against the King of All for that he was not trying to win. The wolf's only goal was to annoy and delay the man in black from returning too soon to the Temple of the Ancients. They had to buy the others as much time as they could and at whatever cost.

But the wolf could only do the dance for so long. Kamira broke away from tangling with Lyon so abruptly, it sent him staggering with the force of a missed blow. He looked up to see Dtu lying on the ground amongst a pile of rubble, with the King standing over him, black claw blazing in flame.

Dtu was about to die. Kamira flew to intercept. Lyon felt as though the world hung on a thread as the question lingered as to whether she would make it in time. But one large, clawed paw swiped at the King of All before his blow could land. He was forced to recoil and point his wrath at Kamira instead. Black spikes shot up from the ground and impaled Kamira through the chest, ending her forward momentum in an instant. Kamira let out a pained and angry yowl that made his skin crawl.

To save her king, she would take the blow. To save Dtu, she would gladly die.

Lyon had to stop this. He could not—façade be damned—stand here and watch his wife perish. As the King stepped forward to destroy her, he suddenly found himself standing there at his side, hand wrapped around his wrist, stopping him. He had not realized he had moved.

Jet black eyes narrowed in fury as the King of All glared at him. Even though Lyon was taller than him, he had never felt so small in his life as he had facing down this man. "Do you dare betray me a second time for her?"

"No, my King. I simply beg that you let me be the one to do it. That I may say goodbye before I send her to the void."

He seemed to consider it for a moment before yanking his

hand out of his grasp and taking a step back. "Very well. But you do it now. No quarter will be granted this day."

The spikes withdrew from Kamira, and she slumped to the ground. Her form changed from the tiger back to the woman he loved. He reached down and, grasping her arm, roughly yanked her up to her feet.

He had a role to play.

He would not live through the night, he knew. Despite the King of All's words to Lydia, this meant the end for him. He knew Kamira well and knew she would wish to blaze the trail ahead and meet him on the other side, grinning and asking him what took him so long.

As she turned her masked face up to him, an idea struck him. He had not realized she had donned her mask again, he was so accustomed to seeing her with it on. The plan that came to his mind was dangerous. It was a gamble... it was risky. It would take precision he did not know if he owned.

But it was his only chance. "I love you, my tiger. You will forever be etched into my mind, every detail, every mark—it pains me to have to take them from you."

There was a flicker in her eyes. *Of course* she understood. Of course, she could see what he schemed. He was transparent to her where all others might find him obscured.

She sneered. "Do it. I am not afraid. But let me keep my mask in death—I do not want that cretin to see my soul."

She trusted him.

"Very well." Tears ran down his cheeks, and he knew they were shed in blood. He pushed her away. She teetered on unsteady legs but stayed standing.

Golden chains shot from the sand and pierced through her wooden mask... and her skull. Puncturing her a dozen times over. She jolted, but the wound was too fast to even hurt her. Lyon knew first-hand how quick a death it was. He recalled the chains as quickly as he had called for them and lowered her to the ground.

Blood pooled in the sand around her dark hair, haloing into the thirsty substance.

Kneeling there at her side, he lowered his head. He had to play his part, and it was not difficult now to let the grief play out on his features. He prayed he had not been wrong and that his aim had been true. He prayed to the Ancients and to any god who may listen to him that his memory of the marks she wore upon her face had been correct. Obscured beneath her wooden mask and oozing crimson, he prayed the marks were still intact.

The King of All did not know his wife's face. Did not know the locations of the ink that kept her soul bound to her body. Lyon leaned down and placed a kiss against her lips.

"Your grief will pass in time."

Lyon looked up to the King but said nothing. The other man was looking down at him with a surprisingly sympathetic expression.

At his silence, the King continued. "I am sorry it came to this. The loss of love is to be mourned." As quickly as his empathy had come, it passed, smoothing back to a cold, hardened expression. "You abandoned your post."

"I came to tell you, my King." Lyon bowed his head. "The throne room has been taken. Maverick was the source of the explosion. He freed the prisoners, and they have Lydia hostage. They wait for you there."

The King of All bared his teeth in rage. Lyon could not help but make a distinctly undignified noise as the other man yanked him to his feet by the arm and, in the blink of an eye, transported them both unexpectedly away.

It was not until he managed to pick himself back up off the floor on which he had been so rather carelessly dropped by the

King of All that he looked up and realized with dread, yet not even a semblance of surprise, where he now stood.

The Throne of the Ancients.

And there, with Lydia at his side, stood Edu in full regalia, his broadsword raised, pointed at the King of All in challenge. Above them loomed the spider queen. Even as they stood four against one... if Ini and Ziza failed in their mission, it would all be for naught.

But it brought his heart a surprising amount of relief to know that come what may, this was soon to be over.

NINETEEN

When Noa appeared in a swirl of black, Lydia wished she had been happy to see him.

How many times had Aon stood there, protecting her against Edu and the others? How many times had her warlock been a shield for her against the world of Under?

The tables had completely turned. Now, she stood *next* to Edu, against *him*. Against the man she loved. And the man he was "meant to be."

His dark eyes went to her, and seeing her standing next to the King of Flames, his face creased in hurt and betrayal. He shook his head as if not wanting to believe it. "I came to rescue you. I, instead, find you all have laid a trap." He turned to glance at Lyon. "You too, Priest?"

Lyon nodded once. "This cannot continue."

"I concur wholeheartedly. This shall not continue. None of you shall live. I had debated it before, but now I am certain. Once my queen is mine, I shall erase this world of all the infectious mold that has grown upon it!" When he looked back to her, his rage faltered, and she saw tangible pain in his eyes. "Lydia... why?"

"You lied to me."

"It meant nothing! They are *nothing!*"

"That's the problem. That's why."

Snarling, he walked toward her and Edu, and the warrior gripped his sword harder, the leather in his gauntlet creaking. Noa was forced to stop. He glared, clearly irritated beyond belief, at Edu. "Get out of my way."

Edu shook his head.

Noa squared his shoulders. Like the fading of a sunset, all emotion left his face. He was once more the cruel, cold monarch. "Very well. Now, you die."

The fight was a blur. Four against one should have been a cakewalk. Lyon, Vjo, Edu, and herself. Four royals versus one man should have ended in seconds. They should have outclassed him by miles.

It wasn't.

And they didn't.

This was the seat of the Ancients' power. This was where they dwelled. They were up against their avatar, their conduit. The King of All was part man, part eldritch creature. He was partly the monsters that were older than time itself. Unlike all of them, he had never once been human.

This was his home. This was his world. This was his throne.

They didn't stand a *chance*.

Vjo was the first to be taken down. The giant spider was sent through one of the massive columns of the room, shuddering the whole of the structure. By the time she landed amongst the rocks and debris, she was in her human form. Dead. Whether it was permanent, Lydia had no idea and didn't have time to check.

Lyon went next, skewered on black spikes and left bleeding out on the ground. Lydia stood over his prone body, protecting him from Noa, who was intent on taking the man's marks and destroying him. "Leave him alone!"

"He dies tonight. One way or another, my love. Either I kill him now or he perishes the moment this sickness is cured from your mind!"

"This isn't a sickness, *King of All*." She spat out his moniker as an insult. "And you'll have to drag me there, kicking and screaming, and let them burn out my mind."

"So be it. I—" He was interrupted when Edu swung for his head, causing him to dodge and step back. "And you. You, above all, I will enjoy destroying. I think I will save you for last, so that I may make it slow."

Edu charged at Noa and swung his sword, meaning to cleave the other man in half. He was the best and oldest warrior in Under. Nobody stood a chance against him in one-on-one combat. Or that should have been the case. But now, like everything else in this world, it meant nothing when Noa was involved.

Black spear after black spear was deflected, until one lucky one caught Edu through the arm. Edu snarled in pain and shattered it with his fist, freeing himself, but not before three more went through his legs and torso. Needle-sharp, and dangerous, they split through his armor and flesh like it was nothing.

Two more, and Edu was trapped. Noa was making good on his word. He was going to kill the man slowly. He was probably going to make her watch as he killed them all, one by one, in front of her.

When he finally turned to her, Lydia felt her grip on her two obsidian swords falter. He walked toward her slowly, the black fabric around his waist whispering on the stone as he moved.

There was no kindness in his features. No love, no pity. There was not even any hate or anger. There was nothing at all. He was the same as this world—immutable, cruel, and unforgiving. Beautiful, terrible, and a hopeless thing to stand against.

She didn't swing at him when he came up to her. It would be pointless to fight him on her own. With a weary sigh, she let her swords vanish into the air from which she had summoned them. Vjo's words rang through her mind. *"Sometimes a noble death with one's head held high is all that you can ask."*

Lydia's body would keep moving. But what would be left of her when all was said and done, she had no idea. Looking up at the cold, black eyes of the man she had loved, she tried one last time. "Don't do this."

He said nothing in response.

Slowly, he reached up and cupped her face in his hands. She didn't even bother pulling away from him. As his hands tightened, she knew what he was going to do. He was going to snap her neck. When she woke up, she would be at the altar, she was certain. This was her last moment of being herself. "Please..."

As tears streaked down her cheeks, he shushed her quietly and placed a small kiss against her forehead. But still his grasp was tight and unwavering. As his muscles tensed, she knew darkness would follow a second later.

She squeezed her eyes tight.

* * *

Ziza had been their oracle. She had been their pathway to the world. The wonders they had shown her—the future, the past, the whole of Under had been hers to see. Hers to understand. But the multitudinous nature of the whole left her unable to fathom anything more than snippets at a time. To see the entirety of it left her incapable of seeing the water drops in the river that raged around her.

To her, there had only been the river, surging and winding through time. Only when forced to do so could she scoop some of the water up into her palms and try to see it for what it was. Still, one molecule of water ran into the next, indistinguishable and indistinct from all the others.

She had been drowned in that river until she learned to

breathe it. Until she could survive beneath the surface. For she could not die.

Then, all at once, she had been yanked away from that raging water and thrown to the shore, left to lie upon the rocks, gasping like a fish. Like the aftermath of an explosion leaving a ringing in the ears, she was left barren by the absence of the noise to which she had been forced to adapt.

Barren, empty, and cold.

How the others had believed her to be all those years, now she truly was.

The void given flesh, many had called her. The same could be said of all the Oracles. She had known the one before her, and she, too, had judged her cruelly, for she could not understand what it meant to have the "Sight." To truly see all that was, had been, and would be.

But like a spent sifting pan, mining for gold in the rocks that flowed by, she was tossed away by those who used her. The Ancients.

She served them.

She loved them.

She had spent just under fifteen hundred years serving as the vessel to their will.

But now, she would do what she could to stop them.

For, unlike them, she had been both the river and the stone upon the shore. She had known both what it meant to see it all and to be one of the many molecules of water amongst the multitude.

She remembered what it meant to be mortal. Scared, frightened, and sick. She had been a pauper upon the streets when the creatures that stalked the night had come for her. Terror was all she had known as a child, and as a woman it turned into a poison that was only matched by the consumption that would have taken her life if the demons had not done so first.

She remembered what it meant to be Ziza.

She remembered Edu.

She remembered what it meant to love and be loved.

The Ancients could not. They could not see, nor understand, that which was so small to them. They were not the river she had been drowned within; they were the very universe in which those things existed. They were the force that made the river, the mountains, and the sod. The trees and the very air itself. They summoned the rain and snow that birthed the river. They could not, would not, know what it meant to be submerged in it. They could not begin to fathom what it meant to be a part of it.

And so, here she stood. Carried by Ini and placed at the foot of the Altar to the Ancients, buried deep within the temple. It had been a fight to get this far, one in which she could not assist. The descent had taken a stretch of time she could not quite contain within her shattered mind. She understood Aon's warped perception. She had always understood the warlock. His pain, his loneliness, his anger and spite. For he was like the Ancients, after all.

When she moved to walk closer to the altar, she stumbled. Ini's hands were on her, straightening her back up. She gently shooed the woman away. "No," she said, hating the sound of weakness in her voice. "I will do this on my own, my queen. Thank you."

Ini let out a wavering breath and stepped back. "You were always the strongest of us."

"I was not strong. Strength is a choice… one I did not have." She turned from Ini and walked toward the altar. She could not see it. It did not matter. She could sense them, burning like a raging pyre within the room. She knew their presence better than any other in this world, save perhaps Aon himself.

"I am so sorry," Ini said quietly from behind her.

"I do not feel resentment for what has happened to me." To whom she was speaking, she was not certain at first. But then she addressed her creators. "I do not weep for my fate. We are all here by your design. By your providence we were given our lives in this world. Your hand may not have guided the knife that made me Oracle—but it was by your agency, nonetheless." She reached the altar and held out her hands, feeling their power crackle over her skin, the charge of a storm the moment before lightning might strike. "You do not have but one child. You have many. *We* are your children. *We* are your playthings. You have made us, and it is your right to destroy us."

She lifted her head. She knew the statues loomed over her, though her sight had been gone from her the moment their Sight had entered. "But hear me, Ancients of Old, and know that the reign of your son must end. It is not for the unkind parentage you have paid us that I deem him unworthy to rule."

Holding her hands out over the edge of the altar, it felt as though there were a raging fire burning beneath her. Like the charge of the electrical devices the House of Words coveted so very much, it roared just inches away. When she touched the altar, it would be like their lightning-conjuring machines finding a path to ground. All that power would flood into her.

She would not survive, she knew.

It was fine by her. She had lived long enough. Over fifteen hundred years now, by her count, although the years had run together for so very long of that it was hard to keep track. Her life had always been on borrowed time. The Ancients cured her of the plague that would destroy her. It was by their will that she would live as long as she had. To love, to lose, to see and know all that she had witnessed.

Let it end.

"No, my Gods. I do not deem him unfit to rule this world for his cruelty. In that, he is your mirror. And it is for that reflection's sake that he should not be. It is for his purity to your image, his resemblance, that now your creation must be undone. For we are a hapless, foolish, bloodthirsty lot. We are unkind. We are unseeing of the grand whole that you could make us be. But know this and hear me now. It is those fallacies, those falsehoods, that give us value. Tragic as we may be in our brevity, our immense stupidity, we are better for our complexities. There is beauty to the rose who has a stain upon its petals. And it, for having grown naturally, is more a miracle than the crafted one of glass in its perfection."

Ziza smiled faintly. She was sad to say goodbye, all things considered. This was her world. These were the people she had come to care for, even if she was merely watching their stories unfold as though through a windowpane. An outside observer, becoming enamored to characters in a play, perhaps, more than an active participant.

"The King of All would rule with purity to your designs. He would be your rose of glass. But heed me, my creators, my Gods, my saviors... we are better for your absence."

Ziza placed her hands upon the altar and felt the river rush over her once more.

* * *

Lydia held her breath and waited for her neck to snap and for everything to go black.

A small *thud* was all she got instead.

Blinking her eyes open, Noa was on the ground in front of her, fallen onto his knees. His metal hand was pressed against the stone floor to keep him from collapsing. The other was tight in his hair, fisting the black strands and clenching tightly.

He let out a long, pained moan as he doubled over, his shoulders caving in. The moan turned into a frustrated snarl, and he straightened, hissing in a sharp breath through his nose. His eyes were wide, and his face was twisted in agony.

Slowly, it receded as he seemed to come around and be able

to focus. "I cannot... even *begin* to describe how excruciatingly painful that is."

"Aon?" She dared to even hope.

"I believe so. Although, to be fair, I am not completely certain." He pushed himself up, trying to get to his feet. He staggered twice, and she had to help him. He leaned on her heavily and looked down at her with a pained, exhausted expression. "Hello, my dragonfly."

She kissed him, hard. She nearly knocked him over with how desperate she was. He laughed against her lips and held on to her to keep himself from winding up on the floor.

She held the embrace for as long as she could. She knew the moment she let go, it meant goodbye. It meant they were all going to die, one way or another. Either by the wrath of the Ancients when they killed their "Only Son" or when Noa finished them all off.

But like all things, it had to end. Aon pushed away from her gently and, looking down at her, lifted his human hand to gently wipe her tears away. "Forgive me for all that I have done."

She could only nod, the rock in her throat far too lodged there to be able to form words. When he took a step away from her, she reached for him.

The look on his face was of pure sorrow as he shook his head. It was clear he wanted nothing more than to stay with her. But this had to happen.

"Do you also have any semblance of an idea how hard it is to play yourself in chess? To be the mastermind of your own demise?" Aon chuckled weakly, obviously sheltering in egotistical humor. He turned to Edu and gestured his hand. The spikes holding the man in place receded into the ground, and the huge warrior stumbled with the sudden freedom. The two men stood opposed on the rock path. Edu and Aon.

"Here we are, two sides of the coin." Aon walked toward the man and, with a flick of his wrist, summoned an ornate dagger to his hand. Why? He had claws. She'd never seen him with a knife, and—as he turned the blade over in his hand, she had her answer. He held it out to Edu, hilt first. An offering. "It was always destined to end this way."

Aon sank down onto his knees as the warrior took the dagger from him. "All things considered, I suppose I should not be surprised. The setting, however, I could not have predicted in a thousand years."

Edu stepped toward Aon and placed a heavy hand on his shoulder.

Aon laughed. "Yes, yes, I too am sorry it has come to this. I would do it myself, but I fear I do not know where on my face my own marks lay. Now, get on with it, you enormous idiot. We do not have much time."

Edu shook his head. Not to say no, but as if he were judging Aon's commitment to snide commentary all the way to the bitter end. He lifted the blade and drew it down Aon's face, severing one of the seven lines of ink he wore.

The warlock hissed in pain but didn't fight back. His hands clenched at his sides, and her heart wrenched. When all seven were gone, he would be as good as dead. It was like watching someone sink beneath the waves. It was like watching someone slowly fade away.

Silent tears trickled from the corners of his eyes as he slipped them shut. Not from pain, but from sorrow. Even after all this time, he didn't want to die.

Lydia was standing beside Edu before she even knew she had moved. Her hand was on his wrist. He looked at her and bowed his head as if understanding how painful this was for her to watch.

Aon reopened his eyes and turned to look up at her. "This has to happen, my love. This must be. I need you to be strong... please."

Lydia didn't even try to fight her own tears. She held out

her hand for the knife. "I should be the one, Edu… it should be me. I love him. You hate him. If he has to die, let it be done by what he thought he'd never have."

Aon's hand found her other one, and she laced her fingers in between his and squeezed it. Edu let out a long, heavy sigh and handed her the knife. He nodded in understanding and took a step back. If there was one man in the world who would understand what it was like to say goodbye to someone you loved, she figured it would be him.

Lydia leaned down to kiss Aon one last time. He kissed her back, his other hand resting on her hip and drawing her close to him. When she broke the kiss, she rested her forehead against his. Just like he used to do with her. "I'm so sorry. I love you, Aon. I love you more than anything. I always will."

His voice was ragged, his emotions raw as he stood on the edge of the void. "That is all I need to die happily. You have given me peace. Real peace for the first time, in all my tens of thousands of years. But the dancers must stop. The music must cease. Let it end."

Lydia nodded weakly. She knew she had to do this.

She knew she had to.

There wasn't a choice.

She had to let him go.

She would be right behind him, anyway. The Ancients would never let their world live, with their precious baby lying dead on the floor. But she couldn't help it. She wanted one last kiss. She kissed him again, this time unable to hold back the sob that escaped her as she did. When she parted from him, she lifted the knife. "Goodbye," she whispered, her lips still hovering over his.

His gauntleted hand slipped from her waist. His lips turned into a sneer against her. "Oh, my starlight… that is a word you will never get to say to me."

TWENTY

Lydia couldn't react in time as he drove his claws deep into her stomach. He yanked, and she jolted as he tore his hand free of her body, taking a decent chunk of her with it. She heard Edu holler from behind her, but whatever had happened had caught him off guard as well.

As she fell, Noa caught her and lowered her to the ground. "A clever plan. A very clever plan. I give myself a great deal of credit for having come up with it. But it seems the candle wick was far too short. It seems the former Oracle was not strong enough."

Noa stood from his knees and brushed himself off. Lydia was left lying there, feeling her life bleeding out onto the floor.

"Edu, for the high crime of treason, I sentence you to death. *Finally.*"

Edu was skewered back to the floor, this time dragged down to his own knees. He was pouring blood from wounds that were too big for him to just brush off this time. And now, Noa was intent on taking his marks and killing Edu once and for all.

No. Not like this. It can't end like this! She pushed herself back up to her feet. It hurt. It was agonizing. It took every part of her to focus to stay awake. Noa was already ten paces away from her. "Stop, Noa. You can't..."

He paused to look at her over his shoulder. He looked impressed that she was upright. As she lurched toward him, he raised an eyebrow at her approach. He did nothing but watch as she managed to close the distance between them.

When her knees almost gave out, he caught her by the elbows and lifted her back up. "You are ever the resilient one." He chuckled as if she had just performed an amusing parlor trick.

This meant nothing to him. Edu meant nothing to him. The *world* meant nothing to him.

"You can't... you can't do this. Please, Noa."

"They all die, now. One by one, I will kill them all. I would make you watch... but I fear I am growing tired of this." He sighed. "You are my queen. You belong to me. And now I fear you will no longer have a say in the matter."

She didn't know what to do. She just stood there, wavering, gripping his arms as he held her up. Everything hurt. She was trapped. Caught in the tidal wave of a demigod.

"Soon, none of this will matter. Your pain will be the memory of a child. You will soon be mine as you are meant to be. You will look upon these moments and feel nothing but shame at your foolishness."

That was enough to give her words. "The man I loved is still in there. He *is* you. You called him your shadow, but you're wrong. You're the imposter and the lie. Strip away everything else, take away the Ancients and all their power and this false righteousness? And Aon is what's left. I love the man you are *in spite* of yourself."

He growled in warning, but she didn't listen to him. She only had a few moments left before darkness would come, and then it'd be too late for Edu and everyone else. She swallowed down the blood in her mouth and tried to find the air to speak.

"When you drag me to that altar, kicking and screaming? When you let the Ancients force their way into my mind and rape me of my free will? I want you to remember something. The woman who comes out the other side will be just as much of a lie as you are. As will the love she'll say she has for you."

It looked as though she had stabbed a dagger into his chest, the way he recoiled in pain. He took a step away from her, leaving her teetering on her unsteady feet. Noa watched her in a strange and muddled mess of fear, anger, and pain. "You cannot mean that..."

"I mean every word."

"Lydia," he said her name through a breath, "we will be happy together."

"If you can be happy living a lie, then so be it. I won't have a choice."

"Do you think I wish to be this way?" Noa howled, his pain suddenly flashing to anger like a spark in a can of gasoline. "I am their servant! I am their slave! I cannot fight their rule. I would have given it all up for you. I would tear the flesh off my bones if it meant you would love me! Do you think I want this?" He closed the distance between them once more and grabbed her by the upper arms. He shook her once, jarring her, and she almost lost consciousness right then and there. "If we cannot be together in truth, then we will be together in a lie. For I will not —I cannot—be alone once more. You cannot give me a taste of that which I have hungered for untold millennia, only then to take it away. For that, I will live a lie, and I will do it with joy!"

This time, when his hands went to her head, she didn't get a chance to think about what was going to happen.

"Noa, please—"

She felt a sickening crunch... and the world went dark.

* * *

"Now, then. Where were we?"

Edu had failed.

It was that simple.

Not because their plan did not work, but simply because he let Lydia take the knife from his hand. Edu had allowed her desire to be the one to kill the man she loved to overrule his own sensibilities. It was once more his fool's heart that doomed him… and indeed, doomed the world.

If only he had not given her the blade.

If only Ziza had held on a moment longer.

Ah, who am I kidding?

Even if Edu had managed to remove a few more lines of soulmarks from Aon's face, it would not have been enough time to finish the deed and kill him. The Ancients had overrun Ziza too quickly for any of them to have succeeded.

They had all failed.

Edu had wished to enter the void alone. To lay down his life to protect those he loved. He prayed that, somehow, in some unfathomable way, Evie might yet live. Yet it gave him some manner of peace to know Ylena and Ziza might greet him upon the other side. They had already walked the trail that lay before him.

His thoughts circled back to his little Evelyn. How he loved the girl. How she had brought him such joy in these past few months. He was so very tired of this life and of the constant and endless struggle against the King of Shadows, now the King of All. His very existence had been defined by it for so very long. He wished to rest. But for her, he would have gone on.

For Evie, he would have continued to walk the road he knew so well. Not for her sake, for she did not need him. She was too strong for that. No, merely because he wished to.

Their love had been a firecracker in the night sky. But it was no less wondrous, no less inspiring, for its brevity. If the King of All did not kill her and in short order, he knew she would live on with the indomitable ferocity she carried with her. The thought of how much hell she would raise for anyone who stood in her way gave him great pride.

His heart hurt for Ini, Vjo, and Dtu. His brother and sisters who would have to contend with more suffering, if the King of All did not make good on his threat to destroy everyone in his wrath. Perhaps they would be following him briefly; he did not know. He almost prayed they would, for death would be a kinder fate than what the King of All could wreak upon them for another five thousand years.

Indeed, there was only one person upon this wretched plane over which he was worried at all. Lydia. She had unwittingly—and in many ways—doomed them all. By her very arrival into Under and on that very first day, she had rewritten the fate of their world. Even if she had not been foolhardy enough to fall in love with the King of Shadows, her arrival would have doomed them to centuries of war and strife as she rose as the Queen of Dreams. If she had risen as such, without her love of the warlock, it would have meant nearly as much destruction.

Nearly.

The Ancients were unfathomably cruel. It was impossible to say what they might have done if the scheme had played out differently. But it seemed, no matter how hard he tried, that their will was immutable, unchangeable, and inevitable.

Edu held no bitterness toward Lydia, even now. She had done the best she could and followed her heart to the bitter end. He understood keenly her desire to be the one to end Aon's life. She was no coward.

His memories drifted to the night he met the Valkyrie who managed to catch him by surprise and bury a bullet in his brain. He remembered the mortal girl who refused him for her own dignity and who had successfully escaped his keep. Such a blazing impertinence! It had been glorious to see. Edu should have recognized a queen, as impossible as she might have been, right then and there. In hindsight, all things seemed so obvious.

Edu respected the girl. More than that, he had begun to grow fond of her. Giving Lydia the knife was a mistake he knew he would make again if given the opportunity. It was her right—her duty—to be the one to end Aon's life.

The Queen of Dreams was now bleeding out, lying on the floor in a heap, neck snapped, her eyes glassy and unseeing as she was taken into her false death. Good. The girl would not have to watch his demise. How valiantly she had tried to spare his life. It was touching that she cared so much for his existence. Her speeches had warmed his heart. He had never done anything to give the girl any reason but to hate and mistrust him until two weeks ago when he saved her from the Priest. It was by her benefit, not his, that she had tried so hard to save him.

Not only that, but Lydia had been willing to do what was needed in ending Aon's life. That willingness to sacrifice her love for the warlock amazed him. He would not have been so strong if their roles had been reversed.

Perhaps she finally understood that Aon was not this man, the King of All, who stood over him.

The one who was endlessly—and tirelessly—monologuing.

Edu had been ignoring him this entire time.

Will you not stop talking and get this over with?

"You know," the King of All interrupted his thoughts, pausing in the speech that Edu was quite simply not listening to, "I think I will release you of your curse. In this, your last moment, I will allow you to speak your last words. As I killed your little empath, it seems the only way. I believe I would like to know what you would say to me in these, our last seconds together."

The King tightened his fist, power curling around his metal gauntlet. Edu hissed in pain as he felt magic course through him like electricity, like the feeling of tendons stretched too far. Edu coughed as he felt something foreign in his mouth. Something he had not known since the Great War.

It felt odd to have a tongue again.

"Come, now, you mindless oaf. What would you say to me before you die? You are too proud to beg, I know that much." The King jeered, superior and confident in his win, haughty as he loomed over Edu's broken body, pinned to the floor by the spikes that were bleeding him dry. Not enough to land a killing blow. Not yet. He would reserve that for the last moment.

Edu laughed.

The King of All's expression faltered if but briefly at the unexpected response. Edu grinned up at the man and felt great pride for the life he had lived. With no remorse, he spoke for one last time. His voice sounded foreign to him now, like that of a stranger.

"Will you please just shut up?"

TWENTY-ONE

He felt anger. No, it was *rage*.

But why?

He should rejoice at the death of his most hated and long-lived enemy.

Edu was ash at his feet, reduced to nothing but dust in the black flame he'd commanded to consume the other man's corpse. Rending the marks from his face would have been too personal a touch. Instead, he let the inferno devour him whole.

There would be no resurrection for Edu. He would not return that putrid pile of flesh to the blood of the Ancients. The "King of Flames" was not deserving of such an honor.

Lifting the red mask in his hand, he looked down at the visage he had come to loathe for so very long. He grasped it in the metal abomination—the hateful replacement for a hand—that he wore to placate his frightened and terrified future queen.

By the dawn, he would heal it and be done with this stain upon his soul. As he would be done with the stain that was this malignant fungus that had grown upon his world in his absence.

Edu. Vjo, Dtu, and all the others. Lyon and all the rest were nothing but bastardizations of the proper way of things. The whole world was warped and confused, clinging to its broken visions as though they were reality, not seeing it all for the sickness that it was.

Anger was still burning through him. Not joy. Not relief. Not pride.

There was an empty pit where there should have been glorious victory.

It choked in his throat. It stung at him like insects.

No... this was not anger either.

Whatever it was, it was a miserable thing. It was caught halfway between anguish and fury, between grief and the urge to destroy something beneath his hands. He turned to look over at the remains of his throne room. At the bodies that lay strewn about at his feet amongst the rock and rubble.

Vjo. Lyon. Edu.

Like discarded toys.

Lydia...

His queen had betrayed him. He had lied to her, yes, but such a harmless lie it had been! It had all been to protect her.

Soon, she would no longer be lost in such strife and turmoil as she was now. She was so young, after all. An infant soul could not grasp at the enormity of what was happening around her.

It did not have to be this way. It did not have to end this way.

Was that the source of the grief that stuck a rock into his throat? He was victorious, after all. He had just dispatched the traitors and undone their careful plot to overthrow him. *No,* he corrected himself. *My own careful plot of self-destruction.*

He did not know what to make of that. His mad self, the shard of his mind that could remember what he was without the Ancients' guiding hand, had sought so hard to bring about the end of it all. Perhaps, now that all hope of such things was dashed, that cretin would wither away and die. He would scab over like a fresh wound and heal.

Why did it feel so futile? Why did it feel so empty, so hollow, to stand over the remains of his greatest nagging annoyance and the bodies of all those who conspired against him?

It made no sense. There was no logic to the pain that lanced his heart.

There was only one cure for what ached in him. One salve that he may place upon the rift he felt in his soul. Stooping down, he lifted Lydia's body into his arms. She was so light, so perfect against him. She smelled like summer grass and the jungle... like dreams.

Qta, of all the bastard children the Ancients brought for him to play with, had always been the most impressive in his power. Creativity was an ineffable thing in its methods. It either was, or it was not. Logic and reason did not apply to its boundaries.

Much like love, it seemed.

He loved the woman in his arms. Loved her more than he could express. It was all he had ever wished for in all his antiquity. Therefore, the cure for his current dilemma would rest within her. He would find solace in her devotion. He would take his joy as she rose from the altar as his proper queen. This inexplicable pain he felt at the death of his oldest usurper would be quickly forgotten when Lydia embraced the Ancients.

He could remember how she smiled at the madman and professed her love to him. How she would hold him in his shattered moments and take his darkest needs with joy. For those briefest moments, even lost in the corridors of insanity as he was, he had been happy. Truly happy for the first time in all his long life.

And he would kill them all to have that back.

* * *

Lydia woke with a start.

Everything just snapped back into focus, all at once. She was lying on the ground, but the stone wasn't the polished surface of the throne room. Wherever she was now was made entirely out of black rock and lit only by blazing fires and an eerie red glow.

A red glow she knew too well.

Well, it wasn't that goddamn lake of blood, for once.

Someone was crying. A young woman. It took her a solid few seconds of confusion to realize it wasn't her. Rolling onto her side, she pushed herself up to sitting and put her palm to her forehead, shuddering at the memory of the pain of Noa's claws digging into her body and the crunch of him snapping her neck. But it was, like all her other deaths, quickly fading.

Looking up, finally, she saw she was on a black stone path that stretched through the glowing red blood of the Ancients on either side of them. It was a mirror of the throne room above them. A stone path lined with columns, and at the end, instead of a throne made for their "Only Son," stood an altar. It stretched up, some fifty feet tall, into the darkness overhead, uplit dramatically in the amber of the fire and the red of the blood.

Stone-carved faces of the Ancients loomed atop pillars, their ghastly and empty-socketed faces split in sick grins or grotesque expressions. Seven of them in total. She shivered again, this time for a very different reason. Their power was *everywhere*. It crackled in the air around her like an electrical storm. This was their home. This was their seat of power. They were *here*.

She felt so very, very small.

"Welcome back."

The voice made her jump. She finally looked away from the massive stone figures down to the base where an altar, carved from the same strange black material as the rest of the room, stretched some thirty feet wide. The King of All stood there, regal and perfect. This was where he belonged. This was where he was made.

At his feet... was Evie.

Clutching Edu's mask to her chest, she was bent over it, weeping. That sent Lydia to her feet, staggering and wobbly as she was, in an instant. She looked to the man who stood there, watching her haughtily.

No. He couldn't be dead. He couldn't be. "Please, tell me you didn't."

Noa stood there, watching her, as cold as the stone around him. "He is now ash."

She put her hand over her mouth and squeezed her eyes tight. She felt sick. It was like someone had grabbed her stomach and twisted. When she managed to choke the rock from her throat back down, she glared at him and tried to take shelter in her anger. "Damn you. Damn you to *hell!*"

He held his arms out at his sides as if to say, "we are already here." There was a red cut still etched down his face where Edu had sliced him, and although it hadn't quite healed, it had stopped bleeding. The soulmarks beneath it were... coming back. *Of course they were. Of course he goes by different rules.*

"What about Lyon and Vjo?"

"Alive, for now. I wanted to tend to this matter, first." Noa shrugged dismissively. His expression was empty—joyless. He wasn't a taunting overlord, a victorious monster.

"I won't let you." She summoned a knife to her hand and held it out in front of her as if she really stood a chance.

Noa raised his clawed hand. She yelped in surprise as the dagger melted without warning. It burned her, the molten gold dropping to the stone with the obsidian blade, now floating loose in the cooling liquid. "You stand at the Altar of the Ancients. Here, their power is absolute. Ergo, so is mine." He frowned. "But in but a few moments' time, you will understand. All of this strife, all of this pain, will be a bad dream."

"Like Aon was to you."

He flinched and glanced at the altar. "Yes. Come to me. Kneel with me. Pray to them and accept their love."

Suddenly, she pieced together why he had brought Evie. But she wanted it to come out of his mouth. "Why is Evie here?"

He looked at her with a cold smile that did not reach his eyes. "To convince you to kneel if you insist on making this difficult."

Shutting her eyes, she swore under her breath. "You don't want them to destroy me. You think they might. You're terrified that if you force me to submit, you'll end up with a drooling lobotomy patient on the other end of it."

He narrowed his eyes, likely not knowing what a lobotomy was, but he caught the gist of what she said well enough. "I want you to accept your fate."

"Only to save yourself pain."

His hands tightened into fists before releasing—clearly trying to hold his temper at bay. "I do it to spare you. I do it to save you. You are correct that I do not know the damage they will cause if you fight them. You are strong, my love. You have a will that would burn as bright as the sun in the sky. It will likely tear you apart if they must force their way in."

"So, what? Either I kneel, or you kill her?"

"Yes."

"Fuck him!" Evie cried. "Don't do it. Don't listen to this sack of—"

A metal claw backhanded her to the face, sending her sprawling to the stone. "Silence!"

Lydia stepped toward him reflexively. "Leave her out of this. Leave her alone. This is about you and me. Nobody else."

"Oh, but it does involve them all. Our world hangs in the balance. It hangs upon your decision. Kneel and spare her life."

"You're lying. You'll kill her the moment I won't care."

"She is meaningless to me. She is a gnat upon the wall. It

makes no difference to me if she lives or dies. She is powerless. Barely more than mortal." Noa reached down and grabbed Evie by the hair with his human hand and yanked her back up to kneeling. He held his gauntleted hand open, palm up, threatening to tear her face off. "Shall I prove it to you?"

She had seen Aon kill one of her friends. And now Noa was going to take another. "Don't do it. I'm begging you. Leave her alone!"

"I will not listen to words alone, my love. Your pleading did not spare Edu, and it will not spare her. Our world cares not for your empathy, and neither do I."

"Don't do it, bunny. Don't do it. He's lying, you know he is!"

"One more word, and she will not have a chance to save you," he growled down at her.

Lydia's eyes met her friend's. She was still clutching Edu's mask tightly to her chest. Her cheeks were stained with tears.

A King would rise to destroy her, and a friend would be her undoing.

That prophecy had haunted her, and it seemed it still would. She had chosen to let her friendship with Lyon send her to the bottom of the lake. And she could choose to let her friendship with Evie send her to her knees in front of the altar.

Maybe this was a pointless moment of grandstanding.

But even though her life was over, one way or another... she couldn't let that prophecy come true a second time. It stopped here, with everything else. "Evie, I love you. I'm so sorry..."

"Nah, bunny, you saved my life. I had a chance to be happy with Edu. I had a chance to make him happy. It was all worth it." The other girl grinned at her, bright and unaffected by her wounds, emotional or physical. "No regrets."

That was the last thing Evie said before Noa drove his claws straight into her skull, skewering the purple mark on her cheek. She didn't even have a chance to scream. For that, Lydia was almost grateful, even as she turned her head and tried not to retch.

A splash snapped her attention back to him. Noa had dropped Evie's body into the glowing moat of blood next to the stone path, where she floated briefly, and then sank. Noa scooped up Edu's mask from the ground, turned it over in his hand idly for a moment, and then tossed it in to follow. "A shame, my love. I truly would have let her live."

"That's the problem with being a liar. Nobody ever knows when you're telling the truth."

He looked back to her. Now, all the distractions were gone. Now, it was just the two of them. "Kneel with me in prayer. Surrender to them."

Lydia shook her head.

He winced and looked down, his brow furrowing, as if he couldn't understand why she kept refusing him. It made so much sense to him. Everything was so obviously correct in his world that she must be a mystery to him. A nonsensical child, screaming at the shadows in the corners of the room and seeing monsters where there weren't any.

"They've taken everything from me. And what they haven't taken, *you* have. My home, my life, my friends... the man I love. It's all gone. All I have left is myself. They can tear that out of my hands, but I won't give it up for them or for you."

Lydia felt as though something were suddenly piercing her skull. Like someone had poured hot iron into her head. Voices, shouting and silent all at once, flooded into her mind.

"We are your masters.
We are your makers.
You are Our Dreamer.
As he is Our Only Son.
Surrender.
Submit.

Know peace."

Oh, yeah. Aon wasn't kidding. That fucking *hurt.*

She was on the ground, holding onto her head. It was like a crowd of people had been screaming directly into her brain with a bullhorn. A bullhorn made from lava.

Someone was holding her, she realized. Looking up, it was Noa. He was kneeling at her side, arms around her, cradling her to him, a look of concern etched on his face.

He reached up to stroke her hair out of her face. "Are you all right?"

"They were talking to me."

"I know. I could hear."

"Why are you worried about me?" She tried to pull away from him, but his arm tightened.

The laugh that left him was incredulous. "Question me how you like, but *I love you.* Judge me unworthy as you may, but *I love you...* and I always will." He leaned down and kissed her forehead. "I do not wish to do this. I wish it had not gone this way."

"I won't. I won't do it." She pushed to her feet, and he followed her. Still, he looked at her with such pain and longing that it made her almost cry for him, even after everything he had done.

"Do it, or they all die. Every single one of them. The whole of this world in exchange for your surrender."

"You'll do it, anyway. I can't trust you."

"But you could trust *him?* The madman, who had come within a hair of murdering you so many times?" He growled angrily and grabbed her by the arms again, refusing to let her turn away from him. "Surrender to the Ancients, or I wipe this world clean."

"Please, Noa... no more. I can't do this anymore."

"You will not have to, my love. This is the end. The end of it all. Submit to them. There is no shame in knowing when you have been defeated." He was dragging her now by the upper arm toward the altar.

She dug in her heels and tried to fight, tried to struggle. She felt as though she were tied to the tracks and watching a steam engine come ever closer. "Please, no. Please!" Terror filled her. Pure, unadulterated fear.

She managed to yank out of his grasp and tried to run away, to run for the exit and never stop. But he appeared in front of her, and she ran into him. He wrapped his arms around her tightly, cradling her head against her chest. She struggled, but he was too strong. He was shushing her quietly, pressing his cheek against the top of her head. "Sssh... oh, my love. Do not be afraid. This is not your death. This is your rebirth. It will be all right, I promise you. I will always be here with you."

"Don't do this..." she begged still, pleading with him to have mercy on her.

"You betrayed me once. You would have taken my life if Ziza had not died earlier than anticipated. I cannot let you betray me again. They have corrupted you. No, my starlight. I cannot spare you this fate. Would that I could." Noa was talking to her in hushed tones, trying uselessly and desperately to console her.

Slowly, like the creeping numbness that came with being outside in the cold too long, she started to calm down. It took what felt like minutes of her hovering on the edge of a panic attack, trying to think of a way out of an unescapable situation. But it began to fade and turn into an empty hopelessness. Not because she was beginning to accept what was about to happen to her, but because she knew it didn't matter.

One way or another, this was the end of the road.

Her muscles start to loosen as she let go of hope. Feeling this, he kissed her forehead. "Good. Come. Kneel with me in prayer. Let them cure you of this pain."

As he went to lead them to the altar, she reached up and cradled his head in her hands and turned him to face her. She rested his forehead against hers and shut her eyes. For a moment, she could pretend and imagine he was the man she loved. "I'm scared…"

Noa tilted her head back and kissed her gently—slowly—trying to reassure her. Trying to remind her of why she was here. When he broke the kiss, he drifted his lips to her ear. "You will know no fear in but moments. All of this will seem like a passing nightmare drifting away in the morning light."

"I can't… I just can't."

The pain of the Ancients speaking returned, and she clung to Noa in a desperate attempt to stay on her feet this time.

"We promised you once that you could always choose.
And so, We will keep Our vow.
Take His place.
We will kill Him, our Only Son.
We will end His suffering, as you wished to do.
Take His throne, as our Only Daughter. Become the Queen of All.
Or sacrifice yourself to Us and him."

She pushed away from Noa, who was now looking up at the altar in confusion. She turned to look as well and felt the power of the Ancients around them. It was ethereal and strange, flickering around the edges of her vision. The shadows of the room were living, shifting and moving things. Every time she turned to catch a glimpse of the pointed, ghastly figures that seemed to hover in the corners of her field of view, they were gone. They were phantoms.

They were the monsters in the corners of her bedroom.

Noa bowed his head suddenly, his hands going into his hair, clenching it in his fists. He fell to his knees slowly, seemingly unable to stand.

But she was distracted by her anger, and the horrifying offer they put in front of her to worry about what was going on with the King of All.

"And what?" she asked. "Be your puppet, same as him? I'd be a curse on this world, same as he is now. It wouldn't fix anything!" she shouted up at the stone monoliths. At least now she had something to shout at and not just at the air in general. "That wouldn't fix—"

A voice, broken and tired, interrupted her. "I would finally be free, my dragonfly..."

Her heart hitched in her chest, skipping a beat. Rushing to him, she knelt in front of Aon and tilted his head up to look at her, pulling his hands from his hair.

The look on his face was one of pain, of hurt, and a weary kind of happiness as he looked at her, his dark eyes flickering between hers. "I said it before, but... your eyes are truly beautiful now that they are turquoise. They were stunning before... now they are quite otherworldly." He moved his hand to cup her cheek. "My queen."

She kissed him with all her hurt, her desperation, her love, her fear. The situation just kept going from bad, to worse, to even worse with every tick of the clock.

When they broke apart, he was crying again, tears mingling with the red slice down his cheek. "You were right not to trust him. He would have murdered them all, regardless. He had no intention to spare them. The only way forward is to take my life and my throne. Let this world continue under you. Even at your worst—even as their puppet—you would be a kinder fate for this world than me."

"No... I..."

"Killing me is the only way."

"I'll lose you too."

"You already have. I am little more than a ghost, haunting the man I really am. I can only return when they deem fit to allow it." A flicker of anger and disgust crossed Aon's face. She had forgotten how quickly his emotions came to him—how accustomed Aon was to hiding behind a mask. "Please, my dragonfly. Let it end."

"Kill us both," she demanded up at the Ancients. "Kill us both and let us go!"

Silence.

That wasn't their bargain. Their bargain with her was either she surrendered or *they* would kill Aon and force her to take his place. There was no way out. There was no just letting them burn out her mind.

Either she gave in or he died.

It took every ounce of will to pull herself out of Aon's arms. But she forced herself up to her feet.

He rested on his knees and looked up at her forlornly but was struggling to smooth his look of pain into one of resignation. She reached down and wiped the tears from his face, careful to avoid the cut along his cheek.

She choked back her tears long enough to speak. "I think I loved you the first time I saw you. The first time I was there in that crypt of yours in your dreams. My villain, my nightmare, my charming demon. You haunted me, toyed with me, and god *damn* it, you always left me wishing you would never stop. You made me feel... as though I somehow made you *happy*. That to you, I was special. You, this ancient, powerful, charismatic, monster. I mattered to *you*."

Aon placed his hand along the back of hers and turned his head to kiss her palm, letting his eyes slide shut. He went to answer her, maybe to profess his own feelings, but he couldn't get them out. He winced, choked, and sobbed once as emotions so visceral overtook him in his grief.

She couldn't stand the sight of him crying. It hurt worse than anything else she'd experienced so far. She leaned down and kissed him again and felt him clutch his hands at the edges of her shirt, twisting the fabric in his fingers. When she broke off this time, she whispered to him, "That's why I can't do it."

Aon opened his eyes to search hers, wavering and unsure. "Lydia, what do you mean?"

She took a step back from him and turned to face the altar. But it was too late. She'd made up her mind. Walking toward the altar, she gazed up at the monolithic structures. They were meant to terrify—meant to strike awe and fear into those who looked on them—and they worked. She took a moment to gather her thoughts.

"You keep giving me the option to give up. You keep giving me the option to say 'never mind' and tap out. You want me to prove you right. You want me to prove to you that I don't love him. You've pushed me further and further, broken me down again and again. It was your choice to abduct me from Earth. Your choice to reject me from the pool. You've had me nearly drowned, and you instructed the others to kill me. You took me back from the dead to play this game of yours. I'm sure you were responsible for Rxa chaining me to the bottom of the lake with you. And now *this*. Now, you ask me to surrender to you, as proof that I'm willing to sacrifice it all to be with him."

"Lydia, please..." Aon tried to call to her, but she ignored him. She couldn't look back at him right now. She clenched her fists at her sides.

"So now, I lose my soul either way. Either as his replacement or as his puppet queen." She shut her eyes, took in a deep breath, and let it out slowly, finding some resolve in that simple action. Opening her eyes, she looked up at the Ancients. At the things that made her, and Aon, and this entire world.

"Here's the thing," she began. There was an odd peace, now that she accepted what she was about to do. "I don't want to live in this world if *he* isn't in it. And I don't mean the King of All. I mean Aon. I mean *him*." She pointed back at the warlock without turning. "You made a creature you thought was too broken to survive. So instead of living with your failure, you plugged up the holes and made him what you wanted him to be. When he betrayed you because he was alone, he was left to pick up the shattered pieces left behind. And you know what he did? That man... that amazing, terrible, cruel, evil, and wonderful man... put himself back together as best he could. He did the absolute best with what he had. He is worth more than all of you assholes added together!"

She was furious now, and it felt cathartic to shout at them. "If I can't live in the world with him, I won't live in it at all! Not really. Not the part of me that matters. If all you want are puppets... so be it. I give up. Have your fucking puppets."

"No, my dragonfly. Don't do this!" Aon pled once more.

"I surrender!" she shouted up at the statues. "I surrender. I'll kneel and let you rewrite my mind if that's what you really want. But I want to make something perfectly clear. I am not surrendering to you. I will *never* surrender to you."

Lydia turned around to look at Aon, who was still on his knees, watching her desperately. She smiled at him faintly, somehow finding the ability to do so. "I'm surrendering to him." She walked to his side and knelt beside him. She took his metal hand in hers and wove her fingers through his.

"Do not do this. Change your mind, I beg you," he whispered, his voice still raw. "Do not join me in my nightmare. Do not follow me down this path."

"I'm going to follow you, whether you like it or not. I'm not going to leave you, and I won't let you leave me either. This is our nightmare now. I won't leave your side." A calm was settling over her now. Her decision was made. "I love you, Aon."

His shoulders slumped. He laughed, a quiet, beleaguered sound. The smile that he paid her was one that she hoped she would never forget. "And I, you, my dragonfly."

Lydia felt something enter her mind, like a claw digging in

through the back of her skull. She knew better than to think it was real. It seared and burned like a blazing fire poker, and she cried out. But she couldn't hear herself anymore. She could only clench Aon's hand as the pain drove all thought out of her mind.

She barely felt it as she collapsed to the floor, her thought slipping away into darkness.

* * *

Our Children.
Our Favorite Ones.
How you have suffered.
How well you have done.
We are pleased. We may rest.
And We shall reward you.
Our Children...

TWENTY-TWO

Once more, Lydia awoke with a start. This time, it felt like she was falling. God damn it, she was sick and tired of this shit! She reached out to gain purchase on anything around her. It felt like she was half lying down, strewn out on stone stairs.

Massive, white stones, roughly hewn and stacked into a step pyramid. She was lying on them, her head on one level, her feet on another one. It wasn't exactly comfortable, and when she had thrashed, she slid unceremoniously down a tier.

It left her looking up at the top of the pyramid... at the Temple of Dreams. Warped and merged with Boston architecture, but... *the Temple of Dreams.*

The moons were high in the sky, each full and triumphantly glowing in the darkness. The stars blazed. No eclipsed sun hung overhead with them. Lydia slowly pushed herself to standing and looked down at herself and at the lines of turquoise-colored ink running down her body.

Lydia climbed down the stairs slowly, unsure as to what to do. Of what to think. Had it been a nightmare? No. It couldn't have been. If it were, she wouldn't have the marks on her arms and her chest. Q would be sitting here, mocking her for having fallen asleep on her front stoop.

Lydia remembered it all. The sand, the ancient city, and the blazing sun. That terrifying altar and the voices.

Walking across the grass toward the reflecting pond, the feeling of it was wonderful against her bare feet. It was cool and slightly damp in the dewy air. The cricket-like insects were chirping in the distance, the flashing multicolored bugs dancing in their patterns in the shrubs at the edges of the clearing.

She climbed onto one of the massive white stones that ringed the reflecting pool of her home and looked around, stunned and confused. She felt just as lost and confused as the day she came to Under.

What happened?

"What game are you playing at?" she shouted to the empty air. "What's your sick ploy this time?"

Nothing and no one answered.

She was alone.

For a moment, she was terrified the Ancients had killed everyone and left her here alone in this world by herself. It was that thought that inspired her. She had to find someone— anyone—and prove the theory was wrong.

There was only one place she wanted to go.

She hadn't ever "teleported" there before. She couldn't have found it on a map if she had tried. But she knew it well. Many of her happiest recent memories came from there.

Stepping through the world in the right way, she appeared in Aon's estate.

The halls were empty.

Panic later. Solve the problem now.

Fuck it.

Now was a great time to panic.

"Aon!"

* * *

Lyon watched the matchstick burn as he held it to the candle's wick. He had been lighting them for the last half hour. He did not know what else to do. Kamira was still unconscious, recovering on a bench nearby. Her heart was beating, but he could not rouse her.

But he had been right, during their battle. He had missed the marks with his chains. She lived. And so, he waited.

Waiting was not a difficult task for him.

The cathedral had returned. Indeed, looking out the front doors—so had the whole city of Yej. Returned from the unmade world as though nothing had transpired. But he knew better. He could feel the weight of the loss on his soul. What had happened in that desert realm had truly come to pass.

Edu was dead. Ylena. Ziza. Evelyn. Aria. Countless more had fallen. Their world had been dealt a serious wound. Their numbers, potentially halved, if not worse. There was no counting the dead.

And yet... here he was. Lighting candles for them, regardless.

Truth be told, he had not expected to survive. He had not expected anyone to live, after their tragic plan had gone so horribly wrong.

But he was here. Alive. Awake.

And with nothing else to do, he tended to the Cathedral of the Ancients, as days that felt so long ago.

He lit the candles in remembrance of those who had died, but also for all seven of their elder creators. For it was in their terrible wrath, and their mercy, that he could find the only explanation for what had occurred.

They had chosen to return to their cage.

They had chosen to *sleep*.

Some great task of theirs was now concluded.

He felt the press of their power against his own. He was the keeper of the chains now. Chains they had willingly donned. And they lay, slumbering and still, in the pool of blood deep beneath the church sanctuary. He could feel them burning away, through the links of the chain that was his power. He was their keeper, as had been his master Rxa before him. As a mirror below, so above. As had the throne room been in the Temple built to their honor, so very long ago and yet so recently still.

The sand and sun burned in his memory too keenly to have been a dream. Part of him had wondered, when he had awoken on the floor of the sanctuary proper, if he had knocked himself silly when he had tried to enter through Rxa's gate of power around the cathedral and had merely dreamed the rest. But it was too visceral, too tangible, too lucid for him to have invented it all.

He was also not nearly so creative. Never in his wildest imaginings could he have invented what he had seen transpire.

As last he had known, he had been assisting in the King of All's undoing and had gloriously failed. Unconsciousness took him, and when he awoke, Edu was already dead. The King and Lydia were both gone. He had only a few minutes to consider his next actions before a piercing pain had struck him, and all had gone black.

Casting his gaze up at the statue that loomed over him, the pale visage flickered in the light from candle flames that were meant to venerate in their paltry glow. He could not begin to guess the answer. But he knew someone—or two, perhaps— who might.

The Queen of Dreams and King of Shadows may know the answers he sought, if the fates were kind and both of them had lived. Turning to look back at his wife, he sighed. He could not leave Kamira here alone. His answers would have to wait.

And so, he turned back to the row of votives and lit another.

* * *

Lydia was running through the halls of Aon's home. It was as she remembered it, with its twisted vine work and soaring, warped, and perverted Baroque details. Once, it horrified her. Now, she would be overjoyed to see it if she wasn't so caught in a panic.

"Aon!"

There was no answer. She ran from room to room, calling his name. No one answered. No one seemed to be home. It was halfway down a different hallway that she nearly tripped over a body lying on the ground. They were dressed in all black, and for a moment she panicked before she realized it was Navaa.

She crouched next to the man and rolled him onto his back. He wore his metal mask over two thirds of his face, as he had before everything had gone to hell. To hell and—apparently, just maybe—back. Putting her fingers to his neck, she felt a pulse. He was alive, but unconscious.

Standing, she went back to her search. He had to be here. He had to be!

People were strewn everywhere, fallen to the floor and unconscious as if they had had just collapsed where they lay. Masked and unmasked alike. All of them out cold as if they had simply dropped there when Aon had killed Rxa.

Did any of that happen? Or is this the dream?

Am I dead?

Again?

It didn't feel like a dream or a vision. She ran her hand along the wall, feeling the woodwork under her hand as if to confirm her hand wouldn't sink through it like it was an illusion.

Turning events over in her head, she tried to think through what was happening but had no answers.

"Aon!" Still no reply. Just the echo of her voice down the arched hallway.

But she didn't stop running. He had to be here. He had to be! Unless... unless the Ancients had killed him. Unless they'd taken his life and put the world back to the way it was, just to taunt her.

No, please, anything but that.

Her steps faltered as she heard something. Something other than the sound of her footsteps and the whisper of wind. It took her a second to register that it was a piano. Someone was playing a slow, mournful tune. She took off in the direction of the sound, which was easier said than done. The twisting architecture made it hard to trace the source of the noise. It might have gone on for minutes before she found the room it came from.

It was a parlor, somewhere on one of the upper floors. Moonlight streamed in through stained-glass windows and cast multicolored shadows across the floors. There, near one wall, was a beautiful grand piano. Black, of course. Light shone off its dark lacquered surface, glinting to match the black metal mask of the man who sat at the keys.

Aon.

His head was partially lowered, his hair pulled back. As he played, he didn't acknowledge her presence.

Slowing her steps, she suddenly felt foolish for charging in, like she was interrupting something. Her heart was pounding in her ears, the result of her running around his house, full-tilt, shouting for him.

Now that she saw him, she held her breath.

She had no idea what she'd find.

Or who.

The King of All or Aon? Or someone new? Had this finally pushed him that last step into madness?

If this wasn't merely a vision or a ghost. Some last, lingering phantasm the Ancients put here to break her heart.

Carefully, she walked closer. She edged nearer to the piano, terrified that with any step he might disappear, vanish into thin air like the ghost she was afraid he was, and she'd be alone. But he still played the mournful tune, crossing his clawed left hand over his right with deft skill.

She had never heard him play before. It was beautiful, mournful, and the notes rang with what she knew he held in his soul. She decided all she wanted to do was sit and listen to him for hours.

She also had the distinct urge to tease him about playing with a metal claw and if he had to pad the keys to keep it from clicking. *Magic,* she answered her own question and tried not to laugh at the absurd errant thought as it came to her.

When she was standing at the side of the piano, he still didn't look up. Didn't even lift his head an inch to see her. He just looked down at the keys and played as if she weren't even there. Maybe she was the ghost. Wouldn't that be fitting?

The urge to reach out and touch him was so strong, but he was caught up in his music, and it felt blasphemous to stop him. And so, she stood there, nearly holding her breath, watching the man she had come to fear and love so very much.

After a few moments, the music wound down and hung in the air until silence reigned in the room. Aon lifted his hands from the keys and turned them over until his palms were face up. He looked down at them, his body tense. His voice was strained and barely above a whisper when he finally broke the silence. "Am I real?"

It took everything in her not to sob at his words. It parroted back to her what she had asked him in the last dream they had shared. It broke her heart. And it gave her such hope that he might, in fact, be the man she knew. "You're real enough to me."

He stood from the bench and took a single step away, standing perpendicular to her. The light shining off his metal mask took her breath away. *He* took her breath away. He looked down at his metal hand once more, turning it over and over, slowly, as if debating its existence. "Edu is dead."

"Yeah…"

"I suppose there is no need to maintain the curse now."

It was a dismissive sentence. A matter-of-fact pondering in the face of the enormity of what had just occurred. He was trying to brush it all off and sink into his armor of sardonic observations.

"Aon."

"I suppose I could let my hand regrow. Although I have become terribly fond of the claw, I must say. While many things may become more convenient without it, I do love the sense of *melodrama* it provides. I think I shall keep it."

"Aon!"

"Yes? What is it?"

Again, acting as though nothing had happened! She stepped toward him and, lifting her hand, twined her fingers with his metal ones and used that to turn him to her. Reaching up with her other hand, she went to remove his mask. She hesitated when her fingertips touched the metal lip.

"It belongs to you." His voice was soft and strained, revealing the truth of his mood for the first time. "As it always will."

Gently pulling the mask away, she was afraid for a moment she might find the King of All, merely masquerading as the man she loved. Instead, she found a man whose expression was a perfect opposite to his previously off-handed tone.

A frantic kind of wild-eyed fear burned in him. Pain, agony, and panic. He was standing on the edge of a cliff. One of despair, of loathing, or of madness, she didn't know. She suspected all three. He stood there, staring over the edge, and chose to speak as if nothing had happened.

One paper-thin scar ran down his cheek, bisecting a line of black ink that had regrown and healed beneath the pale mark. They were slightly damaged, but they were still there. Through the onslaught of emotions that were clearly rampaging through him, his tone still kept it perfectly hidden beneath his sardonic humor. "Tell me, am I hideous?"

Dropping the mask to the ground, it clattered loudly as she threw her arms around his neck and kissed him. Kissed him with everything she had. She had thought she had cried all the tears she could ever possibly create, but she felt them on her cheeks, anyway. He wrapped his arms around her waist and pulled her tightly to him.

When the kiss finally broke to allow them both some air, he nuzzled his head down onto her shoulder. "If you have joined me in my madness, I mourn for you, but I would not part with you given the chance..."

"I'll never leave you."

"You have proven that as fact, without a shadow of a doubt."

"How much do you remember?"

He sighed. "Bits and pieces... shattered glass enough to know it had once been a vase, but not enough to rebuild it. I remember... I remember the deaths. The lives I took. I remember you. Kneeling at my side. Pledging to walk beside me, no matter the cost."

She turned her head to kiss his cheek and didn't know what to say to that.

He let out a wavering breath. "If I am dead, then let this be my eternity. If this is hell, for I do not deserve a heaven, then the reports of this place are sorely exaggerated."

That was her warlock. Quipping his way through the worst

of times. She laughed quietly in relief more than at his badly timed humor, and she squeezed him tighter. "I love you."

"And I, you, my dragonfly." Lifting his head, he ghosted his lips over hers. "I will love you, now and forever."

As he zeroed the distance between them, she knew without a doubt that somehow, for some reason, their world had been returned to the way it was.

But right now, with him, she couldn't care why.

* * *

It had taken Lydia and Aon a day or two to finally venture out of his home and into the world. Everyone was slowly coming around, bit by bit. The servants and masked alike in the House of Shadows were confused and shocked over what had happened. There were far more questions than answers.

Aon avoided them all, locking himself into his library and speaking only to her. He wouldn't even let Navaa into the room.

She could only confirm for them all that Aon was alive, and he was his "old" self. Or "new" self.

Whichever.

He wasn't the King of All anymore.

But he hadn't come out the other side unscathed. He was suffering from a massive migraine and needed to sleep it off. And so, she sat at his side and waited for him to piece himself back together.

He had been, as he put it, "ridden hard and put away wet," by the Ancients. But after many long hours of lying on his sofa asleep with few breaks in between, he seemed to be a bit more with it than before. It was time to venture out.

It was time to look for answers.

And there was only one place Aon knew where they might find some.

It was the last place she wanted to go, but... he was right. She couldn't come up with another idea.

She just *really* hated that place.

As Aon folded the world around them and teleported them away, she found herself looking up at the grinning stone depictions of their creators, perched over a lake of glowing crimson. The Pool of the Ancients was back, and it was utterly unchanged from the first time she had seen it.

Lydia stood next to Aon on its shores, looking up at the pouring water. She reached out to take his leather gloved hand, and he squeezed back reassuringly. Whatever might have happened, they were here together. Everything else was in question, but they had each other.

"Ms. Lydia?"

A voice behind them made them turn. Lydia laughed. "Lyon!" She broke away from Aon to run to the Priest and throw her arms around him. Lyon chuckled and embraced her as well. "You're okay! Is Kamira—"

"Quite alive, if disgruntled. She is napping on the roof."

"Who else?"

"Vjo and Ini have been by in the past day. Dtu has circled the building once or twice but has not come near. That is his way."

But not Edu.

Her heart sank. She pushed away from Lyon to look up at him. Seeing her expression, his meager happiness went back to his default sadness. He shook his head, indicating to her that there had been no sign of the armored behemoth.

"Then who wears the red?" Aon asked from behind her. He had seen the scene unfold and must have read her unspoken exchange with Lyon for what it was.

"I do not know. No one has seen nor heard—"

"I kin' answer that for you!"

"Oh, no." Aon groaned in dismay. "No, *please...*"

A figure bounded up the stairs to the platform that over-looked the Pool of the Ancients. Her fiery red hair was tied back in a messy ponytail, strands escaping here and there from the mop of red. She wore leather and fur. But down her exposed arms were giant swaths of red ink.

And she wore a full mask. Horns, much smaller than Edu's, curled back away from her head.

Lyon's mouth had fallen open.

Lydia didn't know what to say. Finally, after a long moment, she stopped uselessly gaping. "E... Evie?"

"Hi, bunny!" Evie pulled the mask off her face and revealed her broad, shit-eating grin. The girl was having far too much fun with her dramatic reveal. Her face was streaked in red ink, looking like Celtic warpaint. Evie ran up to her and threw her arms around her neck, hugging her. Lydia had the choice between letting the girl knock her over or grabbing on to her to stay standing.

At some point—when, exactly, she couldn't place—Lydia had started laughing. She threw her arms around the girl and hugged her as tightly as she could. "You're alive. *You're alive!*"

"They did t'me exactly what they did t'you and Lyon. They gave me a choice. Said I could go be with Edu or be a queen. I knew he'd want me to keep goin' and wouldn't want me to give up. So here I am, keepin' goin'. I couldn't let you show me up, after all! You came back from the dead, and so did bats over here." She jerked a thumb at Lyon. "Couldn't be that hard, I figured."

"It seems the Ancients truly have a sick and perverse sense of humor," Aon grumbled from behind them.

"And now we know where you get it from," Lydia shot back at him.

Lyon was still standing there, staring.

"Seems we're both queens now, huh?" Evie giggled up at her. "Who'd've thunk?"

"Not me," Lydia admitted with a shake of her head. "Never in a million years."

"So, can anybody tell me what the hell happened?" Evie asked. She turned to look at Lyon and Aon but kept an arm around Lydia's waist as she did. The girl hadn't been particularly shy, and now she had the power of a royal backing her up. But it was at least a friendly gesture and nothing overly personal like Kamira and Ini.

"They are asleep," Lyon replied as he cast his pale ice-blue eyes up to the statues that loomed over the pool. "And they... went there willingly."

"What?" Aon went rigid, clearly not believing what the Priest had said.

"It is true. I do not know what caused this. I do not know what transpired. But they lie in the bottom of that lake, and they slumber. We are... free of them. Ini says no Oracle has been chosen."

Aon walked slowly to a nearby statue and sat down on its base. Lydia slipped from Evie's arm to go stand by him and put her hand on his shoulder. "Are you okay?" she asked quietly.

"They let us go..." He said it in barely more than a whisper. Reaching up, he gently pulled his mask from his face. He turned it over in his hand and looked down at the shining metal surface as he repeated himself. He was stunned. But what she saw in his eyes was... a strange, sharp-edged relief. "They let us *all* go."

Lydia leaned down and kissed the top of his head, and he hugged her close to him with one arm. She was beginning to learn the sign of when he needed her near him. "But why?"

"I cannot say." Aon tilted his head and rested it against her. "Perhaps they think we are no longer in need of their guidance. Perhaps they think we are... better as we are without them."

They all fell into silence for a long time as Aon slipped his mask back over his face, once more disappearing behind the metal that hid his emotions. She realized how vulnerable he must feel without it. Even if they had all seen his face just days ago, that had been Noa, not Aon. As foolish as it was, she didn't have the heart to argue with him about it.

"Well!" Evie let out a rush of air and looked around. "I think I'd like to sit down and talk about what happened. But I think I'm goin' to need a beer to do it. I want to hear all the details." Evie began to walk away and was halfway across the platform before she stopped and looked back to them. "Are y'all coming?"

"Go without me," Aon replied.

"No, champ. It's all or nothin'." Evie laughed. "You have most of the intel, don't you?"

"Must I?" It was clear the warlock wanted to do anything but recount recent events to Evie. "I think I would rather go stick my finger in a live socket." Still, he pushed himself up to his feet and let out a weary sigh, accepting what had to happen.

Lydia chuckled. "C'mon, Spooky. Let's go."

"Spooky?"

"About time you got a nickname for once. It's like 'pookie' but, y'know... more you."

"I think I preferred when you were afraid of me."

Leaning up, she kissed the cheek of his metal mask. "Time and place for everything."

His metal gauntlet curled into her hip, digging the points into her sides. "Of my choosing, if you are not careful..." His mood vanished and quickly snapped into something far more devilish. Far more the fiend she was familiar with. Her mouth went dry, despite herself.

Lyon was shaking his head and began to follow Evie. "Come, my lord, Ms. Lydia. I think it is best we sort out what has come to pass."

"I am your lord no longer, Priest. You are a king, still, by the marks you wear." Aon was following them, although he was lagging, clearly not excited by the prospect of sitting down for "drinks" with the lot of them.

"Old habits die hard." Lyon smiled idly. "Though they do die, it seems."

Old habits died. They might go kicking and screaming into the night, but they went.

But new ones rose in their place, for better or worse.

TWENTY-THREE

Lydia stood and watched the bonfire blaze. The fire licked up into the night sky, where a sun never rose, no matter the time of day. One moon shone overhead, full, bright, and deep red. It was fitting.

They were holding a funeral for Edu.

Well, as much as you could call this a funeral. It was a raging kegger, was what it was. A giant bonfire burned in the center of the field out in front of Edu's keep. It was Evie's keep now. But there, at the base of the stairs leading up to the front door, was a statue of the man himself. It was a spitting image, a gift from the artisans at the House of Fate. A statue of the man who had tried to protect this world and everyone in it as best as he could, right to the bitter end.

They hadn't always seen eye to eye. He had hunted her, tormented her, killed her once, and tried to do it twice. But now that she had seen the whole picture, she knew this world was lacking for having lost him. She'd miss him, as stupid as it was.

Maybe she was just sentimental.

She was standing by the bonfire with a mug of wine in her hand. It reminded her of the night they had all celebrated the

Festival of Moons. She remembered Rxa and how he had seemed like a friend. If only she'd known Dtu was the lesser of the threats that night, things might have gone differently.

Speaking of the dog, he was off by one corner of the crowd, hunkered down, occasionally howling balefully. He and Edu had been close friends, and his death was hitting the wolf hard.

If her sympathy would have been at all welcome, she'd go over and tell him that she was sorry. But their relationship was still... rocky at best. Maybe, in time, it'd smooth over. They had plenty of that now, after all.

There was one man who hadn't yet shown up. Nobody was surprised.

Aon.

Lyon had asked her if he was going to come at all, and she shrugged and said she didn't know. The two of them were in love, but he was still very much his own man. She didn't run his life, and he didn't try to run hers. Predicting him was going to take her a lot longer than the eleven months it had been since she'd shown up to Under.

It hadn't even been a *year*.

She was left reflecting on that as she stared into the flames. The last time she'd seen a bonfire, she also had a cynical snake sitting on her shoulder, popping out insults and bad nicknames at everyone who came within earshot.

She did decide she was going to keep calling Kamira "boobs." That was just funny.

Lifting the mug of wine, she took a sip.

"Getting ourselves drunk without me, are we?"

With a yelp, she nearly jumped a foot in the air. She also nearly spilled wine all over herself but only managed to slosh it onto the ground instead. She flicked it off her hand and shot a glare at the man in black standing next to her. "Screw you."

Aon chuckled. "Later. I have only just arrived, and that would be rude. Although, with his proclivities, Edu might cheer us on from the beyond." He grunted. "No, I take that back. I do not wish to have that image lingering in my mind."

She smacked him in the arm with the back of her hand. "You're late."

"There are no speeches or ceremony, as Edu despised such things, so I do not know precisely what you think I am late *for*."

Lydia just shot him a look.

Aon sighed. "Yes. Very well. I did not know if I would attend at all." He turned his masked face away from her to look into the flames in front of them. The glow cast eerily along the metal surface.

"Why?"

"I am the reason he is dead. I am his murderer. It seemed a bit *gauche*."

"It wasn't you. It wasn't your fault."

Aon shook his head. "We are the same man, my dragonfly. You know that now. I killed Edu. The fact remains that I have the blood of *three* kings upon my hands. I did not think I would be welcome."

Lydia sighed and lifted his arm, ducked under it, and slung his arm over her shoulder. She didn't even give him the chance to argue about it. He looked down at her, and she could almost picture his raised eyebrow. "You're only to blame for one of those. Nobody's holding you accountable for Rxa or Edu."

"Then they are idiots."

"Maybe. Bask in your superiority like you usually do."

"Hmf." He pulled her to stand in front of him and wrapped his arms around her, proof that he wasn't upset with her snark.

She leaned her head back against him, and they fell into silence for a long moment.

"I... find myself grieving for his loss." He sounded confused by the revelation as if it were the strangest thing in the world.

She laughed. "It doesn't mean you secretly liked him, you

know. It means you're going to miss someone who'd been around for as long as he had. The two of you had a familiar routine in hating each other. Of course, you're going to miss that."

"Well put." He squeezed her against him tighter for a moment and rested his chin against the top of her head. "He was always a known variable. The backbone to this world. Without him, it feels… strange." She felt him wince as Evie could be heard hollering from the other side of the field. "And distinctly louder."

"Strange is okay. Strange'll become normal in time." She reached up and slipped her hand along the side of his neck, lacing into his hair, running her nails over his scalp. He grunted in enjoyment and leaned into her touch. She hoped he'd never stop doing that. She hoped of all things that wouldn't ever become *too* normal for him.

"We shall see." He paused for a moment. "But I think… although I despised him with everything that I was, we were as Zeus and Hades, as Cain and Abel, and Osiris and Set. I do not mourn him for he was merely familiar to me." Aon let out a long, ragged breath. "Adopted as though he may have been in truth, I mourn him for… in him, I lost a brother."

"Then I forgive you."

They hadn't heard Evie approach. The girl was standing some five feet away, her leather mask catching the light from the flames.

"My words were not meant for you." Aon resumed his defensive tone. All his vulnerability was lost from the second prior, his armor snapping up the instant someone else was nearby.

"I know. That's why they count." Evie walked up to them and looked over to the statue of Edu at the base of the stairs. "That's why I'm not gonna hold this 'gainst you, Aon. We're here to celebrate the man's life. To miss him. Not to point fingers or start wars."

When Aon didn't answer, Lydia drove an elbow into his ribs. He let out a grunt and sighed. "Thank you, Evie."

"You're welcome! Now. I'm too sober. I'm going to get drunk. You two kids have fun." She giggled and ran off.

Once she was out of earshot, Aon grumbled, "I dislike her."

Lydia laughed and turned in his arms to look up at him. "She's nice. What's the problem with her?"

"She is... *perky.*"

Laughing again, she rested her head against his chest and hugged him close. That was the man she knew. That was the warlock she loved. She was just glad to have him back. For the scent of old books and aged leather that came with him. For the feeling of his layers of black fabric against her cheek. For the feeling of the metal hand against her lower back. "Aon?"

"Yes?"

"I love you."

"And I, you, my dragonfly. Until the stars may burn to dust in the skies overhead."

She smiled. "I think he'd be happy for you, you know. To have found someone, finally."

"I think you may be right."

"Does Under have an afterlife?"

"I have no inkling."

"Where do you think he is?"

"If he 'is' anywhere at all, and not merely returned to the void?" Aon let out a long breath and looked over her to the blazing fire. "Somewhere he may lay down his sword. His stewardship has ended. Either way, he was so very tired. His reign as the shield of Under is over. He is at peace, and that is all that matters."

Nuzzling into him again, she shut her eyes. She let herself

enjoy the warmth of the fire at her back, and the warmth of the man in front of her. "I'm sorry, Aon. I'm sorry he's gone."

After a long pause, he quietly admitted, "As am I."

* * *

It was the first time they had all been in the same room officially since everything had gone to hell and back.

The first meeting of the royals. The "conclave," as Aon had called it. It hadn't happened in over fifteen hundred years, seven kings and queens sitting around a table, discussing the fate and politics of Under.

They all met in Evie's keep. She had offered to host, and it only felt right to accept. There they all were, sitting at a round table, each section carved and decorated with sigils and colors for their Houses. It hadn't been used in so long that dust was still caked into the grooves, even though it was clear that someone had gone to great lengths to try to clean it off and give it some fresh varnish.

She was the only one without a mask. She refused. Valiantly. And she was going to keep refusing as long as she could before Aon finally wore her down.

It was inevitable, like everything else, but she was going to enjoy being without one for as long as she could keep it up. Even Lyon had donned a full porcelain mask. She had teased him that she couldn't tell the difference.

Kamira, Maverick, Oanr, Navaa, some guy named Yuandi who was now the Elder of the House of Fate, and even Otoi were all in attendance, standing at the edges of the room. She was the only one without an elder. Her House was still empty, besides her.

It was getting a little lonely, if she were honest.

She spent most of her time in Aon's estate. Not because she didn't like her Temple of Dreams; she loved it there. She could really stretch out and cut loose. She could summon monsters and let them run amok without Aon complaining about how she was ruining the upholstery.

But it was empty.

There wasn't anyone to talk to. It hadn't felt so bad when Q had been there. She still wore the glowing turquoise feather in her hair in memory of him. He hadn't been real, but... he had mattered.

"Someday soon," Aon had told her, "you will wish all the rabble would simply go away and will yearn for the time your home stood empty."

She doubted it. But what did she know? She was staring down the barrel of eternity now. Who knew what would happen to them? But she wasn't afraid, to be honest. She had faced down her death and worse. It might come tomorrow, or it might come in ten or a hundred thousand years. She was just hoping she could enjoy the journey there as much as possible.

"Now," Aon interrupted her thoughts, "do you not feel foolish being the only one here without a mask?"

"Actually, I feel like the only smart one, thanks." Lydia raised her glass to him and sipped her wine. She was the only one besides the elders in the room who could drink. And she had a feeling this meeting was going to be long and boring. "And they're still stupid. I saw all your faces six months ago. No point in hiding them now."

"She does have a point," Ini pondered. "And a glass of wine does sound lovely. Oh! Posh." Ini pulled her mask from her face and put it down on the table in front of her. She ran her hands through her hair and over her face, giggling. "It does feel nice, I must say, for a change of pace!"

"Sister," Vjo scolded her.

"Which one?" Ini smiled beamingly back at the spider. "We have so many now. Perhaps we are now the queens and kings of Under and not the other way around! How wonderful. Come.

All of you. Let us sit together as friends. Let us show each other that which we hid for so very long. Let there be peace, for once."

The room sat silent for a moment. Lyon followed suit next, taking the porcelain from his face and placing it on the table. "It feels foreign to me to wear it."

"Then go without it." Lydia grinned. "*Viva la revolución. No pants Friday.*"

"While my sentiment to agree with you is strong, so is my adherence to culture and duty. I will wear it in public. I will happily go without when I may." The Priest smiled back at her gently, and she grinned back at him. Good enough.

Evie took off her mask and plonked it onto the table without much fuss. She whapped her hand on the table, and with the gesture, a mug of beer appeared next to her hand. She cackled in excited laughter. "I love that trick!"

Shockingly, Dtu followed suit next. He took off the wooden, wolven mask and placed it face up in front of him. He looked down at it, and his jaw twitched as he then cast his orange eyes up, catching Lydia's gaze. "Peace. I would like peace. I have had enough of the death and loss."

Lydia nodded to him and smiled. She very much liked the sound of that.

Vjo sighed and shrugged, then took off her own mask. "Very well... there is no harm in it."

Only the warlock remained.

Aon was sitting perfectly still, his emotions unreadable underneath the metal mask. Lifting his clawed gauntlet, he went to pull it from his face and hesitated before lowering his hand. "I killed Qta. I killed Rxa. I killed Edu. I took countless lives when I reigned as the King of All. I should be your prisoner of war. I should be on trial."

Ini, who was sitting to Aon's left, reached out and smacked him. Literally decked him upside the head. The whole room went into a gasp and then went silent. "Don't be a damned fool, warlock!"

Aon turned to look at the woman and, for once, seemed to have nothing to say.

"The war is over. *Your* war is over. Let it *be* over." The pixie pointed at him. "Do not look for strife where there is none. You have lived your whole life searching for meaning in the darkness. You have it now. Do not keep looking. There is nothing left there except to destroy what you have found."

Aon went to defend himself. "I—"

"And for once in your miserable life, listen to my advice!"

The room fell silent once more. Aon seemed to consider her words. Lydia sympathized with him. She knew he must simultaneously feel guilt for the lives he had taken, rage for what he had suffered, and the haughty superiority of a man who felt he was always right.

He was the King of All, who had given up his throne to pretend he was like them. Because what he was as a broken, shattered madman was better than the creature he was designed to be. He must be balancing on the edge between declaring himself victorious and begging for them to put his head on the chopping block.

Lydia slipped her foot behind his underneath the table. He didn't move, but she knew he noticed. He needed a lifeline. That was what she would always be for him.

With a long, beleaguered sigh, he reached up and slowly pulled the metal mask from his face and placed it down before him on the table. Seven lines of ink in perfectly straight lines ran down his sharp features, one marred just slightly by a paper-thin scar.

Something was missing, though. Lydia smiled sadly and lifting her hand... made herself a mask. Summoned it out of thin air. Acting on instinct, she just created whatever felt right.

It was more Q than Qta. A tribute to the friend she had

never had and yet had lost. Made of a solid piece of polished turquoise, it resembled a snake. Or really, the skull of a ghost-snake. Ghastly and bizarre, it suited her. She wouldn't ever wear it unless she had to. But it felt right, now, to complete the circle.

She put it down on the table in front of her. It took Aon's hand atop hers to break her gaze from the polished surface. He was smiling warmly at her, and there was such love in his spilled-ink eyes that it made her heart skip.

"Well, then…" Lyon interrupted the silence for a moment. "Shall we begin?"

Lydia sat back in her chair and looked at the masks on the table, each one twisted and warped in its own way. Each one representing a kind of fear or monster that hunted the darkness. Green, white, red, purple, blue, black… and turquoise.

The Masks of Under.

Lydia looked at the swirling black gate that stood before them. It had been twenty-five years since she had come here to Under. Twenty-four since the events they had dubbed "The Rise." There were many, *many* thousands of them ahead of her.

But she wouldn't walk them alone.

Aon had his arm slung around her waist, the thumb of his clawed gauntlet fed carefully into the loop of her golden belt. She wore black pants, a turquoise tank top, and the gold that Qta favored had slowly found its way into her wardrobe over time.

Aon had decided to keep his claw. Honestly, she'd miss it too, if he got rid of it. It was a part of him, and it suited his personality. Although he'd never admit it, she suspected he kept it also in his own remembrance of Edu. Only once had he ever said he was sorry for what he had done. The rest of the time, it was "good riddance." Or he would complain that he preferred Edu over Evie, as Edu was quiet. They knew the truth, so nobody felt the need to bother him about it.

Leaning against his side, she let out a breath. The world of Earth and Under had come back into alignment for the first time since all those years ago. The hunt was on. There were humans to collect and bring back to replenish their ranks. It was how things had to be.

Twenty-five years ago, she had been terrified on the streets of Boston, running from a gigantic man in armor alongside her best friend. She had struggled against the enormity of it all. She had done her best to protect herself, but it had been utterly futile.

Now, she was on the other side of things. Now, she would be the monster hunting the streets, seeking the prey that called out to her even now. She could sense them—the marked—on the other side of that portal. Calling out to her blood, demanding she take them home.

Home.

That was what Under really was to her now. She had come to accept it, to embrace it... but it hadn't been easy for her. Her, less so than most.

She felt guilty, knowing she was going to be terrorizing people, robbing them from their lives and throwing them into that god-awful puddle of blood. She still wondered what had happened to her mortal family, even after all this time. The reminder of them, like the loss of Nick and Q, always left her melancholy.

But this is how things have to be. That was how Under worked. It took souls because it couldn't make them. The people she would be stealing were meant to join them. The fear would be short-lived. Maybe, just maybe, she could try to talk some sense into them. Lydia almost laughed at the thought. *Lyon and Ylena tried to talk sense into me. Didn't exactly take.*

It was the law of nature. The cycle moved on. But it still stung to know that she was going to be the harbinger of the same fear and pain she had experienced. She could only do her best to try to soften the blow.

But there was another odd thought that was pulling at the

back of her mind. For the past twenty-four years that she had been the Queen of Dreams, her House had been utterly empty. She had been the only one.

That was probably about to change.

She was going to get some people in her own House, she was sure. She didn't know how to feel about that. Somebody out there—some poor, sorry son of a bitch—was going to get chucked in the pond and come out her "elder."

Her laugh ended in a sad sigh.

"What?" Aon asked.

"I'm going to have a regent."

"You will likely have many to share your home."

"I guess that means I have to pick my socks off the floor now."

Hugging her tighter to him, he chuckled. "Whatever it takes to make you clean up after yourself."

Lydia slapped him in the chest playfully. But looking into the gateway, she felt her humor deflate like a bad balloon.

Earth.

"Given the choice, would you go back?" Aon asked, correctly reading her. He always could. He shifted to stand behind her, pulling her into his arms. Lydia leaned back, resting against his chest. "Undo all that has happened, and go live out your mortal life, would you?"

"Nah. It'd be super awkward. I bet there's self-driving cars and all sorts of weird shit I don't know what to do with."

He rested his masked metal cheek against the top of her head. "What if you could turn back the clock? As though none of this had transpired at all?"

"Of course not." Her life was here, with him. The moment that mark appeared on her arm so long ago, that had always been the simple, unavoidable fact. The first time she had laid eyes on him, she belonged to him and vice versa. "But it's strange, to be on this side of things."

"I can only imagine. You do not have to take part, you know. There are plenty of us to seek out those who have been marked." He tightened his arms around her and let out a small, contented sound. "Many skip their first alignment of the worlds, for the pain is still too new."

"Where would be the fun in that?" Lydia turned her head and kissed the metal surface of his mask.

"Bah! How am I to hunt prey with lipstick on my mask?" Aon complained and pulled out his black silk handkerchief to wipe the turquoise smudge off the metal surface. "I would hardly be terrifying to my victims with that, now, would I?"

Grinning cheekily, she decided to be done with her melancholy. "I'll tell you what. Catch more of them than me, and we can see how much lipstick I can get on something *else*."

Aon growled and wrapped his arms around her tighter. "Well, then. The game is on."

Taking a step away from him, she gestured and summoned magic to change her clothes. This was an occasion, and while she refused to dress "fancy" in her daily life, she was slowly coming to terms with being a queen. Now, she was in something that was a mix between ancient and new—just like her. Feathers and gold chains and turquoise silk fabric. It felt silly, but over time, it became less so.

One last thing and she'd be ready to go. It had taken her twenty years before she'd given in to Aon's argument about culture and formality.

Flicking her hand, a mask appeared in her palm, with its visage still reminding her so much of Q. She smiled, remembering her brief imaginary friend. She still missed him, truth be told. She missed everyone they had lost.

Nick. Her mind clicked back to her friend as she remembered how they had run from Edu in terror that first night and how much had happened since then.

If he could see me now. She tried not to laugh.

Maybe he could. Maybe he was part of this place now. Another soul, fueling the whole of Under. She slipped the mask over her face and tossed its feathered headdress back over her hair. She had felt so dumb the first time she put it on, she had refused to come out of the room. Aon insisted she was beautiful. She suspected he was just being nice. Taking a breath, she let it out.

Earth was on the other side of that gate. The last time she had been there, she was a terrified little mortal girl.

Now... she was very much not.

Aon had watched her in silence, respecting the emotions that were running rampant in her head. Finally, seeing that she was as ready as she'd ever be, he held out his metal gauntlet to her, palm up.

How many times had he done that? Offered her his hand? Offered to lead her into the darkness and into their future together?

"Come, my dragonfly."

Fin.

A LETTER FROM KATHRYN

Dear reader,

I want to say a huge thank you for choosing to read The Masks of Under series. This was my first series I ever officially published out into the world—and the tale of Lydia, Aon, and all the rest will forever be near and dear to my heart.

If you'd like to stay in the loop for all my future series and releases, just sign up at the following link. Your email address will never be shared and you can unsubscribe at any time.

www.secondskybooks.com/kathryn-ann-kingsley

There are several kinds of writers out there in the world—those who are happy to tell their story to a blank page, and those who thrive on hearing about how their readers engage with their tales.

I'm the latter.

I absolutely love hearing from my readers – you can get in touch through social media, my website, or even join my Discord (the link to join is on my website) to interact with both me and other fans.

Stay Spooky and Happy Nightmares,

Kathryn Ann Kingsley

KEEP IN TOUCH WITH KATHRYN

www.kathrynkingsley.com

X x.com/vodriel

instagram.com/kathrynannkingsley

PUBLISHING TEAM

Turning a manuscript into a book requires the efforts of many people. The publishing team at Bookouture would like to acknowledge everyone who contributed to this publication.

Commercial

Lauren Morrissette
Hannah Richmond
Imogen Allport

Cover design

BRoseDesignz

Data and analysis

Mark Alder
Mohamed Bussuri

Editorial

Jack Renninson
Melissa Tran

Proofreader

Catherine Lenderi

Marketing
Alex Crow
Melanie Price
Occy Carr
Cíara Rosney
Martyna Młynarska

Operations and distribution
Marina Valles
Stephanie Straub
Joe Morris

Production
Hannah Snetsinger
Mandy Kullar
Jen Shannon
Ria Clare

Publicity
Kim Nash
Noelle Holten
Jess Readett
Sarah Hardy

Rights and contracts
Peta Nightingale
Richard King
Saidah Graham